Imbroglio

The Ties of Love and Lies

Heather Dawn Robin

Imbroglio
© 2015 by Heather Dawn Robin

Second printing *Imbroglio: The Ties of Love and Lies* © 2016
All Rights Reserved.

No part of this work may be used, reproduced, distributed, stored in a retrieval system, or transmitted in any form by any means—electronic, mechanical, photocopy, recording, or otherwise—without the author's prior written permission, except as permitted under U.S.A. copyright law.

This is a work of fiction. Names, characters, businesses, organizations, places, events, and incidents either are the product of the author's imagination or are used fictionally. Any resemblance to actual events, locales, organizations or persons, living or dead, is entirely coincidental.

ISBN 978-0-9965089-0-2

Central cover art by SAPR © 2015
Cover design and additional artwork by BookCoversLab.com
Makeup by Drini@EyeDreamOfDrini.com
Photography by Diondré Jones@Jonesnphoto.com
Styled by Nicci Carr

For more information, visit HeatherDawnMedia.com or HeatherDawnRobin.com

Printed in the United States of America

Published by Heather Dawn Media

Acknowledgements

Most importantly, to my Lord and Savior, to Whom I owe my life. You blessed me with the creativity and ignited the spark. It was just You and me for three years, hammering, sculpting, and chiseling this work which You gave me a glimpse of back in high school. I'm amazed at how You orchestrated the pieces together. I hope You are well pleased.

To Mommy, Daddy, Sis, and my Suga'man, thank you for your immense love and support. You all are my backbone, my raison d'être. Literally and figuratively. When I finally shared this story for the first time three years after its revived inception, your responses made me soar from the doubtful place I was. Collectively, you allowed me to pick your brains, helped tremendously with story development (loved the volunteered reenactments,) and gave me the space I needed to get this vision accomplished. I love you all more than you can comprehend. Y'all ready for more?

A special shout to Mom for the beautiful cover art and to Sis for coming with it when we redesigned the synopsis style and concept. You both are so wonderfully talented.

To those who willingly lent their eyes, ears, and/or wisdom to this work, I feel inadequate in expressing how much I appreciate you. Angela Caldwell (the clever and fastidious debater), Desiree Taylor (Mrs. I have questions), Aaron Grider (picking up on the little details and strong-arming me into making this a trilogy), Ray Hawkins (who had to "get out the room") and my informants: LaSalle Culpepper, Marcella Esparza, Jeff Lemond, Saul Martinez, Angel Gonzalez, and the cultural vloggers and bloggers on the Internet, you fueled my passion.

To the sharpest editor I know, Brady Rhoades, my polisher. Common misspellings, authorial intrusion, and punctuation boo-boos have a hard time getting by you. Your valuable insight added more heat, richness, and fun to the journey. Let's not stop at this one!

(A big thank you to Dennis Freeman for connecting us. One of many great referrals.)

To La Donna Lewis, thank you for being a sounding board and coach for my social branding ideas and grabbing the torch when I floundered in the fog.

To the mystery man who helped smooth the frazzle of getting my bio, synopsis and other marketing elements together, thank you. Glad we're friends.

To Nicci Carr, how your call came so right on time! Thank you for blessing me with the make-up connection and your sense of style.

To Todd Kausen, thank you for embellishing my titles on the revised design to give them that beautiful 3D effect.

To LaTara Bussey, for seeing the picture clearly, taking me under your wing, and willingly getting me up and running on my website. You share life.

To Christine Walters, for sharing your marketing savvy and your drive.

Last, but not least, to you, the reader, for picking up my book. Thank you. I hope you won't be able to put it down.

Imbroglio

(im-brohl-yoh)

Act I
Contact

[1]

It occurs on a busy evening at Hartsfield International Airport in Atlanta, Georgia, as another cold January comes to an end.
Shannon Moore idles curbside, fuming, after dropping off her girlfriend to catch a flight for a so-called "business" trip. She ponders the argument they just had and the sad realities in her life. *We cannot seem to get along anymore about anything.*
Shannon exhales roughly, trying to still her emotions. Having this week off work will serve no purpose since Gina had decided that an impromptu trip to Hawaii was more important than using this time intended for them to iron out some personal matters. Once again, the priorities are placed on the back burner, and she comes to the difficult conclusion that she has had enough. She can no longer be plagued with all the drama, heartache, and confusion that Gina brings.
    Her thoughts are interrupted when she catches a glimpse of a distant traffic cop in her side-view mirror patrolling the long line of vehicles behind her. Since he's heading in her direction she figures he will be shooing her away momentarily, so she puts the car in drive, rolls down the window to let in some cool air, and looks over her shoulder to merge into traffic.
    Out of nowhere, a man's torso materializes at her window. *"Jeezus!"* Shannon huffs, stunned. Slamming her foot on the brake, she shrinks away from the man and, instinctively, her fingertips touch the weapon concealed at her waist.
    She regains her senses quickly, realizing it's the same guy from the limousine in front of her who had been accompanied by an elderly Caucasian couple of wealthy stature and feeble health. Just moments ago, she'd absently watched them say their goodbyes.

Irritated, Shannon canvasses the scene, her almond shaped eyes dotting about in search of a viable reason for him to be at her door. There isn't one. *Here we go again*, she thinks, bracing herself for the flirting she assumes is on its way.

"Yes?"

The man leans down to the window and speaks in a pleasant baritone. "Hello. Lost in thought?"

Shannon can't help but notice how extremely good-looking he is, with rich caramel skin, long, thick eyelashes, and silky, black, deeply wavy hair. From what she can tell, he is about 6-feet-tall. A black trench coat overlaying a slate gray crew neck sweater and dark slacks hang from his proportionate musculature nicely.

However, unaffected by his looks and not one to be sold a bill of goods or a sorry old pickup line, Shannon responds tersely, "Nope! Excuse me." She inches the car forward, hoping he gets the hint.

"One moment, please!" he expresses, moving to impede her progress. Flashing a flawless set of teeth, he continues, "I know you've heard what I'm about to say probably more times than you can count, but I'm going to say it anyway. If you would get to know me, I guarantee you whoever put that frown on your face would be miserable to see you having so much fun."

His statement has to register. A second or two later, Shannon's face cracks. "Nice one," she comments, dropping her guard a tinge. *It surely isn't what I expected to hear. No typical drag about being beautiful. Nothing sleazy.* It was kind of clever and somehow soothing in her present state of mind.

The man extends his hand. "I'm Carlos."

Before anyone can say another word, the ill-tempered traffic cop arrives on the scene, yelling at them from a car length away. "You two! Move it. Now!"

Carlos looks at the cop and rubs his neatly groomed French cut goatee. He tells Shannon, "Please, don't leave yet."

She watches as he approaches the cop and doesn't know why she's actually waiting. *Curiosity,* she supposes, shifting the car into park. Carlos and the cop exchange words, and he returns to her window. To her surprise, the cop plods on to other cars.

Intrigued, Shannon asks, "What did you say to him?"

"I... told him you rear-ended me, and we were exchanging information."

Shannon's jaw drops. "You did *what?*"

He raises his eyebrows guiltily and responds, "Yep." Reaching for his wallet, he pulls out his driver's license and a business card, then hands them to Shannon. Mischievously, he tells her, "Play along now. He's watching us."

She eyes Carlos with comical defiance. "I'm not showing you my driver's license."

"Why not? I showed you mine."

Shannon laughs, a succession of vibrant ha-yucks that conclude with a breathy inhale, and the cop, now a few cars ahead of them, looks sternly in their direction. Carlos turns and projects his voice. "A little difficulty here, but I believe we're almost done."

The cop starts to walk toward them, and to thwart his advancement, Carlos says, "Sir, we have it! Don't need any help." He turns back to Shannon, very amused by his own shenanigans. "I need your help here. Please don't let me go to jail for lying to this officer."

The antics and audacity of this guy... But, a smooth way to get my number, for sure. On impulse, she pulls out her driver's license and begins writing her *real* number on the back of his card. For the second time in just a few minutes, Shannon is wondering why she is cooperating. Perhaps it is because she's feeling spiteful. Or perhaps it's because Carlos is already proving himself to be quite the man of his word. *Truly entertaining.*

She hands the license and card to Carlos just as the cop approaches the car.

"What's going on here?"

This time, Shannon collaborates. "One minute, officer. I just need to get my license back, and we're done."

The cop observes the driver's license in Carlos' hand and hangs back, motioning to other cars. Carlos' contrived look of surprise at her participation prompts Shannon to return a look of her own. She mouths, "See what you got me doing?"

Carlos reads the license briefly before she snatches it back. Smirking, he schmoozes, "Okay, Shannon Moore. *Very* nice meeting you—"

The now angry cop is at Shannon's door. Carlos straightens and backs away swiftly toward his limo, calling out, "Please! Be more careful next time!" As he approaches, a man, also tastefully attired and cloaked in a trench, opens the limo door. Before Carlos steps in, he looks back at Shannon and winks.

She tries to stifle her laugh.

"Miss, you think this is a joke?" the cop demands.

"No, sir," Shannon blurts, muttering, "It is time to go," under her breath as she pulls off.

Amused, she wonders if Carlos will actually call, but isn't desirous for him to do so. Given her current troubles, his efforts wouldn't even get him to the "friend" category. She just wishes Gina could've seen her giving the handsome new acquaintance, Carlos Antonio Romero, her number. *Invoking jealousy is the sweetest revenge.*

Shannon maneuvers the ruby red Camry onto the I-85 North freeway entrance and her phone rings. She presses the bluetooth button on the steering wheel.

"Hello."

A familiar voice. "I just wanted to make sure this was your real number."

Shannon shakes her head in disbelief. "Oh, my gosh. YOU are a piece of work."

Carlos chuckles fondly, a low throaty staccato. "Oh my gosh?"

Shannon just smiles, used to people teasing her about her reluctance to curse—especially in her line of work and the practices she has no problem engaging in.

He continues, "I think we got out of there just in time. Did you see the look on that man's face? He was so furious!" They laugh.

"For sure he was," Shannon says.

"I love the sultry, southern drawl. Alright, little lady. I'll talk to you again."

Hanging up, Shannon smirks at the fact Carlos has no idea she doesn't remotely consider him (or anyone like him, for that matter) her type. She has to admit, however, that he seems to be a lot of fun. Unlike her other half these days.

Fifteen minutes later, Shannon parks in the lot behind a small, unpretentious apartment building speckled with the needles of two Dwarf Loblolly pines shading the front lawn and makes her way through the breezy corridor where her ground-level unit is located. She flops down on the couch, reminded of her problems and surrounded by photographed memories of better days. Her eyes rest on the one of a loving hand reaching for hers. *It's over. I suppose I'll start looking for a new apartment in the morning.*

"No!" Shannon says out loud to pump herself up. "I'm going to find something fun to do for the next five days. This vacation will not be a time of pragmatic responsibility, self-pity, boredom or moping!"

She picks up the TV remote and within seconds puts it down. She isn't sleepy, but decides to go to bed.

It's only 8:10 p.m. So much for not moping.

One Time

[2]

Shannon's eyes open sleepily and stare into the bedroom she keeps darkly draped. "Oh, man," she mutters as she looks at the clock on her nightstand. It's just after 11:00 a.m. *There went my plan to get up early and get some laundry done before the Saturday laundromat crowd got too heavy.* She sits up stiffly. *I must be really tired. Or really depressed. Whatever the case, I'm sure of one thing.* Shannon swings her legs out of bed and saunters to the kitchen. She stands with the refrigerator wide open, staring at the half empty shelves before closing the door with her foot and spinning around. "Subway, here I come," she groans and heads for the bathroom, hoping that a hot shower will help get her going.

Twenty minutes later, Shannon emerges from the stall feeling refreshed from head to toe. She carelessly smooths her long, wet ringlets into a ponytail, twisting the ends into a loose bun, then quickly throws on a light blue V-neck T-shirt, a pair of jeans and her favorite white, faux-fur–lined, hooded puffer jacket. She grabs her purse and keys from the nightstand, then walks to the Subway restaurant just a short block from her apartment.

Yet another reason why she is dragging her feet to move: Her apartment's prime location. With so many places close by that she often frequents, she doubts she will be able to find another spot like it for the money.

Shannon orders her sandwich, trying to dismiss her thoughts. Her purse begins to sing an indistinct tune. She pays for the 6-inch tuna on wheat and digs to retrieve her buried phone as she heads out of the shop.

It's her partner.

"Gohmes. What's up?"

"You still on vacation?" he garbles into her earpiece.

"Why are you bothering me?" Shannon asks in mock frustration.

"You won't believe the crap I've been dealing with the last two days. Louis lit the whole squad up when he found out Robbins and Eddie blew that D.I.N.O case. Missed a 48 hour. And this new sub I have? Ditzy. Can't stand trainees. When you comin' back?"

Shannon responds like an old woman. "Never! You be careful out there, sonny," and hangs up on his comeback. She unlocks her apartment door and her phone rings again. She doesn't recognize the number.

"Hello."

"Shannon Moore."

The deep voice sends an unaccustomed, yet unmistakably delightful chill up her spine as she steps into the living room. "Carlos Antonio Romero," she returns.

"Using the middle name. Okay. You're up one. So, Shannon *Lizette* Moore, would you be able to meet me downtown by 1 for a quick lunch?"

Hearing her middle name spoken aloud causes her to cringe. *This is exactly what I get for showing him my driver's license. Now, he is going to be using it—and whatever else he'd managed to read on there. Like my address*, Shannon reckons, disgusted that she of all people hadn't thought her actions through.

"Okay, you win," she says, "Don't ever use my middle name again, though. Please."

"Why not? It's a nice name," he remarks.

"It's not. Just forget you know it, okay?"

Carlos laughs at Shannon's exasperation. "Understood. Now, what about lunch?"

Let him down easy, Shannon. He seems like a decent guy. "Actually, I'm just getting back from picking up something to eat. If you had only caught me sooner..."

"I think you should put that away for dinner or an evening snack and come grab a bite with me."

Shannon looks down at her sandwich indecisively. "Uh..." She dilly-dallies, conflicted by her blossoming intrigue with the man trying to persuade her on the other end of the line.

"It will be a win-win for you. Think about this: I have an obligation at 2, so I won't be able to take up as much of your time as I would like. If you are miserable in my presence, you at least know it won't last long, and you'll get a free meal out of the deal."

Shannon bites her lower lip, considering, all the while asking herself why she is.

"I would really enjoy your company," he adds, earnestly.

I don't want to bother with having to blow this guy off in the end... She stalls, then decides the company perfect for taking her mind off her sorrows. *It beats staying home. And, it will be harmless. Guaranteed.* Shannon slides her weapon back into its holster.

"Where am I meeting you?"

Carlos laughs heartily. "That's what I wanted to hear."

***

Shannon arrives at La Cucina Lunga at ten minutes to 1 p.m. It's valet only parking and her stomach sinks. By the looks of it, she is grossly underdressed for this place. She feels like turning around, but she's blocked in from behind and forced to pull forward as directed. She puts the car in park, and immediately her door is pulled open by the attendant. Stepping out of the car, Shannon takes the ticket being handed to her and plans to let Carlos have it for not giving her a heads up about the dress code.

She is shown to a seat at the table where Carlos is sitting, attractively outfitted in a cream sweater and tan wool slacks. Now that she is out of the car, he observes her 5-feet-six or so shapely, athletic frame walk toward him. He stands when she arrives.

Shannon chides, "Why didn't you tell me this place has a dress code?"

Carlos casts an unimpressed glance around the fancy room at the restaurant patrons. Looking back at Shannon, he replies, "Dress codes are for people who need help to be seen in public. You don't need any help."

"Yeah, yeah," she tosses back, trying to hide the fact that she's flattered by his quick wit. Rushing to beat Carlos to the punch, she quickly pulls out the chair across from him and takes a seat. With an amused look on his face, he returns to his own seat.

Indeed, just as she originally perceived, Carlos is a natural comedian, but she quickly learns he is also a refreshingly unusual gentleman. He inquires what foods she enjoys and then asks if he may order something for her since she hadn't eaten there before.

Shannon is not used to this. Chivalry had been foreign in her neck of the woods. Accepting his offer, she watches him speak with the server and tries to figure his age. *He looks mid-thirties, but he's too seasoned to be anything less than forty-five.* Try as she may, she can't recall the birthdate on his driver's license. *My skills must be slippin'.*

Every so often during their conversation, Shannon hears the lilt of an alluring accent that she can't place. She finally inquires, "Do you speak another language?"

First, he tells her that he speaks Igbo.

Innocently, Shannon asks, "Igbo? Where's that from? Nigeria or Kenya or someplace like that?"

"Someplace like that."

Shannon presses. "Where were you born?"

"In a city called Sancti Spiritus."

"What state is that in?"

"Not a state. A country. Cuba."

"Oh!" Shannon laughs at herself.

Carlos waits for the signature inhale then continues to tease her. "In that *country*, we speak Spanish." When she finishes cutting her eyes at him in a non-verbal warning, he asks, "And you?"

Replying with emphasis on each word, Shannon says, "I am a Decatur–Georgia–born–Negro."

Carlos claps his hands with delight. "You don't hold back, do you?"

Amid their cachinnation, he takes in her radiant maple syrup complexion and the wispy coffee brown curls peeking out from her hairline and through the unrestrained bun. He remarks, "You look like you could be from my country."

"Is that so?" Shannon nibbles her bottom lip. "I'd like to go there someday even though I haven't heard too many good things about it."

"I plead the fifth," Carlos responds, his chestnut irises glinting with invitation.

Again, Shannon comes alive inside. *This is crazy.*

The food arrives. Out of habit and not so much due to a relationship with God, Shannon bows her head to say a quiet prayer. It is one of the things drilled into her while growing up in the Moore household that she never shook.

Carlos interrupts her apologetically. "Excuse me—"

He pauses, looking up to the Heavens. "Forgive me, Lord, for interrupting her." Then he looks back at Shannon, quizzically. "Wait, you are praying to the Lord, yes?"

Her mouth puckers in indignation. "Yes. I was."

"Okay, good. Can we bless the food together?"

That teasing bite in her smile is so infectious... Carlos can't stop himself from wanting to keep her amused. He recalls how captivated he'd felt the first time her face lit up for him at the airport.

Although she'd caught his eye from a distance, he had not been prepared for how gorgeous she is up close. He waits for her to sample her first morsel and watches the elation spread from ear to ear. *Yes,* he thinks. *Looks. Personality. She just may be a winner.*

In the midst of their meal, the Maitre D' comes to the table and informs Carlos that his car is waiting for him. Carlos acknowledges him, but makes no move to leave. They had just begun eating.

Shannon tells Carlos, "I understand that you need to go. You warned me. Just don't be offended if I stay here and finish my food because it is too good to leave behind. You have good taste."

"I'm curious," Carlos begins, finding her enjoyment of the food adorable. "What had you picked up for lunch today when I called?"

She snickers at how silly she knows it will sound. "Subway."

The grin on Carlos' face stretches halfway and stops, full of mischief.

"What is so funny?"

"I'm just thinking, of all the things you could have been doing today, how wonderful it is that you were willing and able to have lunch with me. I beat out Subway. This has to mean something."

Shannon tosses back her head. "Ha!" she says. "Don't get the big head. It's only because I'm off from work and have nothing else to do... today."

"Ouch!" Carlos grabs his chest like he'd been sucker punched. She shakes her head at him, and he follows up, cunningly, "Off from work tomorrow?"

Lie Shannon, she thinks. What comes out is, "Yep."

Beaming, Carlos concludes, "How fortunate."

He is about to say something else when the same man who assisted him at the limo the day before approaches the table. It is obvious Carlos has delayed leaving far too long, and is now being summoned.

"I have to get to this meeting. I'm very late now," he says, ignoring the man's presence.

Shannon reminds him, "I tried to let you go—"

Carlos stops her mid-sentence. "Oh, no. Whatever repercussions I suffer, it was absolutely worth every minute."

Looking deeply into her distinct, russet colored eyes, he reaches across the table for her hand and assists her to her feet. Shannon cannot help thinking, *He's good.*

When they reach the parking valet, he hands her ticket and some cash to a valet driver, then informs Shannon, "I really need to get going. Please forgive me for not waiting here with you while they bring out your car. Je t'en dois une."

Perplexed, Shannon says, "Wait a minute, that's not Spanish. What is that? You speak French, as well?"

He eyes her with an air of mystery. Shannon can't tell if he's fooling with her or not. She rolls her eyes playfully. "Goodbye, Carlos."

He backs away to his waiting limo. "Au revoir."

She shakes her head again, grinning at how uncommon he is. As the limo drives away, she observes the fleet number printed on the bumper and wonders how much it must cost to hire a private car each time he travels around the city. *Has to be a pretty penny,* she thinks, pulling out her phone. She types a note with his plates for future reference. *Just in case...*

Returning home to her quiet apartment and the growing mound of laundry she has waiting there for her to tackle, Shannon squats beside the hamper in her bedroom with the intention to start sorting. She stares at the clothes spilling over the edge onto the floor. Ordinarily, she can't stand a mess, but she looks around for something else to do. *It can wait. Doesn't matter that I'm running out of clean clothes.*

She piddles around the apartment aimlessly, losing track of time, until she starts to feel hungry. Happily, she remembers her Subway sandwich—and the man who had been a nice distraction for her today. Sitting down to eat, she flips through cable channels looking for something entertaining to watch. Her phone rings. A telemarketer. No sooner than she hangs up, the phone rings again.

"I'm not buying anything," she proclaims.

"I'm not selling anything," comes the pleasant retort. "Hello, Shannon Moore." His voice is a welcomed sound.

"I thought you were a telemarketer calling back. I'm so sorry!" Shannon explains.

"I see. What are you doing?"

"Avoiding what I should be doing."

In a hushed tone, Carlos conspires, "Don't I know it. I snuck out to call you right now. If they find out, I'm in trouble."

"So, you speak French?" Shannon rallies.

"Everything I could learn on TV from Pepé Le Pew."

"Where do you live, Pepé?"

Not caring too much for this line of questioning, Carlos continues to jest. "In the air. Matter of fact, tomorrow I will be on a plane headed to Wisconsin. What is in Wisconsin, you might ask? Cheese. Lots and lots of cheese. Really."

Does this guy know how to be serious at all? "Ha ha. Very funny," Shannon says aloud.

"What? That's not a euphemism for money among the brethren?"

"Un huh. You still didn't tell me where you actually live. I need the city of your physical address." Trained to get to the facts, Shannon can't help her approach for gathering information. Awaiting his response, she thinks, *If he doesn't give me a straight answer, I'm hanging up the phone.*

Carlos does answer, pensively. "Oh. Well, let's see. I have a home in Miami. Sometimes I stay in a flat in downtown Chicago. But, my heart is in Havana. I'll let you pick."

Interesting, Shannon contemplates. *And so very different from my humdrum.*

Despite desiring to know what he does for a living, she doesn't ask. Questions about her job would probably volley in return, and she isn't inclined to deal with that right now. Unbeknownst to her, Carlos is feeling the same way. Very much liking the natural way they had been interacting with one another, he would prefer that the typical intimidation not arise about his complex occupation.

"So, you're not in my city much then?" Shannon surprises herself with that question. She hopes that it hadn't come across like she really wanted to see him again.

"I am. Are you about to say you'd like to see me again, Ms. Moore?" Carlos didn't miss the intonation.

Shannon begins to squirm and is grateful that he isn't there to see it. She stumbles over her words. "I didn't say... I was just asking a question."

"Ah. You don't want to see me again."

"That is..." She tugs at her ear. "...not what I said!"

Carlos relishes her flustered responses. "Good. I'm glad to hear that. I'll talk to you again."

When he hangs up, Shannon jokes out loud to herself, "Okay, girl. What's up with you?" She heads to the hamper. *Time to get started.*

Inner Views

[3]

Buzz. Buzz. Buzz.

Shannon lies motionless, face down under a heap of blankets in the middle of her bed. Suddenly, the covers stir and she exposes an arm reaching toward the sound coming from her nightstand. Refusing to poke out her head from under the blankets, her hand gropes around futilely, trying to catch the cell phone vibrating across the surface.

Unable to locate it, Shannon snatches the blankets from her head in frustration. Propping herself up onto her forearms, she snags the elusive phone as it slowly dances its way past the red L.E.D. lights glaring 6:58 at her.

She moans, hoping there isn't bad news on the line. Everyone who knows her knows better than to call at this time of day, so this isn't a good sign. To Shannon, anything before 11 is ridiculously early, which is the main reason why she works the afternoon shift.

She taps the screen to answer and whispers groggily, "Hello?"

A familiar baritone responds, "Time to get up, Ms. Moore. You don't want to miss breakfast."

Irritated at being awakened by a non-emergency, Shannon mumbles into the phone, "You have no idea how much of a morning person I am not."

To Carlos' astonishment, she hangs up. *Hmm. She's a bit grumpy in the morning*, Carlos muses, as he dials her again. *Maybe she won't make it to the finish line after all.*

Shannon answers curtly. "*What?!*"

"You know, I'm getting a little leery of calling you. I seem to be closer and closer to getting my head chopped off."

In spite of herself, Shannon has to lighten up, envisioning the impression she is giving off. "Listen, I was asleep!"

"Okay," Carlos responds. "And now what?"

Shannon lets out a loud sigh before exclaiming, "I'm not going to breakfast with you. I'm going back to sleep."

"That's a waste of time, you see, because you're already up," Carlos replies. "Get out of the bed. You said yourself you didn't have anything to do... today." He delivers "today" the same way she had said it to him the day before.

Even though Shannon is sitting up by now, she chirps, "I am not up, and I said that I didn't have anything to do *yesterday*."

Faking bewilderment, Carlos responds, "Is that what you said? Anyway, you're going to need to eat at some point. Why not with me? I'll have you back home in time to catch the morning church service."

Church? Shannon hasn't stepped foot in a church since she lived in her parents' house. "That's okay. Thanks for the offer."

"What a shame. I was hoping to enjoy one last meal with you before I leave this afternoon."

This rouses her. *He's leaving?* Shocked at the disappointment she feels, she refuses nonetheless. *He's just a temporary plaything. Get it together, girl.*

"Carlos, I just don't feel like going."

"Alright, then," he says, giving in. "Enjoy your rest."

He hangs up.

Shannon plops back onto her pillows and closes her eyes. *Maybe I should have gotten up*, she ponders, recognizing a hint of foreign remorse. The phone vibrates in her hand and "Blocked Number" illuminates on the screen. Secretly pleased, she answers.

"Here's your last chance," Carlos offers, not waiting for a greeting.

Tucking the corner of her lower lip under her upper teeth, Shannon groans. *Apparently, I've met someone more stubborn and persistent than I am.*

"You know—fine!" she concedes. "But, I'm meeting you there."

"Le Ivoire Petit. 15025 Piedmont. Let's say... eight-thirty?"

"Yeah. Okay."

They disconnect. Shannon rolls out of bed for a quick shower, wondering why she continues to entertain his advances and determines that today will be the last occasion she does.

Before dressing this time, she searches for the location he'd given her on her phone and along with the map appears a picture of the swanky looking cafe. She decides against her typical V-neck shirt and jeans. Instead, she pulls on some black jeggings, tucks in a white, button-down, long-sleeved shirt, and dons a gray and black tailored vest. Clipping her long, thick curls off her neck, she grabs her black, low-cut Chucks, her purse, and her coat. With Gina's car keys in hand, she heads for the front door.

Carlos is waiting for her outside in the public parking lot when she arrives. She greets him jovially as soon as he opens her car door. "I figured I'd better join you for breakfast before you harassed me to tears."

"You're a smart lady," he quips, gesturing toward the restaurant. "This way."

As they walk toward the French cafe, they pass a storefront window with a multitude of snow globes on display. Shannon stops abruptly and stoops to marvel at them.

"I take it you have an affinity for these... shaky things," Carlos remarks.

"I absolutely love snow globes. They remind me of warm and cozy holidays in front of the fire, and family and friends, and you know, good times," she confesses.

Carlos remains silent, watching her. She stands up, and they proceed to the cafe. A thin man appearing to be in his mid-twenties stands somewhat anxiously by the door of the entrance. He gives Carlos a spirited nod and grins broadly at Shannon as he holds the door open for them. "Enjoy!" he tells them energetically.

They enter the eclectic eatery which Shannon soon learns specializes in French African cuisine. The place is empty and minimally staffed, giving off the impression the establishment was opened solely for the two of them.

Accorded carte blanche, Carlos selects a specific table with a nice view of the avenue and moves to pull out a chair for Shannon.

Rigidly, she waves him off. "I got it. Thanks."

In a deliberate over-reaction, Carlos snatches back his hands, holding them up emphatically as if he doesn't want any trouble. Shannon smirks, but appears to Carlos to be a little embarrassed, making him wonder why she's determined to be so independent.

After ordering salt cod beignets, omelets and caramelized banana and mango tarts, they discuss unique food palettes and traveling around the world. This segues into Shannon sharing her past as a sibling-less army brat unable to grow any real roots for the first part of her youth.

"My parents had me late in life, so fortunately my dad retired before I reached high school. I could finally start making some real friends."

In turn, Carlos talks about his life growing up in Cuba.

"When we were teens, my brothers and I did all sorts of things. We would torture animals, steal cars—"

"Whaat!?"

"Oh, yes," he continues, "I wasn't a good kid. I'm probably going to pay for it whenever I have some of my own."

"You're kidding me. You don't have any children?"

"Why do you ask like that is so hard to believe?" Carlos crosses his arms and leans back against his chair with finesse.

"I mean, a good looking guy like you who seems to be doing well in life..." She trails off intentionally.

"If good looks are a prerequisite then I don't want to know how many offspring you have running around." He adds quickly, "Yes, I do want to know. How many?"

Shannon indulges him by holding up a goose egg.

"Why don't *you* have any?" Carlos asks.

"Mmm, not in the cards, I guess."

The conversation takes a serious turn when Carlos shares his mother's untimely death and how it was for him as the third of six kids. "My only sister, the second oldest of our bunch, eventually became very mothering of us all after our mom passed. And then our stepmother arrived on the scene."

Shannon gapes as Carlos confides how his stepmother took an interest in him as a pre-teen, ultimately coercing him into being intimate with her, until his suspicious sister caught them one day and blew the whistle.

"What did your father do?"

"He got rid of her and never said a word to me about anything."

"Did you two start having problems after that?"

"No. In fact, I think we got closer."

"Wow."

"Indeed, Ms. Moore, I've seen a lot of things in my lifetime to dismantle the innocence of childhood."

"I'm so sorry. I can't stand to hear of children growing up like that," Shannon says ruefully.

"All of it made me who I am," he asserts. "I think I turned out extraordinary. I'm not crazy or dysfunctional. At least, I don't think. Hopefully, you'll say the same about me one day."

His smile is magnetic, and Shannon giggles, a nerve-racking reaction far beyond her customary disposition.

"So, you say you like snow globes because they remind you of warm and fuzzy family time during the holidays. Is that what growing up in your household was like?" Carlos inquires, shifting the spotlight to Shannon.

"Certainly wasn't like that for me," she begins, the painful memories evoked by his question easily wiping away her giddiness. "Unlike you, my dad and I didn't get along. He kicked me out as soon as I turned eighteen."

Carlos' brow furrows. "Really? Why?"

Tussling with the temptation to hide the truth, Shannon rubs her earlobe. "We... couldn't agree on the type of people I wanted to date." At Carlos' dumbfounded expression, she punctuates, "That's right. Haven't seen my dad—or my mom—in seventeen years."

"I'm sorry to hear *that*," he says. "Such a long time to be at odds about childhood choices. Are you still trying to date the same hoodlums?"

Here it comes. The game breaker. Having enjoyed his company immensely these past couple of days, she is strikingly sad. She gets ready to confess her sexual preference just as the waitress arrives with their food. Carlos turns his attention to their order, and Shannon decides, *If he inquires further, I'll tell him.*

The waitress leaves. Carlos asks, "So, you don't even know if your parents are still around?"

"Nope."

"Have you thought about paying them a visit?"

"Actually, I have thought about it a few times, but... there's a lot of pride and hatred between us."

Carlos studies her. "I am familiar with both," he says, and much to her hidden gratitude, he changes the subject.

They consume their delicious delicacies, chit-chatting about a variety of topics until Carlos playfully feigns concern at having awakened her.

"You would've missed all of this," he teases, before regretfully cutting their time short once again. "Ms. Moore, I have to take off, and unfortunately, I cannot be late this time."

"You're always ending the fun," Shannon declares.

"If you'll tolerate me another time, I promise to drag out the fun as long as you can handle it."

Feeling her face flush, Shannon takes a sip of water and quashes the thoughts that his statement just awakened in her mind.

Okay. So, I'm out of control and should definitely keep my distance from this guy, she thinks as Carlos regards her curiously.

They rise to leave, and to Shannon's surprise the same person who assisted them outside the restaurant joins them when they exit the doors. The man is all smiles and jitters, and he shrugs away a nervous, low-grade electrocution every few feet. She turns to Carlos.

"Is he with you? I thought he worked for the restaurant."

"Yes, he's with me," he says.

Assuming the guy is his bodyguard, Shannon perceives Carlos may be someone famous she's unaware of. She clicks the remote's unlock button when Gina's car comes into view, preparing to make a quick departure. *If he is famous, I don't need to be seen in public with him. That's a sure-fire way to get caught.*

Carlos opens the car door, and Shannon slides behind the wheel. *Don't try anything, dude.*

He squats beside her seat.

She offers him her hand. "It was worthwhile getting up. Thanks for breakfast."

In silence, Carlos takes her hand into his much larger one. He brushes his thumb gently across her knuckles and in spite of her resistance, lifts them to his soft lips. A sensation shoots between Shannon's legs, making her thighs contract and knees meet. Her narrowed eyes swing upward and connect with his.

"Whoa, now," she warns, searching his face for recognition.

Carlos' mouth moves to one side in contemplation as Shannon reclaims her hand. *Yep. He saw my reaction.* She gives her earlobe a tweak.

"Enjoy the rest of your day, Ms. Moore. And please...drive safely." In full grin, he closes the door.

Homeward-bound, Shannon mulls over the events of the past few days, unable to deny her intrigue with Carlos. *Who am I fooling? It's attraction—an oddity considering I haven't had any desire to date a man since freshman year in college.*

She reflects on the last time she and that Alpha Phi Lothario tried having sex and winces. It was a catastrophe, culminating with clumsy groping and nothing more, and she broke it off with him a few days later. Shannon pulls into the driveway, purposing to downplay this allure with Carlos as simply a product of rebound.

She's unsuccessful. Curiosity veers her straight to her computer. "Okay, Carlos Antonio Romero, let's see if you're on the World Wide Web," she says aloud, typing into the search engine.

Aware that his name is too common to narrow effectively, she takes a chance anyway to see if she will stumble across a nugget. As expected, a myriad of social media profiles, articles, and pictures show up. She browses entries with photos, but none are a match. One particular article about a venture capitalist does catch her eye, but since it contains no photos, she passes it over.

I'll check him out at work. Wait—What does it matter anyway? I'm 'bout to end this stringing him along the next time he calls. If he calls.

***

By Monday evening, Shannon is so bored she lounges on the sofa ferreting her hair for split ends, snipping off the ones she finds individually. *Two days left to go on this raggedy vacation and not one exciting idea to snag my interest.*

Strangely, the more time passes, the more her thoughts roam to Carlos and what he's doing or if she will hear from him again. This time around, she's hoping she will.

Gina calls instead.

"Hey, girl! I'm at the airport. Think I can get a ride home?" she asks in her chipper, extroverted fashion.

"If you would've told me when you were coming back, I could've been there to pick you up. I'm in the middle of something," Shannon lies.

"It's all good," Gina says, deflecting. "I'll see you when you get here. Delta."

The line goes dead.

She is so presumptuous, like I'm just gonna drop everything for her, Shannon ruminates. *I should leave her tail out there.*

Nevertheless, twenty minutes later Shannon arrives at the airport. Gina hops in the driver's seat and immediately starts complaining.

"You been drivin' my car? Look all these miles you put on here," she says, her distinct, high-pitched, lazy drawl grating on Shannon's nerves.

She looks at Gina. "How you been? Good. How 'bout you? Good, thanks."

Gina rolls her eyes and flips back the blond highlighted bangs of her short hair. "Whatever! I ain't gone let you ruin the wonderful time I just had."

Shannon stares at the narcissist next to her. "I'm so over you."

"What the hell does that mean?" Gina demands.

Ordinarily, Shannon would tell her off, engage in an argument and deliver scathing remarks, but in her epiphany, she marvels, *I have nothing left to say.*

It only takes about a day of Shannon's silent treatment to pass before Gina accuses her of cheating and not acting right. "You so nonchalant and distant. You never even asked me what I was doing in Hawaii," she complains, trying to instigate a fight.

Keeping her lips buttoned, Shannon practically locks herself in the bedroom, hardly able to endure the wait until she can return to work. *In less than thirty-nine hours and twelve minutes.*

***

Thursday afternoon, Shannon revs her lime green and pearl-white Kawasaki Ninja ZX Supersport into the station's parking lot and backs it into the stall. She dismounts and secures her helmet to the bike just as Gohmes ambles toward the entrance doors in her direction.

"What have we here! Excited about coming back to work?" he greets her.

He has no idea how much so. "Yeah, yeah. I'll meet you inside," she grumbles, sneaking in a smile as she gathers her belongings.

Ritually, Shannon stops by the detective's desk area first to say, "Hello" to Officer Bryne, one of the ladies who picks up calls to the department. Often, when Shannon is starting her shift, Officer Bryne is getting off, and since she likes to leave "a few minutes early," many times Shannon doesn't catch her. She hopes that's not the case today.

In Shannon's estimation, Officer Bryne is one of the sweetest ladies on the planet. Elderly and deeply southern, "Mama Bryne" as she's lovingly called, greets everyone with a warm smile and a big hug whether you are a friend or a stranger. Despite the negativity she's surrounded by on the job, somehow she manages to keep a positive attitude. Shannon craves that type of energy so lacking around her, especially today, which is why she came in early.

Packing her bedazzled eyeglass case into her pocketbook, Bryne greets Shannon in her motherly way. "Hi, Baby!"

Shannon soaks up her hug. "You getting ready to head out?"

"Yes, Baby. In a few minutes, I am gone!" Mama Bryne bats her extended eyelashes, stylish even in uniform.

"Shoot, I wish I was leaving, too. And I'm just getting here."

"You'll be okay. Just keep yo' eyes open out there and keep doing the wonderful job you do. You have a good heart and God's favor is still on you," she says, glowing from the inside out. "He's the One blesses you, Baby. Remember that."

Shannon's head bobs politely on the way to her desk.

Their dialogue is pretty much the same every time, but it's sincere. Mama Bryne makes it no secret that she fervently prays for Shannon. Occasionally, she even invites her to her church. Shannon never takes her up on it, typically responding with a non-committal, "One day." Even with Shannon's own admission that she has been away from church for too long, Mama Bryne never pressures her, only encourages, "Okay, Baby. Just come on back, hear?"

The unopened case files filter back into focus as Shannon stares in front of her. She doesn't feel like pursuing criminals today. Truth be told, she really just wanted to get away from the apartment. Her partner, noticing her lackluster attitude, slams some more papers onto her desk.

"Come on, let's get to it! Spa time is over!" he barks.

Shannon throws her pen at him. "I was right at a breakthrough, Gohmes. Now, you'll have to figure out the next move all by yourself 'cause I just lost my train of thought, jerk!"

"Yo, Moore!" Detective Robbins walks by her desk, swirling his freshly refilled coffee mug. "Taking another vacation already?"

Gohmes cracks up, his rotund belly bouncing at each guffaw.

"Robbins, how're those knuckles feelin'?" Shannon retorts. "That whuppin' you got from the Captain over that PCD had to hurt. By the way, thanks for screwing up while I was off."

Several snorts echo around Robbins as he tries to maintain a straight face. He knows it was funny and grapples for a riposte.

"How was your eleventh vacation of the year?" he chides.

"None of your business. As usual."

Robbins struts to his area, his coffee cup carefully poised while his eyes plot retribution.

"Why you so private? He wants to *know*. Tell the man," Gohmes taunts, grabbing his coat from his chair as Shannon sniffs. "We got a follow up filed yesterday. Let's go interview some witnesses." He looks at Robbins, still within earshot. "There will be no protocol violations on *this* team."

Shannon high-fives Gohmes, and they head for the squad car.

Formalities

[4]

Nearly assaulted by a suspect during an interrogation, Shannon sits tensely on her sofa sipping a Caramel Macchiato from Starbucks. The apartment is silent and dark, just like she likes it when she's trying to relax. With February underway and Shannon back to her stressful, never-ending, daily investigative grind, she concludes it's not the job that's most distressing. It's the tension at home.

At least Gina stays away from the apartment most of the time, she thinks, happy for *some* reprieve. Having to constantly ward off the woman's unfounded accusations, caustic tirades, and dramatic, public flare-ups is both mentally and physically draining. It's because of such repeated spectacles that Shannon has to give up her beloved apartment in the first place. After the last complaint, the landlord made it crystal clear there would be no lease renewal. Frankly, Shannon couldn't blame him.

She pushes out her angry, negative thoughts, and markedly, her mind drifts to fond memories of Carlos instead. Almost a week has passed since their last encounter. Shannon is doubtful he'll call again.

In the midst of wishing she had held onto his business card, the phone startles her out of her reverie. The number is blocked. Anticipative, Shannon answers, and Carlos' greeting envelopes her like a euphoric hug. She sits upright, but downplays her excitement.

"I was just thinking about you. Literally."

His reply is seductive. "I love that I'm in your thoughts."

"Well, I can see I was on your mind first."

Carlos lets out a lengthy, rich laugh, then offers a proposal. "We've had breakfast and lunch together. Now, it's time to have dinner. I have to warn you, though. It's a last minute invitation."

He informs Shannon of the small function he must attend that evening. "I would be honored if you would join me. I have to be there for some networking, but I'm more interested in having dinner with you."

Without any of the resistance of the past, she accepts, grateful she had taken off a half day. For some bizarre reason, she agrees to let him pick her up at her apartment—on the condition that she meet him at the car, of course.

While locking the apartment door, Shannon checks out the limousine waiting in the front. As she crosses the lawn's walkway, the same man seen twice previously with Carlos exits the front passenger side and opens the rear door. Carlos steps out to greet her. He's dressed to the nines.

Having been told to wear jeans, Shannon blurts, "You did it to me again! This is obviously not a jeans affair."

"Don't worry."

"I'm not going," she says and turns to go back.

Carlos stops her. "Not so fast—"

"Oh, no. I don't own anything that formal, and I'm not going to be embarrassed tonight."

"I've got you covered. Get in." Shannon hesitates, a quizzical look on her face. "Trust me."

Taking a chance, she climbs inside and is alarmed to see someone else sitting on the opposite side. He is also dressed formally, but it doesn't disguise his bearish demeanor.

"Oh. I didn't expect anyone else to be in here," Shannon remarks, distrustful of their intentions. Hoping she hasn't made a mistake getting into the car, she sits on the edge of the seat making quick assessments in the event she has to take someone down.

Sensing her uneasiness, Carlos introduces her to his party. "This is my brother, Ocho. He works with me, and up front—the guy at the door—is my brother, Beto."

Beto turns slightly and waves at Shannon through the interior window. Ocho just looks at her. The brothers hardly resemble each other.

Carlos calls out to the driver, "Adam?"

"Where to, Jefe?"

"5th Avenue," Carlos instructs as he pulls out his phone. He informs someone named Violet, "We're on our way."

The limo slows to a stop in front of a small, stylized boutique. The sign above reads, "5th Avenue Designs." An older, poshly dressed, sun-scorched woman opens the shop for Carlos, Shannon and Ocho to enter, then locks the curtained door behind them. Ocho surveys the room casually and sits down on a cushioned velvet love seat while Carlos introduces Shannon to Violet, the shop owner.

After a few inquiries, she begins fitting her from head to toe, selecting all articles including shoes and accessories. Having never experienced anything like this, Shannon doesn't know how to act. Carlos is thrilled and takes immense pleasure in intervening.

When Violet reaches for Shannon's hair, he directs, "Leave it pulled loosely back the way she has it. I like it like that."

"Oh, come on. Seriously?" Shannon asks.

"Absolutely."

Reluctantly, Violet heeds his wishes, but not without first tweaking a few hairs into place here and there. She leaves the two bantering by the counter and disappears into a rear storage area. Although the hour is getting late, Carlos doesn't seem to mind.

Shannon voices her concern. "This is becoming more than a notion. At this rate, we may miss the dinner entirely."

"This is much more enjoyable," Carlos insists. He spots Violet returning with the makeup kit she had been searching for, and immediately discourages the need. "Also not necessary! She's already outshining anyone that will be there."

"Pah!" Shannon and Violet exclaim simultaneously, neither one buying the line. Both boisterously insist that she needs makeup.

Overruled, Carlos continues to intrude, picking up a random lipstick tube. He hands it to Violet. "Here. That's all she needs."

Snatching the tube of midnight blue lipstick from his hand, Violet's eyes widen and she shoos him off in her gravelly voice, "Away! So I can work!"

Forty-five minutes later, the shop owner swings the dressing room curtains apart for the reveal. Shannon steps into the room clothed in a sleeveless, knee-length, lace sheath dress by Valentino, the delicate lace-overlay bodice framing her neckline with charm while the daring tangerine color complements her skin tone exceptionally. She is stunning.

Carlos' eyes gleam as he bows with flair. "Wow," he utters, transfixed on Shannon. Violet clears her throat.

He turns to her. "Violet, I think I've lost my words."

"Not likely," she grumbles.

Carlos turns back to Shannon. "Wow! You are dazzling. I didn't think it possible you could look any better than you did before. Violet, well done. Well done!"

Violet waves them away. "Carry on before you miss the reception."

Taking Shannon by the hand, Carlos grins. "Let's roll."

The event turns out to be a political soiree with quite a few power players and government officials that Shannon readily recognizes, many of whom seem irritated by Carlos' late arrival. However, they quickly mask their feelings and make no mention of it to him. It appears Carlos' presence here is particularly revered.

An announcement is made. "Ladies and gentlemen, we will begin shortly. Please, take your seats."

As they meander through the crowd, Shannon's conscience screams she's out of her league. She leans in to Carlos and whispers, "I see you like to grossly understate things."

Placing a guiding hand on the small of her back—a touch that ignites Shannon yet again—he inclines her ear. "I didn't want you to not come or to start worrying about what was in your closet or being uncomfortable. Relax. We are going to have a good time. I'm not concerned about these people. Neither should you be."

Some introductions, some schmoozing, some business discussions. Throughout, Carlos has a way of making her feel comfortable. In the crowd, Shannon spots the same couple Carlos had been with at the airport on the evening they met. She points them out.

"You remember them?" he asks, rubbing his chin. "So then... you were watching *me*." He grins.

"If that's what you want to believe, go right ahead."

Shannon enjoys watching Carlos' grin convert into full delight and suspects he has never had a cavity in his life. He takes her hand and says, "Let me introduce you to one of Delaware's finest Supreme Court justices and his gracious wife..."

Politely, they break away and discuss a few of the conversations held and some notable reactions. Several people clearly desire to earn Carlos' support or business partnership, but he humorously expresses his disinterest to Shannon, and they stifle more laughter at the inside jokes.

A second announcement disrupts the hum of dialogue in the room. "Once again, ladies and gentlemen, kindly take your seats. Dinner is now being served."

Hampered by social interactions, Carlos and Shannon eventually locate their table. As they dine, Shannon occasionally inquires who this or that person is and finds Carlos' characterizations of them hilarious. She's at ease, and the fun is genuine.

Across the room, a man looks in their direction often, garnering Shannon's attention. His hair, eyeglasses, and overall style fail to blend, and he makes eye contact with her unintentionally one too many times.

"Who's the nervous guy with the toupee that can't pass up a drink tray?"

"Him, I don't know," Carlos answers, but his tensing jawline doesn't elude her. Discreetly, she joins him in keeping an eye on the man. Their conversation lulls.

"Excuse me for a moment," Carlos tells Shannon abruptly. He disappears from her sight into the crowd of people who have yet to take a seat. Vacillating between scoping out the guy and panning the room for signs of Carlos, she finally pinpoints her escort talking to Beto and another man resembling house security. Both men nod in affirmation before dispersing.

Wondering what the dialogue was about, Shannon watches Carlos make his way back. He is detained by casual greetings and a few conversationalists, but at last, returns to the table.

"Some people don't know when to stop talking," he tells her, replacing the cloth napkin onto his knee. "Hopefully, we will be able to continue our meal uninterrupted."

Picking up his fork, Carlos proceeds to eat without any explanation or excuse for why he stepped away. Shannon takes a bite.

"Now, it's my turn to be curious... especially being here at this function. What do you do, Carlos? What has you flying from place to place so much and hobnobbing with big shots?"

Carlos finishes chewing, then takes another forkful. Continuing to chew, his expression is that of someone carefully considering his words. He swallows.

"I'm an entrepreneur. I own a few businesses, some of which involve international contracts. I don't typically talk about them when I first meet someone, for various reasons, but I guarantee, if you stay in my life long enough, you'll know." A pause. "I must admit, one of the many things that intrigued me about you is that it took you this long to ask me what I do. I usually get that question within the first hour of meeting someone."

Pricked by his arrogance, Shannon asks, "Is it poor etiquette to ask what someone does for a living?"

Carlos' retort is swift, his intonation difficult to decipher. "I think it is. *I* don't want to know what I do. Why should you?"

Shannon sets down her fork in exasperation.

"Smarty pants," he states. "You must know that wasn't what I was implying." Laying his knife and fork across his plate, he redirects. "What about you? What do *you* do for a living?"

Shannon is reluctant to share about her own line of work, but she retorts, "Oh, I'm not so complicated. I'm an officer of the law."

A strange look passes briefly across Carlos' face. Taken aback, he sizes her up. "Really? You're not kidding me?"

Not liking the direction their dialogue is taking, Shannon grows more agitated. "What? Is that a bad thing, too? To be a cop?"

Carlos studies her for a minute, and her defense mechanism propels her to scoff, "Hmm. I usually get one of two responses from people when I tell them I'm a cop: apprehension that I might arrest them for something or hope that I'm going to get them out of paying some tickets. But this one is new: Appall. I guess you don't fraternize with blue collar workers very much."

Carlos reaches for her hand and calmly declares, "Appalled? I hope I wasn't looking appalled. It's just very hard for me to envision such a beautiful señorita brandishing a gun and chasing after bad guys. I can't process it. And please don't try to intimate some socio-economic prejudice on my behalf. If that were true, I would've never tried to talk to you. You and I both know you were homeless. On the street. Begging for my attention."

Shannon softens at his exaggeration and contagious humor begins to bubble up between them. The tension eases, but Carlos' homeless comment does remind her of someone. She looks around the room. A few obstinate attendees still mill about, but most have obediently claimed their places among the tables. Servers busily make their rounds in preparation for the next course. However, the man tossing back drinks is nowhere in sight.

"Hmm. Mr. Toupee seems to have disappeared," she comments.

"Really? Maybe he needed to be somewhere else."

Shannon finds it strange that Carlos doesn't bother to look around, especially after having appeared so discomfited when she'd initially brought the man to his attention. Riveted on Shannon, he waits for the server to finish clearing his plate before continuing to speak.

"What precinct are you out of?"
"Southwest."

Carlos contemplates her response briefly. "That's Jaxson Parks' division, isn't it?"

Shannon is surprised. "You know our Chief of Police?"

"Why does that shock you?"

"Well, for one, you don't live here and two, you didn't strike me as one who follows police politics. A lot of residents here can't tell me who our chief is."

Their server places dessert before them.

"I've known Jax for a few years," Carlos states. "Have you ever met him?"

"Actually, I have. I know him better than most."

"You must be a pretty high ranking officer then to be buddy buddy with the Chief of Police."

Shannon explains, "Long before the military or police force, he and my father were good friends. He's actually my godfather and really more like a father to me than my dad—you know, with my dad disowning me. Not many people know this since I've always wanted to avoid any rumors and accusations of nepotism. You can rest assured all my achievements are my own."

Carlos raises his eyebrows at her commentary, and she clams up. *Girl, you just got too cocky and shared too much.* Not many people know half of what Carlos now knows about her, and she really has no idea of the extent of his connections. She hopes her work environment won't start getting messy.

"Tell me about that," he says. "What are some of those achievements?"

Shannon restrains her loose lips. "Mmm... I don't want to sit here and talk about that. I can't stand promoting myself."

"Okay. Well, tell me about your typical day, what it's like, etcetera."

"What's it like? You're basically on call 24-7. It's non-stop. You have to be ready to move on a lead at any time. It's challenging, dangerous, but rewarding when you put that creep that, say, took some innocent child's life behind bars. I've always had an affinity for the daring, for speed, for justice, so it's a perfect fit for me."

"What about safety and being around for family?"

Shannon smirks. "Never given that much thought."

Enlightened, Carlos asks, "What other unusual qualities would I be surprised to know about you?"

There is one in particular he'd truly be shocked to learn, but I won't dare share it with him now. "I think that's pretty much it."

Feedback reverberates from a rustling microphone, causing most of the eyes in the room to search for its location.

"May I have everyone's attention, please," the host petitions from her elevated lectern. "On behalf of all the committees represented here, we'd like to thank you for coming and do hope that you have enjoyed your dinner. At this time, we would also like to thank a few key people for their tremendous financial support and advisement over this past year. Dr. Moskowitz, Mr. Burnside, and Mr. Romero, would you please come to the stage."

Carlos rises. Surprised, Shannon turns excitedly to cheer him on. He winks at her and makes his way through the applause to center stage, converging with the other man and woman at the podium.

The host presents each honoree with a plaque, and when it's Carlos' turn to step to the mic, she says an immensely favorable blurb about his business savvy, generous benefaction, and integrity of character. Shannon is impressed. *Now, the interactions, the responses, the hovering sycophants make sense.*

Returning, Carlos places the plaque on the table and reaches for her hand. "Why don't we take a walk?"

"I guess congratulations are in order," Shannon remarks along their stroll into the rotunda. "You could have told me."

"That's no fun." His eyes meet hers.

Melodic notes from an accomplished pianist waft over their ears as they near her vicinity. Without warning, Carlos pulls Shannon to him and begins to dance.

"Oh, no, no! I'm not a dancer," she exclaims, trying to scooch away.

"You don't have to be. Just follow me." To the pianist, he requests, "¡Rumba, por favor!"

The pianist transitions. The dancing starts off playful, with Carlos leading Shannon in graceful Latin dance moves, spins, and dips, but then he draws her close.

Stirrings she has never felt before—with anyone—tingle through her body. His firm, masculine embrace feels undeniably right and so secure. His face is close to hers, his mouth inviting. He's staring at her succulent, shapely lips...

Realizing the precarious position she's in, Shannon grips his biceps anxiously. Forgoing the kiss, Carlos spins her back out and comes up from behind to whisper in her ear. "Don't think I didn't want to," he teases. "But your eyes got as big as a school girl, and it made me nervous."

Laughing through her embarrassment, Shannon relaxes, but she avoids his tickled gaze. *This will DEFINITELY be the last occasion that I entertain his advances,* Shannon declares inwardly. Not even her inner voice is convinced.

It's obvious they are increasingly enjoying one another's company. As the evening comes regrettably to an end, the couple move back into the main hall and prepare to leave. Saying a few goodbyes, they pick up their coats from the cloakroom and are escorted by Beto and Ocho to the limousine.

The vehicle brakes in front of Shannon's apartment, and the moment she thanks Carlos for a wonderful night, her thoughts collide with reality. *I should've figured he would insist on walking me to the door.*

Unsuccessful at persuading him otherwise, Shannon exits the limo, searching discreetly for an indication that Gina may be home. By the time they halt in front of her door, her nerves are frayed, due both to the quickening desire she's feeling for Carlos and the fear of being exposed.

Hurriedly, Shannon says, "Okay, I gotta go now."

Carlos leans forward, breathes "Goodnight" in her ear, and presses a tender kiss on her cheek. He backs away. Shannon scoots behind the door, thankful for an evening that ended well.

Later that night, she receives a text. "I hope you enjoyed yourself tonight."

She types back. "It was terrible. Please don't ever invite me out again, Prince Charming ;)"

Immediately, a new notification pops up. "That's King. King Charming."

King he very well could be, but I am no Cinderella by any means.

Internal Affairs

[5]

What had begun as an act of spite and a careless diversion is now throwing Shannon into an emotional tailspin. Restlessly, she sinks into her pillow, her mind telling her to leave Carlos alone, that her head hadn't been in the right place and she had taken her "game" too far, but she is unable to get off the ride. She has fallen for this guy, drawn to him by something more powerful than her logic, and if she would be honest with herself, she'd admit that she wants to experience all of him—every part.

Inside his hotel room, Carlos finishes his text and swivels around in the bar chair, deep in thought. This new bit of information about Shannon has him between the proverbial rock and hard place. Dating a cop would pose some inherent difficulties for him that he'd prefer not to deal with. They are from two different worlds, and although she assimilates into his world nicely now, the likelihood that a relationship between them would survive in the future is slim to none. Still, he cannot stifle this overwhelming desire to pursue her. He calls Ocho into the room. "Dig up everything you can on Shannon Moore," he instructs. "She's a cop in the Southwest division."

At work, Gohmes inquires, "You're in a good mood. What's been up with you?"

"Why you always in my business, Gohmes?" Shannon deflects, unable to refute feeling in wonderfully high spirits from the night before.

Gohmes, her partner for the last three years and probably the only person on her job thus far she'd ever consider confiding in, smacks his gum, itching for the scoop. Nonetheless, she can't bring herself to share this latest adventure. *Couldn't explain it if I tried.*

More than intrigued by Carlos, Shannon is energized, and evidently it is showing. Every day, she anticipates a call from him, but, as life would have it, five long days drag by without a word.

***

Carlos rolls his chair away from his desk and listens intently as his sources report their findings.

"She's an undercover Detective Sergeant in a specialized homicide unit," Ocho explains repugnantly. "Not just a cop like she said."

She's low-level rank, Carlos thinks. *Not a concern. But still, if she was trying to be deceptive...* "Go on."

He listens stoically as the brothers continue. The next piece of information is far more difficult to accept or dismiss. To his shock and dismay (and his brothers' amusement) they divulge the rumor that Shannon is also a lesbian. Carlos looks at them suspiciously, waiting in vain for the "just joking."

"The story is," Beto elaborates, "she hasn't been known to date anyone since she's been on the force, and the only person she's really ever seen with is her—" He draws quotes with his fingers. "Roommate."

Carlos' skin begins to crawl at the possibility that he was conned. "So then, she could have been a plant for me to meet," Carlos presumes. "And if that's the case, who put her on me?" Silently vowing to find out, he tells his crew, "Keep an eye on her."

Ocho blurts out, "We're wasting time on this chick! My guys have better things to do than be chasing—"

"I said, keep an eye on her."

Ocho looks away, but doesn't say another word.

A few days later, Carlos visits the Chief of Police. He walks boldly past Jaxson's secretary directly into his office and takes a seat before she can finish announcing his arrival. Quickly, Jaxson quells his slow to respond staff by waving them off and closing the door. He doesn't greet Carlos, not too thrilled to see him barge in unexpectedly.

"Thought I would see you at the Werlinghouse Fundraiser," Carlos says, breaking the ice.

Jaxson folds into the seat behind his desk and responds faintly, "Ahh... I was in Aruba working on... another project of interest, if you know what I mean."

Carlos is unimpressed. "We have an agreement. I provide you with the goods and services. You provide me with my income. You're not holding up your end of the bargain. I'd hate to have to end our agreement, if you know what I mean."

Tiny beads of sweat creep onto Jaxson's receding hairline. "I'm aware of that. Give me three days. I'll make good on it by then."

Carlos slams his hand down on the desk and proclaims, "Done!" Catching a subtle reaction from Jaxson out of the corner of his eye, he smooths his tie and says, "See? I'm a reasonable man. In exchange for my leniency, however, I require some information in return."

Arriving at the principal reason for his visit, Carlos looks directly into the dour facial expression opposite him. Jaxson issues a slow nod to continue. "There is an officer by the name of Shannon Moore in your precinct. What can you tell me about her?"

The lines in Jaxson's forehead deepen. "Moore? She's one of the best D2s on my squad. Highly skilled, superlative work ethic."

Carlos restates, "A Detective Sergeant."

Jaxson folds his hands in front of his face and presses his forefingers together against his lips. "Why are you asking me about her?"

"Whoa, Jax. I know you're her godfather. Let me assure you, I don't mean her any harm." Carlos chuckles and digresses, "She did say that you were like a father to her." He stares unflinchingly at Jaxson. "I'm just... intrigued. Anything I should know about her personally? Is she, let's say, secretly married?"

"Oh, I see," Jaxson says, chuckling a bit himself. He leans back into his chair, shaking his head "no." Proceeding carefully, he offers, "Married to her work. I think you'll find it very challenging to get her attention."

"I should consider myself honored then," Carlos comments. "I trust that our acquaintance has been unassisted, as well."

There's a strained silence as the two men study each other and Jaxson comprehends the implication. "I introduced her to the gun club some time ago. Anything other than her membership there is not my doing. But, I can look into it."

"She's a member of my club? Oh, this just gets better and better. I'll have to make sure she gets special privileges now that I know this," Carlos boasts. He rises to leave, and Jaxson berates himself inwardly for potentially sharing too much. He calls after Carlos.

"Wait! You said you two talked. This wasn't at the gun club?"

"No. That particular conversation was over dinner."

Jaxson's eyes bulge. "You and Detective Moore?... I'll be honest. I can't say that I approve."

"Oh, come on," Carlos retorts. "She can't be that bad."

The door closes. Jaxson hunches over the desk.

Shannon's phone vibrates as she and her partner cross-question a gang member suspected of narcotics trafficking. It's her least favorite type of interrogation, so the interruption is welcomed. Hoping it's Carlos giving her a reason to sneak away, she takes a peek and recognizes the number. It's not one that she sees often.

Shannon turns to Gohmes and excuses herself. "I gotta go. You got this."

The chief escorts Shannon into his office and closes the door. Apprehensively, Shannon inquires, "What's up?"

"I'm just checking on you. How's everything?"

"Good," Shannon replies. She waits. "I'm in the middle of an interrogation. What'd you call me in for, Chief?"

"What is going on between you and Carlos Romero?"

Shannon's breath hangs in her throat. "How do you...? Wait, what...?"

"He came in here asking about you."

Masking a smile, Shannon asks, "He did?"

"He did."

She looks at Jaxson uneasily. "So, what did you tell him?"

"I told him you're a workaholic and he probably doesn't have a chance in hell to get close to you."

Shannon continues to look at him, anticipating more.

Jaxson responds, "That was it. Your turn. How do you know him? Are you two involved in something?"

Inhaling noisily, Shannon says, "Okay. Time for me to go." She stands and heads for the door.

"Moore!"

Stopping in her tracks, she turns to look at Jaxson, who's clearly expecting an answer. Irritated at his intrusive questioning, she snaps back a response. "No. We're not."

"Then is it work related?"

"No."

"How did you meet?"

"Why are you grilling me like I'm some twelve year old?"

"I'm curious what your interest is in him."

"Interest??? Listen, Jax, if something changes, you'll be the first to know, okay?" She turns to head out.

"Be careful, Moore. Don't get involved in something you really don't want to be a part of. I mean it. And one more thing. This conversation never happened."

"Yeah," she mumbles scornfully as she wrenches the door open.

What is Jax's problem? Shannon's stomach knots at the awkwardness of their conversation. Feeling there is much more to the exchange than what was said, she returns to her desk and immediately accesses the database.

No criminal information shows up for Carlos. In fact, nothing at all shows up, as if he doesn't even exist. Shannon picks up the desk phone and dials a friend in the federal building.

"Andrew, you have a moment? I need to know everything you can pull up on this name and associated plates."

"Always have a moment for you, Sweetness," he says.

"Thanks, Drew," Shannon says and hustles to hang up before he starts.

"Hey, wait!" he calls out. "When are you going to take me to dinner?"

He tries so hard to be suave. Shaking her head, Shannon exclaims, "You never quit. Amazing."

"Well, how 'bout I take *you* to lunch?"

"Drew!"

"You can't blame a guy for trying. I'll call you back."

Shannon puts the handset back on the cradle, tittering about his dependable persistence. Too riled up about Jaxson and Carlos, she eschews returning to the interview and opens a folder on her desk, preparing to wait awhile. Not twenty minutes later, Andrew calls back.

"Uh oh. That didn't take you any time at all. You got something?" Shannon asks.

"Do I!" he retorts and proceeds to relay his findings.

Shannon hangs up the phone bewildered. *An active member of the NRA? Sanctioned dual-citizenship functionality? Multi-million dollar commodities corporation owner and stockholder?*

She's grateful there isn't any criminal activity, but this is almost worse. Now, she's battling new thoughts of intimidation. Carlos truly is way out of her league, and she has no idea why he has entertained *her* company. Concentrating at work is no longer an option, so she pulls a "Mama Bryne" and leaves "a few minutes early," a soothing Caramel Macchiato calling her name.

In Starbucks' parking lot, Shannon dismounts her bike and looks around vigilantly. Lately, she's had this eerie feeling of being watched. She hustles inside the shop and plans to take an alternate route home. Although she personally never had a disgruntled ex-con come after her in retaliation, she knows of one too many detectives who have.

Later in the evening, with Carlos at the forefront of her mind, Shannon can no longer resist picking up the phone. She dials the number from the text she'd received from him previously. His call service answers. She hangs up and shoots him a text instead.

"I'd love to hear your voice. Having a rough week. CMB." After a beat, she adds, "I think I miss you," and presses send before she can change her mind.

She never receives a response.

***

"I spoke with both Detective Moore and the Division Captain—discreetly, of course. She doesn't appear to be involved in anything work related regarding you," Jaxson contends.

"That's good news," Carlos replies.

"You'll hear from me if anything changes." The chief hangs up.

So far, none of the tails on Shannon have revealed anything questionable, either, Carlos ponders. *In fact, she and the roommate appear to cross paths like ships in the night.*

He finishes reading Shannon's text and turns off the display. His instincts tell him that their blossoming feelings are sincere, but his mind isn't convinced. It will take a lot more proof for him to let go of the reins. It's evident he didn't get to where he is by being careless. *If our acquaintance is indeed a ruse, I will see just how far she is willing to go.*

Gifted

[6]

On Valentine's Day, Gina hands Shannon a fairly large package wrapped in plain brown paper. "What's this?" Shannon asks, standoffishly.

Gina shrugs and snaps back, "I dunno! It ain't from me."

Shannon scans the box. There is no return address listed, just her name handwritten neatly across the top. "Who delivered it?"

"Some guy!"

Shaking her head at Gina in disgust, Shannon holds the box closer to her ear. She is leery of opening it, especially with her heightened sense of being followed, and Gina's lack of cooperation isn't helping. *It would be so much easier if she would just give me some details about the delivery person.*

As Shannon stands there staring at the package, Gina backs away.

"Yep. It might be a bomb. Wouldn't surprise me."

"Being blown to smithereens would seem like Heaven compared to being here with YOU."

Flashing a fake smile, Shannon carries the package to the bedroom. She locks the door and bravely tears the wrapping.

Inside is a beautifully decorated box with a note of instruction taped to the top lid. It reads,

Shannon,
When I think of you...

Signed capital C, scribble, S.

Squealing with delight (and relief), Shannon lifts the lid from the box. Inside are four boxes labeled with instructions. She opens them in order.

The first box reveals a triangle shaped snow globe with beveled edges along the top of one side. At the bottom is a narrow pie-slice base with an inset magnet on both sides. The contents of the next two boxes are seemingly identical. The last triangular globe, however, has no water or snow inside it, just a lone cubic zirconium.

Intrigued by its unique design, Shannon connects the four pieces as labeled, forming a large square diamond. She shakes it. As the snow settles, Shannon notices the particles magnetically pool on the flat surface inside each of three sections of the diamond.

She takes a closer look at the entire globe and reads the words spelled out. "I Think...You Are... A..."

Shannon gasps at the fourth section. *Is that a real diamond?* Discovering a button on the base beneath, she presses it. The section opens. Carefully, she removes the jewel, and as she pulls, the chain it's attached to snakes to the surface. Holding the globe up for further inspection, she reads the inscription broken up along each section of the base. "So... should... everyone... else. 1.00 carat."

It takes away her breath. Never in life had anyone listened to her likes and customized a gift just for her. Clasping the necklace around her neck, she repeats the message aloud. "I think you are a diamond. So should everyone else..."

Overwhelmed, she calls Carlos and can hardly speak when the call service lady asks for her message. Within a few minutes, he returns the call.

"Were you calling to wish me a Happy Valentine's Day?"

"Carlos..." Shannon can't find the words. "You are amazing!... It's the most thoughtful gift I've ever received."

"Gift? What are you talking about?"

"Stop, I'm very serious," she insists, not in the mood to be played with. "Thank you. Thank you very much. You have no idea how much everything about the gift means to me."

"You're welcome, Beautiful. I wish I could have been there to see you open it up. Hey, why don't you send me a selfie with it on when you get a chance?"

Shannon laughs, inhales, bites the lip.

"Listen, I gotta go," he says, pleased with himself.

She hangs up.

Not even Gina yanking on the door handle can ruin the moment.

***

Shannon rapidly finishes off a round and pauses to reload. She always seems to perform her best target practice at this gun club, perhaps because of the sense of gratitude she feels being here. The equipment is state of the art and the amenities private, allowing her to focus peacefully. *Unlike the places where the rest of my squad practices,* she gloats. *One of the perks of knowing the chief personally that I don't mind cashing in on.*

Sensing someone step beside her, she turns to look.

"Carlos! Hey!" Shannon's adrenaline surges from his presence. *What is he doing here?*

Calling the target forward, he views the placement of holes in the silhouette, then presses the control to send it back. Shannon snatches the headset from her ears in time to hear him say, "Impressive."

Dismissing the initial thoughts of being stalked, she hugs him warmly. Still, she needs to know. "What are you doing here?"

"Just checking out a few things." Noticing the necklace, he comments, "I see you're wearing it. You make it shine."

Shannon hugs him again, showing more affection than she wanted to express.

"Wow," Carlos declares playfully, but he doesn't appear his normal self. His demeanor makes her wonder what's up.

"What are you checking on?"

"You, for one." He chortles at Shannon's perplexed expression and glances at the time on his wrist. "Please, continue with your practice. I have to run. Hope to see you again soon, Señorita." A peck on the cheek and he leaves.

Shannon watches through the glass partitions as Carlos strolls down the elegant halls of the facility with Ocho leading and Beto in tow. She expected more from him, with this being the first time they'd seen each other since the dinner two weeks ago. Her mind races. *Our phone conversations have been minimal, as well. Is something different now or is it really just his busy schedule creating the distance?*

She resumes her practice on a few more sheets, but the effort is fruitless, his clean smell lingering on her clothes as a constant, stimulating distraction. On her way out, she's stopped by a staff member who beckons her to the membership desk.

"Ms. Moore, we have a new credential for you. Congratulations on your upgrade to our VIP Premier Membership." The man hands Shannon the updated card. "I'll just take that old card from you."

He waits for her to retrieve it.

"But I didn't upgrade my membership."

The staff member smiles reassuringly. "It is compliments of the owner."

"Who is the owner?"

"That would be Mr. Romero."
Shannon stands there, dazed.
"Is there something else I may help you with, Ms. Moore?"
"No. No. Thanks. Have a nice day."

Consent

[7]

Nearly the entire month of March passes like an unrelenting smear of disappointment. Gina continues to pop in and out of the apartment every so often to harass Shannon whenever and however she can, especially once she learned of Shannon's plans to part company forever at the end of the lease. It takes everything within Shannon to not lay Gina flat out each time, and she gleefully counts down the days remaining until her contract is up.

Moreover, Shannon hasn't seen or heard from Carlos since the day at the gun club. Her attempts to reach him have been unsuccessful, and, believing he has moved on, she maintains the pretense that she's not heartbroken. But the truth is, she can't shake him from her heart or mind.

I have no one else to blame but myself for letting it happen, Shannon laments, absently fondling the pendant around her neck. She makes a self-declaration that if Carlos ever calls again, he won't get past hello. *I'm done with him, too.*

However, the day he calls, he irrefutably destroys her resolve. As the palpitations in her chest fail to submit to her mind, she does manage to greet him with reservation instead of joy, at least.

"I know it probably seems like I dropped off the face of the earth these last few weeks, but my plate has been unbelievably full," he tells her. "I want you to know there hasn't been a day that's passed that I haven't thought of you. Please believe that."

"Yeah, right. I've hung around too many guys not to be able to recognize nonsense when I hear it. You couldn't've at least called, or returned my calls, or shot me a text?"

"If I told you the truth, you wouldn't buy it," Carlos asserts. "So, how about this? Allow me make it up to you. What are you doing this weekend?"

"This weekend's my birthday, so I probably will have plans."

"I see. Well... at least let me call to wish you a happy birthday. What day is it?"

"April 2nd," Shannon replies. *Don't think I'll be holding my breath waiting for your call, either.*

On April 2nd, Shannon moves about the apartment organizing her belongings and supplies. At the end of the month, she'll finally be able to move away from the crazy chick who seems to live just to make her life miserable. *And today is as good as any to start packing. So what if I haven't found a place yet, and so what if it's my birthday.*

She turns down offers from her partner and fellow officers to hang out and grab drinks, claiming she isn't in the mood. But when the evening draws near, and Carlos finally calls (as promised) to wish her a happy birthday, she reluctantly divulges her "sudden" availability.

Carlos is pleased to hear it. "I just so happen to be in town," he says, knowing he made a special trip to her city for one purpose. "I'm wondering, could you tolerate me taking you to dinner?"

As they valet park at the Ritz Carlton, Shannon eyes Carlos. "Why are we going to a hotel?"

"Don't get any ideas of trying to take advantage of me, Belleza. We are just going to *eat* in this *restaurant*. Which just so happens to be *at* the hotel where I'm staying. Let's get this straight right now."

Shannon gives her lip a little nibble and slips her hand into his as the uniformed staff welcome them to their destination.

A bottle of chilled Nonino il Moscato di Grappa arrives with grandeur to their table. Per instruction, it is uncorked and placed on the cloth. Carlos pours her a glass. Sipping the delectable grappa with ease, Shannon wants desperately to ask about her dialogue with Jaxson and her subsequent discoveries, but she knows that both subjects are out of the question. Relegated to Carlos initiating information on his own, Shannon resolves to enjoy the dinner conversation, wherever it may lead.

During a quiet moment, Carlos confesses out of the blue, "You make me smile..." He gestures to his heart. "In here."

He says that to all the ladies, I'm sure, Shannon thinks, blushing just the same. Nervously, she finishes off her latest glass and holds it out for Carlos to replenish. His is barely touched.

"It's true, Shannon. I like the way I feel when I'm with you. I feel... I can trust you." His eyes seem to search out her deepest secrets.

Shannon swallows. He pours her another. Then another.
She can't remember how many glasses she's emptied so far, but soon, he's ordering a second bottle. When it appears, the waiter places an accompanying dessert tray before them. Shannon examines the array of cannoli, custards, and cheesecakes and unwittingly puts her foot in her mouth.

"I love to bake desserts," she shares.

"You bake?"

Shannon nods confidently.

Carlos holds out his hand to the waiter. "Give us a moment, please." The tray disappears. "So, you would go into the kitchen and make something special just for me?"

"I would!"

"Really?"

To her dismay, he challenges her to prove her ability (or lack thereof) and despite her resistance, proceeds to hire out one of the smaller kitchens for an hour. After much negotiation, a member of the cooking staff provides Shannon with the ingredients and utensils she claims to need and steps aside. Utterly confounded, she registers the bind she's gotten herself into without her recipe book.

"Show me what you got," Carlos taunts.

"After all this, I reckon I must!"

Tentatively, she begins a baking adventure. She preps, guesses, mixes. He stirs. Soon, she offers Carlos a taste of the mixture from her finger. He sucks tantalizingly, sending mutual frissons throughout their bodies, then grimaces when the flavor hits him.

Confused, Shannon gives what is supposed to be an orange soufflé a try, and she too looks around frantically for something to spit into. With tears of laughter streaming down her cheeks, she tries to make excuses, but Carlos isn't going for it.

"Un-uh, that's a wrap. We don't even need to put that in the oven."

Shannon wipes her hands clean and tosses the kitchen towel into the air in surrender. Carlos fakes a move to catch the towel, but catches her into his arms instead. Unexpectedly, he pulls her close and kisses her. His lips are soft and his movement expert. She stiffens, as a wave of revelation washes over her, but quickly her lips melt instinctively into his.

The forgotten staff member clears his throat to get their attention. Shannon rapidly gathers her composure, attempting to stifle giggles at the onlooker's intrusion, while Carlos unabashedly thanks him for his service.

Ocho awaits the couple as they emerge from the restaurant, and Carlos turns to Shannon. Slowly, he rubs his supple lips together, causing her blood to surge faster. "I hope you've enjoyed your birthday, Ms. Moore. I'm certainly glad you agreed to spend part of it with me." His tone becomes more influential. "You're not ready to leave me now, are you, Belleza?"

Meeting his heated gaze with her own, Shannon isn't thinking about leaving. *I'm equating the likelihood that anything else done with you will be as amazing as that kiss was.* Having had too much to drink, she throws caution to the wind and responds with a sultry, "There is no other place I'd rather be."

Raising one eyebrow, Carlos offers Shannon the crook of his arm for support, and she intertwines hers with his.

"What does 'belleza' mean?"

"It means beauty," he says, running a finger gently along her jawline. He lifts her chin for a kiss.

Just like in the pages of a fairytale, Shannon feels as if she's floating on a cloud—albeit a tad bit wobbly.

The elevator doors open onto the floor of Carlos' suite. Ocho joins Beto waiting in the hallway, and both brothers stare at Shannon presumingly as she follows Carlos into the room. Suddenly embarrassed by the judgment she feels, she wishes she could disappear through the floor.

She promptly seeks out the bathroom. Carlos directs her to the one closest. Safely behind the door, Shannon rests her head against it fretfully. *What am I doing?*

Habitually, Carlos quickly surveys the suite, assuring no one else is inside. In the bedroom, he places his phone on the nightstand, removes the gun and holster from his leg, and stashes it in the nightstand drawer.

Shannon washes her hands and evaluates herself in the mirror. She's as nervous as a virgin about the path she's heading down and inhales deeply to settle her fluttering stomach. Fairly composed, she exits the bathroom just as Carlos walks back into the living room, pulling his dress shirt free from his slacks. Unsure of what to do next, she stands there. He winks and waits for her to do that special thing with her lip. She doesn't disappoint, admiring the subtle way he has of releasing her inhibitions.

The look in his eyes beckons her. When she approaches, he leans down to kiss her, drawing her in gradually, gently sucking each lip before transitioning into a more vigorous union. He begins backing her slowly into the bedroom, undressing her little by little. Abruptly, she stops him.

"Hold on," she says, reaching for the small of her back. Carlos tenses, his eyes transforming into distrustful slits. Shannon removes her gun. "It's okay," she assures him as she places it carefully on the dresser. *I can only image how awkward this must appear to him right now.*

He gives Shannon an inscrutable stare. Suddenly, he too reaches behind him, removes his gun, and places it on the dresser. They smirk at each other.

The last of their clothing hits the floor, freeing up every inch of their bodies for exploration and discovery. Shannon is mesmerized by the masculine perfection before her, a masterpiece surpassing Michelangelo's illustrious David. She traces her fingers along the fine, sleek hairs forming a V above Carlos' sculpted abdomen and stops at the faint birthmark right below. Similarly, his eyes devour her voluptuous hourglass lines, resting briefly on the peek-a-boo bellybutton residing in the flatland between her hills and valleys.

Their eyes meet again. Carlos guides her hand to his mouth. Pressing a kiss into her palm, he lifts her into his arms and carries her to the bed. Unhurriedly, he travels across her body, making skillful visits with his hands and tongue until every nerve-ending from her hair follicles to her toes cries out with desire—audibly.

"Shhh," Carlos whispers. "No need to invite anyone else with handcuffs to the suite."

Shannon squeezes a hand over her mouth.

In the dimness of the room, their bodies thread an illicit, hot-blooded tapestry crafted by precision and decorated with multiple climaxes Shannon didn't know existed. No desire is left unfulfilled. Ignored, Carlos' phone buzzes repeatedly on the nightstand.

***

You've got to be kidding me, Shannon thinks, the afterglow quickly fading as Carlos slides his arm from around her to reach for his phone. She watches him check the call history, dial, and have a brief conversation in Spanish. Seeing how disturbed he looks when he hangs up, she ventures, "Is something wrong?"

Absently, he responds, "Not for long."

She decides not to inquire further. "I'm thirsty. Want something to drink?"

"Water. Please."

Shannon moves to get up, but remains seated on the edge of the bed, seemingly unable to stand.

Snapping out of his preoccupation, Carlos teases, "What's the matter? Weak in the knees?"

She rises from the bed, tugging the bed sheet with her.

"Can't stand you," she mumbles.

Entering the sitting room, Shannon tries to justify her underlying uneasiness. Carlos' response to the late night call he received was both troubling and strange, almost ominous in her opinion. It wasn't so much what he said, but how he said it.

It's probably nothing, she tells herself, but to appease her nerves, she takes a quick peek through the peephole to see if the brothers are still on guard.

Seems Ocho has a solo shift now. Wondering if that was Beto who called, Shannon shakes her head dismissively, unable to comprehend the need to have bodyguards around constantly. *But, this lifestyle of the extremely wealthy is so very foreign to me anyway, why should I relate?*

She grabs a bottle of water and pours some into two glasses at the bar, concluding that with great privilege comes great sacrifice—and strange responses to phone calls, apparently.

When she returns, Carlos is sitting up in bed, holding one arm around his bent knee while the other leg rests over the side of the bed. He watches as she drags the sheet wrapped around her across the floor, then pats his hand on the mattress, motioning for her to sit between his legs.

Shannon purses her lips at his teasing expression before handing him a glass. Still clutching the sheet in front of her, she takes the seat offered and leans back into his enticing caress.

Carlos strokes her hair for awhile before brushing it forward over her right shoulder. He begins kissing her left shoulder and gently moves up her neck to her earlobe, his cool breath adding to the electrifying sensation each time he exhales. She eyes him over her tingling shoulder.

"You are... absolutely breathtaking," he declares.

"I feel the same about you."

Carlos looks away, turning to place his glass on the nightstand, and immediately Shannon's insecurities rise. *He just withdrew from the intimacy of the moment like a man who's only interested in a one night stand.*

She watches him questioningly, on the verge of turning away in disappointment, when he says, "Go ahead. I'll let you get a good look." He stretches out among the surviving pillows without inhibition, lacing his hands behind his head.

Shannon scoffs, "You actually have the audacity to pose?"

"Come here."

Carlos' command is low and seductive, breaking into the levity of the moment. As she leans toward him, he pulls the sheet away, brazenly watching her spread herself across his warm body. She lays her head on his chest, aching with arousal, and can't describe in words how simultaneously conflicted and titillated she feels, reveling in the arms of a man who she knows very little of. Her brain tells her to get up, salvage some dignity and make her way home, but her body says otherwise.

At Shannon's prompting, an encore performance begins. Overpowered in an orchestral vortex of ecstasy, the two unite, foolishly unprotected this time, and Carlos' intent to withdraw from the swelling accelerando is derailed.

Collapsing with the finale, his mind churns. He glances at Shannon sprawled across the bed, equally exhausted. She doesn't seem to realize what just happened. Like someone drugged, she rolls to her side whispering, "Happy birthday to me."

Carlos chuckles. "Si, Belleza, happy birthday to you."

Lying behind Shannon, he toys with the springy curls of her hair until she falls asleep. *I may really be in love with this woman.*

As he watches her, he replays their initial encounter and the events leading up to this moment. For the first time, in light of his suspicions, someone has him struggling against his better judgment to keep his distance—and his self-control.

I'm in too deep, Carlos muses, rolling onto his back. *If she is an undercover lesbian investigating me, she's certainly willing to go the extreme.*

***

Carlos is awakened by his phone vibrating on the night stand. He looks over. Shannon is sleeping like a rock. Silencing his phone from vibrating, his hand brushes the package of condoms they hadn't used the second time. Rising from the bed, he shakes his head with disapproval, petitioning God to dodge the bullets of consequence. Usually, he was so careful, never wanting the drama his brothers go through with having kids scattered around the world—and certainly not wanting to contract a disease.

Not bothering to answer what he knows is just a wake up call, Carlos gets in the shower, dresses, and packs. All the while, Shannon remains knocked out.

***

Distantly, she hears her name being called and feels a gentle nudge. Shannon lifts her head groggily to see Carlos sitting in front of her on the bedside. Pulling her wild hair back from her face, she scrambles to a seated position, clutching the sheet with embarrassment. Carlos is fully dressed with his belongings poised to leave the hotel.

She looks to her left. Her gun is still on the dresser. To her right, the clock on the nightstand reads 5:43.

"Good morning, Sleeping Beauty. I never would've guessed you were such a... sound sleeper."

Shannon's head drops with dismay. "Please tell me I wasn't snoring."

Carlos shrugs indecisively, pinching his thumb and forefinger together. "A lil' bit."

She covers her face with her hand. "Oh, my God..." *Now, I feel cheap AND silly.*

Removing her hand, Carlos is reassuring. "I think all of it is quite adorable." He stands to his feet. "I must leave. I would've let you sleep, but I didn't want to be that guy who takes off without saying goodbye."

Shannon jumps up from the bed, still clutching the sheet. "I'll just put my clothes on..."

Carlos stops her. "Take your time. Have a shower. I had brand new toiletries brought to the bath for you. You don't have to rush. There will be a car waiting at the valet when you're ready to leave."

Shannon looks away, thoroughly ashamed.

Carlos turns her face back to him. "Don't ruin an incredible night with unnecessary regret." And then, as if reading her mind, he says, "I promise you, as long as God allows me to live, this will not be the last you see of me."

The mention of God makes Shannon dip her head again. *How can he bring Him up after what we've just done? From what I know of God, He can't be pleased.*

Carlos asks for a kiss, and Shannon pulls the sheet in front of her mouth, shaking her head. "Nope. Morning breath."

He snatches the sheet. "Give me a kiss, woman."

They peck and he exits.

In the stillness, Shannon looks over to see her clothes placed neatly on the chair. Shirking the twinges of guilt, she smiles and heads for the shower.

***

Carlos calls Shannon on the plane on his way out of the country. Eliciting the watchful eye of his brother, he calls again later that evening to make sure she is still okay. When he finishes the call, Ocho mentions, "Los, if there's one thing I know, it's jineteras.[1] This is one you should eliminate, cobio.[2] She's trouble, and you're falling, bro."

Carlos snickers and calls out to the front of the plane, "Beto!"

"¡Si!"

"Ocho is trying to teach me how to choose a woman."

"¡Oye! That will be a short lesson!" Beto counters.

They all laugh, including Ocho, but not before he gives them all the finger.

"I'm serious, Los," he says, displaying one of his rare smiles. "I'm serious, man."

---

[1] A Cuban colloquialism for women who seek assistance from tourists for personal advancement; prostitutes

[2] Brother

The Turn

[8]

Two weeks before the lease is up, Gina returns to the apartment to retrieve some of her belongings. Shannon doesn't ask where or with whom she's moving the items. She no longer cares. These days, her thoughts and spare time are occupied solely by Carlos, her affections fostered by every wonderful, entirely too brief moment she had spent with him since her birthday before becoming irrevocably sealed by their recent, mutual confession of love.

Heavy with another confession of her own, Shannon is driven to put Gina in the past. But, as usual, the woman refuses to be congenial and her behavior is capricious. All morning long, when Shannon's phone would ring, the probing, jealous questions would soon follow. Consequently, when Shannon sees the most important person in her life attempting to reach her, she doesn't dare answer. She responds with a text instead.

"Can't talk right now. Call you back later?" she types.

Carlos replies, "Are you at work?" To which Shannon sends back, "No, trying to pack. Getting ready for the move in a couple weeks. TTYL, k?"

Shannon reads his "Okay," and lays the phone on the counter. Heavy drops of rain pound against the roof as she and Gina stand eye to eye in the middle of the kitchen and resume their yelling match over who owns the toaster.

Thunk, thunk, thunk.

Is that the door? Shannon pauses, granting Gina full liberty to run her motormouth non-stop.

It is probably just the rain, she presumes, but leaves her ex in the kitchen to check it out.

"That is NOT the toaster you bought," Shannon continues to quarrel. "That is the toaster *I* bought to replace the one you had that broke!"

Gina smarts off, "You mean the one YOU broke!"

"You know what? This is stupid. I don't even care. Take the toaster!" Shannon retorts, squinting casually through the peephole. She freezes. *Oh, no he didn't! Not right now!*

Caught in a quandary, Shannon detaches from the pleasant sight of her unexpected visitor and rapidly processes how to handle the situation. Carlos' timing could not be worse. He knocks again.

Hoping Gina hadn't noticed, Shannon cracks the door and says quietly, "Carlos. Hi."

Smiling, he tilts his head to peer inside and asks, "Everything okay in there?"

No, it is not.

Shannon's smile is lopsided. She can see Ocho standing a few feet away at the entrance of the corridor. She steps outside, pulling the door closed behind her. "I have something very difficult to tell you," she begins, but the doorknob is snatched from her hand.

"So, this 'who you're cheating on me with?" Gina demands.

"We're not together, Gina. Don't even try it."

Gina turns on Carlos. "You've got a lot of nerve, showing up here at our place."

Initially, Carlos is shocked, then his expression changes to one of seeming amusement.

"Gina, SHUT UP! I'm so fed up with your lies!" Shannon yells.

"I will not shut up!" She struggles to push past Shannon toward Carlos. Ocho steps over protectively, making Gina rethink her intentions.

Calmly, Carlos lifts his hand and waves him off, and Shannon capitalizes on the moment, snatching Gina back inside the apartment so violently she slides across the hardwood floor.

"Come over here again, Gina, and I swear I'll be going to jail today," she threatens from the doorway, then pivots apologetically to Carlos. "I know how this looks, but it's—"

"While most men would find this exciting and worth their time, I don't. Looks like your cover is blown, Ms. Moore. I hope you've gained what you were trying to achieve at my expense."

In the blink of an eye, Carlos' expression changes frighteningly from amused to repulsed. Walking away, he coldly ignores Shannon's cries to stop or listen and says haughtily to Ocho, "Think she will like what happens next?" Ocho slides in front of her, signaling her to keep her distance.

So stupid, Shannon! Why didn't you tell him before? She presses her palm against her forehead, willing herself to think productively and get beyond her self-derision. *I can't let him leave like this.*

Running into her apartment, she shoves Gina out of her way and grabs her bike keys and badge from the counter.

With no safety gear on but her helmet, Shannon zooms hastily onto the street. She spots the hired Grand Marquis heading in the direction of the freeway and races to catch it. Keeping a keen eye on the vehicle, she speeds through traffic in the rain.

Ocho calls back from the front seat, "Think we got a tail."

Carlos whips around for a view out the rear window, and he and the guards scrutinize the green and white motorcycle maneuvering closer to them. As Shannon closes in, Beto expresses aloud what everyone else in the car is thinking, "She rides a motorcycle?"

Carlos turns around, unwilling to give her any more of his attention. *I let her get to me. Stupid move...*

"What do you want to do, Los?" Ocho asks.

"Keep driving."

Shannon follows the vehicle until it pulls into a private airport entrance. As the gate arm drops down behind the Marquis, she blows past the security shack and the flustered hollers of the guard inside who immediately raises his radio. She paces the car as it slows near a white and gold trimmed Bombardier Global 6000. Drenched and freezing, she flips back her visor and raps on the tinted window.

"Carlos, let me explain. Roll down the window."

The car is still.

Shannon removes her helmet and the rain pours down her face. She leans closer to the glass. "*Please*, give me a chance."

Inside, Carlos angrily watches what has to be the sexiest display of supplication he's ever seen. A single raindrop clings to the tip of her nose then releases, sailing past her glistening collarbone before it disappears into the jeans hugging her wet thigh astride the bike.

His desire flares. With his brothers' eyes adhered to his every move, Carlos refuses to give in to weakness. Beto whistles for his attention, and his eyes skate from Shannon to the flashes of blue, red and white lights halting beside her bike. When the cop gets out of the car, Shannon calmly turns to him with hands raised.

"Detective Sergeant Moore, APD Southwest Division. My badge is clipped to my waste if you'd like to see it."

Hand on his weapon, the yellow-caped cop lifts the edge of her shirt with his baton to read the badge.

Shannon continues, "This is not a police matter, but a personal one, and I'm asking you, one officer to another, for five minutes."

The cop begins, "Officer Moore—"

"Detective Sergeant."

"Detective Sergeant Moore, I don't know what's going on here, but I can't just let you crash through security or endanger our patrons—"

She looks at him. "I need five minutes. Please."

Carlos and his guards sit uncomfortably inside the car in disbelief. Ocho remarks, "See, this is what you get for getting involved with a cop."

Beto whistles antagonistically as the cop gives in.

"Five minutes. And don't move from where you are."

Fed up, Carlos motions for them to get moving. Simultaneously, the front and rear passenger doors open. Ocho exits the front as Beto gets out the rear with an umbrella. He walks to the opposite side of the car and opens the door. Carlos steps out, shoving the umbrella offered to him away, and walks stonily toward the plane.

Knowing the danger in trying to run after him, Shannon remains still, her storming emotions camouflaged by the rain as the love of her life heartlessly ambles away from her. "Won't you at least listen to what I have to say?" she calls.

Carlos stops. Expectation hangs in the air as he stares straight ahead, the brothers watching with deprecation while Shannon alone wills him to turn around. Sliding his hands inside his coat pockets, Carlos looks up into the rain.

He keeps walking. Ascending the stairs, he boards, and the doors of the private aircraft close. The Marquis pulls away.

"Detective?"

Her five minutes are long over. Numbly, Shannon thanks the officer and inches the bike around, barely able to see her way across the tarmac.

Somehow, she makes it back to the apartment. Stepping irately over Gina's possessions stacked neatly near the front door, she heads toward the singing she hears somewhere in the back. Wholly prepared to throw punches without restraint, Shannon slams down her helmet onto the bar counter in passing, knocking over one of Gina's prized stemware into the kitchen sink. The delicate glass shatters unrecognizably, and Shannon gets another notion.

Returning to Gina's pile, she grabs the 26-inch flat screen TV and rushes outside to the parking lot. Tossing the TV into the air as high as she can, she steps aside to watch it crash onto the asphalt and break into exhilarating pieces. Next, it's the stereo, then the jewelry box, followed by two pairs of designer suede pumps.

On a roll, Shannon stands in the dwindling pile, smiling impishly just as Gina prances into the living room. Oblivious to the goings-on, Gina starts in softly, "Guess you really had feelin's for him, huh?" Then, in her Jekyll and Hyde kind of way, she transforms. "Ew. I did you a favor. Now you won't have to deal with a dick."

She laughs obnoxiously. To her surprise, Shannon snickers, too, and picks up her purse.

"What are you doin' with my purse?" Gina demands, looking around suspiciously. The moment she notices that some of her items are missing, she rushes toward Shannon, questioning frantically, "What have you done with my stuff?!"

Shannon responds, "You might want to check the parking lot."

As Gina flies out the door, Shannon tosses her purse after her and yells, "I just did you a favor! Now you won't have to deal with so much *stuff!*"

Hearing the screams, Shannon slams the door and drops the keys she secretly removed from Gina's keyring into the trashcan. *Evidently, the banshee has reached the parking lot. This is not going to go over well with the landlord.*

Aware that the problem she now has banging at the apartment door and cursing her out is not going to leave quietly, Shannon proceeds to the bathroom to take a hot shower. Without a stitch of remorse, she starts the water flowing and dials.

"APD Southwest. Officer Bryne speaking."

"Mama Bryne, this is Moore. Can you get a sergeant over here. I've got a domestic."

***

After the police, the landlord and a belligerent Gina clear out, Shannon sits compulsorily at the computer and types into the search engine, "apartments for rent." At the persuasion of the sergeant, the landlord was kind enough to give her and Gina a whopping three days to move before reporting the notice of eviction publicly. *Which translates into very little time to submit applications before the negative rental history surfaces, an issue that wouldn't have been a problem had I not been dragging my feet to start looking in the first place.*

The search results populate. Shannon stares at the browser. *Be realistic, girl. Three days may be better than an immediate "get out," but it's still too short notice to find a place of my liking—even IF I take off from work.* She types in another search for storage units instead and reluctantly presses the speed dial on her mobile phone. Gohmes answers.

"Yo!"

"Hey, I need a place to crash for a few days," Shannon discloses.

"What? Your girlfriend kicked you out?"

"No. She didn't kick me out. The landlord did. What else do you need to know?"

"I need to know she not gon' be bringing that mess over here!"

Shannon can picture Gohmes' eyes bugging and his mouth stretching wide as he speaks. It almost makes her laugh. "Gohmes, you have a gun. If she shows her face, just shoot her."

"Daaaang! It's that bad, huh? Wonder how long it's gonna last this time. You know y'all like magnets. Can't stay apart."

Shannon snaps, "Are you going to let me stay or what?"

"Come on over here, girl," he says playfully, "I'll make some room on the psych sofa and we'll figure out what's been going wrong."

Shannon smacks her lips. "That's why I don't like telling you stuff. You don't have a clue."

Gohmes laughs maniacally. "Don't forget the entrance fee!"

A few hours later, Shannon pushes a large sausage pizza into Gohmes' stomach as he opens the door. Chortling with approval, he steps aside to let Shannon pass and calls after her, "I don't want to hear none of your bachelor pad comments either!"

***

In the wake of suffering with Gohmes' filth for ten days, Shannon unpacks the last of her stored belongings into her new apartment in Marietta with gusto. As she collects the remaining broken-down cardboard boxes from her small studio space, she appraises its minimal furnishings, elated simply to see visible floors and countertops again.

It's not much, but it's so much better than where I've been. That alone calls for a celebration, she thinks, dropping the boxes in the outdoor trash bin. *A celebration... Alone.*

With a desultory glance at her new building, the loneliness creeps in and the thought of spending the evening there spurs her straight inside to strap on her gym bag and helmet.

Passing under the moving bubble-eyes and beak of the huge Big Chicken landmark, Shannon detours on a whim and heads to the gun club. As the wind whips around her along the freeway, she rehearses in her mind several motives for the decision. *I haven't been in awhile. Need a change of pace. A little practice will help me relieve some frustration...*

The excuses continue, but by the time her Kawasaki whizzes on the lot, only one reason encompasses them all: her desire to run into Carlos for a chance to clear up their terrible misunderstanding.

She hands the staff member her card and watches with humiliation as it's confiscated. She barely hears the woman say, "We regret to inform you, Ms. Moore, that your membership has been revoked."

Shannon doesn't bother asking why. *If the ignored phone calls and text messages weren't enough of a confirmation for me, this one is.*

Carlos had cut her off.

***

Taking a sip of strong coffee, Shannon muddles over the paperwork spread in front of her like she does every day lately. She's relishing the burn as it travels down her esophagus when her desk phone rings, interrupting her thoughts. It's the captain.

Aw, naw.

His tone is taciturn. "Moore, in my office."

Doubtless as to what the meeting is about, she pops a couple of breath mints to mask the alcohol and rises from her chair deliberately. *I know I've been slipping, and I don't need to be reminded of it again. For the second time this month.*

At first, there were just a few occurrences of oversleeping. However, those turned into regular tardies and became compounded with forgetting crucial information in her reports, flubbing interviews, avoiding those closest to her and, most recently, spiking her coffee to deaden the emotional pain of losing the man who had left his indelible presence in her thoughts.

With a steeled countenance, Shannon enters the captain's oppressive den, secretly hoping he will put her out of her misery this time and suspend her—indefinitely. Not so. She's ordered to—
"Mandatory behavioral assessment!?"

Emerging from his office in a whirlwind of fury, Shannon attracts everyone's attention along her path as she shoves chairs and kicks over trashcans. Returning to stand defiantly at her desk, she glares at the captain poking out his head, his eyes slashing the room in search of the fracas. They land on her. She senses someone approaching.

The voice is quiet and calming. "Don't keep telling those closest to you that you're okay when it's clear you ain't, Baby," Mama Bryne says. She peers lovingly at Shannon before pulling her into a consoling hug. "It's time to come on back, Honey."

As the fortitude in Shannon's chest caves in, she understands exactly what those words mean.

Revelation

[9]

"Church," the pastor pauses to wipe a folded hand towel across his perspiring face. Shannon listens intently to the man of God standing at the end of her aisle as he continues his sermon. He looks out compassionately to the congregation, many still enraptured by the joyous praise and worship led by the music ministry.
"Today, sadly, a lot of people are unwilling to call sin, sin. They want to be politically correct and not offend anyone. But, if you are a believer in Jesus Christ, you must call sin, or unrighteousness, the same thing He calls it. In 1 Corinthians 6 verses 9 through 11, God says, 'Do you not know that the unrighteous will not inherit the kingdom of God? Do not be deceived. Neither fornicators, nor idolaters, nor adulterers, nor homosexuals, nor sodomites, nor thieves, nor covetous, nor drunkards, nor revilers, nor extortioners will inherit the kingdom of God. And such were some of you.' Church, has *anyone* besides me been on this list?"
The room buzzes with random expressions. He continues, "*'But,'* the Apostle Paul writes, 'you were washed, you were sanctified, you were *justified* in the name of the Lord Jesus and by the Spirit of our God.'"
"Amen! Thank ya, Jesus!" Mama Bryne hoots. Shannon sneaks a peek at her friend rocking gently beside her in the pew.
Returning to his podium, the pastor picks up his Bible and instructs the congregation, "Turn over to Ephesians Chapter 4 verse 20 with me, please." It takes Shannon a minute, but she does.
"Here, God says that you have not so learned Christ. Reading further, He says that you should put off your former conduct—that old corrupt person you used to be—and be *renewed* in the spirit of your *mind*. Now, some folks will say that's just the way they were born. Others will argue such behavior is learned. Listen, when my ten-month–old son told a lie to cover his behind and he couldn't even talk in sentences, I didn't ask, 'Where did this

originate? Was he born with a propensity to lie or did he learn this from my wife's side of the family?'"

The congregation roars with laughter. The pastor smiles at his wife. "Honey, okay, I confess. It's on my side. Too." Another swell of cackles. "None of that matters though, church. Whether that corrupt conduct is learned, chosen, or genetically predisposed, God says, 'STOP IT! Renew your mind with righteousness!' The Lord tells us something else in this passage: 'Let all bitterness, wrath, anger, clamor, and evil speaking be put away from you.' Uh, side note, friends. That means forgiving those who've hurt you. We've all been hurt by someone, some of us very deeply."

Gina and Carlos' faces aren't the first Shannon recalls to mind. It's her father's. Memories surface of the day she came home from elementary school excited to make her daddy her Valentine and hand him the heart she'd made especially for him. He'd rejected it, told her it was foolishness, then yelled at her for not mitering the corners of her bed. *Never able to show me love...*

Shannon fans away the pre-summer heat along with the emotions brewing inside as she looks back to the pastor. He continues, the towel mopping the top of his bald head and the back of his neck.

"So, someone might ask, 'Pastor, what am I supposed to do with my feelings or with these temptations I have?' Well... if you have the urge to lie, you fight it. Got a bad attitude? You fight it. Want to sleep with someone outside of God's holy design of marriage between a man and a woman? Do like Joseph did and flee!!!"

"That's right! Amen, Pastor," Mama Bryne exclaims, buried by the other murmurs of support from the congregation. Conviction grips Shannon like a vice. *Seems like I'm guilty of just about every category. A lost cause. I should leave.*

"Ladies and gentlemen, this battle against our sinful selves is real and difficult," the pastor says, descending the stairs to draw nearer to the congregation. "And we must fight to live upright before God. Make no mistake, sin breaks God's heart, but I'm here to tell you that we have a loving, forgiving God who knew before the foundation of the world the very lowest you would sink. And knowing this, He still gave His very best to redeem you because you are worth it. He sent His only Son, Jesus Christ, to die on the cross for you so that you may have an eternal Heavenly life with Him and never know the eternal suffering of Hell. Won't you give *Him* your best today? Won't you give Him you?"

Waves of sorrow and remorse pour over Shannon, and she cries out internally, *Please forgive me, Lord. I am so broken, hurting, and lost right now. I need help... I need You.* Oblivious to those around her, Shannon rises from her seat and walks to the altar.

***

With teeth gleaming as Shannon approaches the pew, Mama Bryne is pleasantly shocked to see her revisit the church on her own the following Sunday. "Looky here! God is good!" she exclaims, throwing her arms around Shannon in a warm embrace.

"I hope you don't mind me taking up some of your elbow room again this Sunday," Shannon jokes.

"Young lady, I'm so happy to see you back I could fold up into this tissue box! I don't need much shouting room."

A woman on the other side of Mama Bryne peers over the rim of her glasses at Shannon. "*Hmph.* Yes, she do."

***

After church, Shannon lays her Bible on the pew and turns another befuddled look toward Mama Bryne. She hadn't planned on taking up so much of the woman's time with her questions, but most of the congregation had dispersed long ago.

"I don't get it. How can the Father, the Son, and the Holy Spirit be different, but the same? It doesn't make sense."

"Well, lemme ask you a question. How many forms does H_2O come in?" Mama Bryne collapses her silk hand fan, invitingly.

Shannon scrunches up her mouth, hesitant to answer.

"Go on, Baby. It ain't no trick question."

Chuckling, Shannon says, "Liquid, solid and... vapor?"

"That's it! Ice, water, mist... each serves a different purpose, yet are made of the same substance. The Divinity of God is one, but each has a role in our lives. Romans 1 verse 20: 'For since the creation of the world God's invisible qualities—His eternal power and divine nature—have been clearly seen, being understood from what has been made, so that people are without excuse.'"

The room is quiet as Shannon absorbs her words. "Whoa."

"Whoa is right," Mama Bryne says, using the pew in front to pull herself up. "Ain't He good? Now, let's get out of here 'fore they lock us in!"

In Jesus Christ, Shannon found a redeeming love like no other. Week after week, He surprises her—wooing her with His unfathomable forgiveness, charming her with His wisdom, comforting her with His enduring faithfulness, and uncovering her priceless worth—making her crave more of Him.

Thirstily, she draws nearer to the Savior, the One who had pulled her from the doldrums of rejection and changed her life. Never did she imagine that one day the person she was would no longer hold the same appeal.

Encouraged by Mama Bryne and her new church family, Shannon explores the Jesus she had never met growing up in her parents' ultra religious home. Her tender faith blossoms, and she begins to feel a newfound hope and freedom from the bondage and mistakes of her past. Things start to look up.

That is, until two words flip her world upside down.

"Thirteen weeks?" Shannon asks, astounded.

The gynecologist nods, solemnly. "You didn't miss those periods, I take it?"

Shaking her head, Shannon replies, "I've been under a lot of stress and... didn't pay much attention." *Not to mention my previous sexual encounters were usually free of this risk, so instinctively the thought didn't even register.*

"Is this a desired pregnancy?" the doctor asks.

Shannon looks at her.

***

Sitting on her couch in the dark nursing what's left of her coffee, Shannon remembers her mother's ominous words, "If you fornicate, it will catch up to you, one way or another. God hates sin." To Shannon, that always meant catching a disease. She never expected this. *And now I'm being urged by an OBGYN to make a decision quickly if I want to terminate safely.*

She scoffs. Her recent decision to pick up her cross and walk with Christ seems to have been all for naught. Angrily, Shannon crushes the disposable coffee cup in her hands and lashes out, "Is this punishment for my sins!? What else am I going to get hit with, Lord? What else!?"

The phone rings. Shannon stares at Gina's face on the screen. *Don't answer it, Shannon.*

Hardheaded, she presses the green button and blurts, "Don't call me."

"Wait, Shannon, don't hang up!" Gina beseeches her. "I want to apologize for how I've been acting. I know I was wrong. Can we grab a coffee and just talk?"

I never should have answered. "I already grabbed a coffee."

"Then, let's meet up."

"I'm not in the mood to go out."

61

"I'll come to you," Gina offers eagerly. "Please? I just want to right some wrongs, girl."

God, You must not be real. Or You simply don't care about me. I can't believe You are letting this happen right now. So, whatever.

In her present mental state and tempted by the company of someone familiar, Shannon gives Gina the address. *Maybe things will be different. I could use someone to confide in.*

It doesn't take long for her to realize that person is not Gina. Within the first few minutes of her arrival, Shannon is certain what she thought was there before isn't there now. In her spirit, she cannot bring herself to accept Gina's pathetic attempts to reconcile, much less share her present troubles. Suddenly, she wants her gone.

"Listen. I forgive you, Gina, but it's over," she says, holding the door open for her resolutely.

No sooner than Gina exits the door—surprisingly without a scene—Shannon is conflicted. It takes all of her willpower not to call her back.

"Lord, why is this happening to me, just when I started to get my life on track?" she cries out.

Desperate to ditch this emotional roller coaster, she picks up her Bible. Flipping it open, her eyes are drawn to Proverbs 3: 5 and 6. "Trust in the Lord with all your heart, and lean not on your own understanding; In all your ways acknowledge Him, and He shall direct your paths."

Shannon lays her head against the headboard and murmurs, "Lord, I'm acknowledging You, but I still don't know what to do."

The Bible slips from her hands to the floor, exposing the handwritten note on the inside cover. Shannon reaches to pick it up and reads it again. "A gift for you, my sweet Shannon. I'm here to walk with you. Call me anytime! Mama B."

At 2:48, hesitantly, Shannon dials. *She said, "... anytime."*

Sleepily, Mama Bryne answers. "Umph, my Lord. What you doing up so early, Baby?"

"I haven't been to sleep yet." Shannon clears her throat. "Mama Bryne, I... really need someone to talk to."

"What's the matter, Baby?"

"For one, I'm pregnant."

Mama Bryne moans deep and slow, sharing in Shannon's distress. Gingerly, she inquires, "Is the daddy around?"

Shannon bawls. "No. And I don't know what to do!"

"You have a way to get here?"

"Yes," Shannon manages.

"Well, you come on. Be safe. And Baby, it's gon' be alright."

Shannon sits her coffee mug onto the round kitchen table, warmed inside and out from both the coziness of Mama Bryne's home and the transparent story she just heard. "Really?" she asks in amazement.

Mama Bryne nods her colorful head-wrap and the matching satiny robe billows as she returns to her chair with two slices of sweet potato pie. "Yes, the guilt and remorse I felt from that decision took me years to just be able to come to grips with."

"Mama Bryne, I wouldn't've thought you..." Shannon's voice falters, realizing her words might sound callous.

Smiling, Mama Bryne says, "We all make mistakes. How you handle them is what matters in God's eyes. What you did to get that baby may have been a mistake, but know this, what's there in your womb is not. Honey, don't kill that baby. The Lord will make a way for you both. He really will. He doesn't promise that it will be easy. But He does promise to walk with you through it every step of the way. You just have to trust Him."

Which is precisely what Shannon promised herself she would do whenever she faced trouble or opposition from that day forward. *The problem is, the two greet me every day*, Shannon reflects grimly while handcuffing the suspect she and her partner just apprehended. She turns to Gohmes, upset by the unnecessary expletives flying from his mouth.

"You really don't need to curse like that," she says as they begin walking the suspect to their squad car. "Granted, this kid is ignorant and seemingly worthless in my opinion, but I don't feel like hearing the two of y'all cursing back and forth at each other like you BOTH are immature teenagers."

Gohmes lights into her. "Oh, I'm sorry. That's right! Since you're all into Jesus now. I better stop because, you know, He's real concerned about me cursing out this MURDERER."

They shove the kid into the back of the car. Climbing into the driver's seat, Shannon snaps back, "Gohmes, I was telling you about your cursing long before I accepted Christ so quit with all the religious comments, hear?"

He shuts the passenger door. "Yeah, but you're a super saint now and can't nobody do nothing around you. I'm not walking on eggshells around you, Moore. You ain't all that!"

The look on the suspect's face as he watches from the backseat is priceless.

"Whatever, Gohmes. I don't know what's gotten into you."

"No, I don't know what's gotten into *you!*"

***

"He and I argue like that most of the time now. I haven't even tried to talk to Gohmes about the Lord, but as soon as he found out about *my* salvation it seems like he's making it his personal mission to get me to renounce Him!" Shannon complains into the speaker phone, pacing the floor of her apartment. "On top of this, Gina hounds me with her incessant calls at least two or three times a week. As if I don't have enough to deal with right now. I don't think I can do this. I don't think I should have this baby, either. I'm not going to make it."

On the other end of the line, Mama Bryne listens, patiently awaiting her chance to speak. "You can. And you will. This is no surprise, Honey. The enemy doesn't want you to have the victory and leave all the mess behind. When trouble comes, it's time to be strong in faith, not give up. Put on that full armor and keep moving forward, Shannon."

No sooner than she hangs up, Gina calls. Exasperated, Shannon decides to answer the woman's repeated question of "why not" in a different way.

"I'm pregnant and going to have the baby. You still want to be with me now?"

"Very funny, Shan."

"It's the truth, Gina," Shannon says and allows reality to sink in. She has to hang up on the rant that ensues. *Seems I just can't get away from the foul language,* she thinks as she climbs into bed, mentally exhausted.

***

A terrifying sound of shattering glass startles Shannon awake. Reflexively, she reaches for her firearm. In the darkness, she can see the window blinds swaying. Moving stealthily to the window, she peeks outside. Someone had taken a bat to her apartment window. There's no question who it was.

Another week passes, and each day Shannon slips deeper and deeper into an abyss of despair. With Gina calling her a lying whore and her partner teasing her mercilessly about becoming a Jesus freak at every chance, coupled with worrying about her pregnancy, she finds it difficult to escape from her emotional slump. The department shrink doesn't even touch on the problems, probably because she refuses to share anything with her, and the lifeline Mama B. willingly extends that used to revive her is fading.

Shannon murmurs tearfully, "I need to hear from You, God. It seems impossible to trust You or know what to do when I'm constantly being reminded of my past."

Hearing herself say this strikes a chord. *The Pastor said something like that in one of his sermons. A sermon about starting over...*

Like a light bulb turning on, Shannon gets the answer she's been waiting for. The following morning, she walks into the captain's office.

"I'd like a transfer, Sir. Perhaps lateral."

***

The following year, Shannon types, "A few days ago, on January 11th, I delivered a beautiful baby boy. Meet Carlos Antonio Moore. He is truly my absolute joy and an answer to my prayers. Thank you for everything you've done for us. Love, Shannon."

As she snaps a selfie of her and the baby to send with her email, thoughts of Atlanta and everything with it from her past—the disjointed relationship with her parents, her past lovers, her old job, her reputation—come to mind. All are 2,500 miles behind her.

I do miss YOU dearly though, Mama B., Shannon ponders wistfully, uploading the photo to her desktop. *Sometimes, I feel so confused and conflicted. But, thanks to you, I'm finally able to look forward to what the future holds. Right now, that's enjoying my newborn and my maternity leave from the Las Vegas PD.*

On impulse, she drafts a second note to which she attaches the same photo. *He should probably know, too.*

Shortly thereafter, two recipients open their emails with salutations from Lake Las Vegas, Nevada. One smiles with glee and immediately picks up the phone to call, while the other stares in disbelief. Printing the picture, he jots contact information on the back and inserts it against the framed picture of Shannon he already had sitting on the hutch behind his desk.

Act II
The Visitation

[10]

In mid April, a queenly woman in her late sixties opens the oversized stained glass double doors of her home and attempts to greet the unheralded visitors on her stoop pleasantly. However, each of the three callers can sense that their presence there is unnerving. One smirks when the woman's eyes drop to their gloved hands.

"Hello, Candace," Carlos says charmingly and steps inside uninvited. Beto and Ocho advance behind him, and the door clicks closed.

"It is Candace, correct?"

The woman stands petrified.

"You don't remember me, I take it." Carlos shifts his sights across the room in search of the person he came for. "I apologize for disturbing you, but I need to speak with your husband right away."

Slowly, Candace recovers and attempts to speak. "Oh. Let me go—"

"Yes, why don't you take me to him immediately."

She looks skittishly at Carlos and nods her head. "Please, follow me."

Candace leads the three men around the baby grand piano through the meticulously arranged Victorian parlor and knocks on her husband's office door. When he appears stone faced in the doorway, she takes a seat in the parlor. Beto remains in the room with her as Carlos and Ocho enter the office and close the door behind them.

As the two outside the office watch each other stoically, inside, the other three stand balefully by the door.

"Sit down, Jaxson," Carlos commands and begins a slow pace across the floor. Casually, he surveys Jaxson's office while the chief takes possession of his oversized desk chair.

"All these years we've known each other and I've never been inside your home. Lovely place you have here," Carlos comments.

Jaxson hardly opens his mouth to express his thanks before he's berated.

"I strongly dislike having to track you down for my money, Jaxson—"

Abruptly, Carlos stops talking, his breath catching noticeably in his throat. The Chief is inattentive to the occurrence, consumed with concealing his own trepidation and reclaiming some sort of authority.

"You know I always get it to you, Los...." he starts, but soon recognizes that Carlos isn't listening. He follows his eye-line and sees it glued to the picture of Shannon and the baby displayed behind his desk. Dropping his head in consternation, he tries to continue. "I'll get it to you. Just give me forty-eight hou—"

Jaxson shrinks back in fear as the hand reaches across him without warning.

"Who is this?" Carlos asks, picking up the picture.

Exhaling angrily, Jaxson answers, "That's Det—"

"In the picture with her," Carlos snaps. "She has a kid?"

"Apparently, yes."

Carlos' squinted eyes shoot daggers at Jaxson, and he rushes to clarify his statement. "She took a leave of absence. Several months later, I get this picture in the mail of her and her new baby." He forces a laugh, trying to lighten the mood. "I guess that's how a godfather is supposed to find out."

Still staring at the picture, Carlos is ruminative. "So, this was recently taken," he states, more to himself than anyone else. He loosens his tie with one gloved hand and replaces the picture onto the hutch with the other, his mind drifting back to what he'd felt that night. *Her new baby and probably mine.*

Jaxson and Ocho watch intuitively, but neither one says a word.

Carlos breaks the silence. "Where is she?"

Jaxson tells him very little, hoping Carlos doesn't flip over the picture and catch him withholding information. He mentally prepares to call Shannon with a heads up, but his thoughts are quickly manipulated with a warning.

"I'm feeling generous," Carlos says, smiling spuriously. "It's a lot of money so, I'll give you a week. You just make sure *NO one* outside this room mentions this visit or this conversation—any part of it—ever took place. And... this *will* be the last time I come looking for my payment."

Carlos flashes his full, multi-million-dollar smile and continues. "How quickly the protection from exposure can be lifted, unveiling the numerous assets you've acquired from illegal trade that affords you the gratuitous lifestyle you enjoy—which enables you to sustain the heinous addictions you'd like to keep secret. Of course, those will be the least painful of your worries. You do understand what I'm saying, don't you, Jaxson?"

Jaxson's flinty nod indicates he clearly gets the picture, his typically commanding countenance shaken.

"Now. Where *exactly* is she?"

Pressed between shielding his goddaughter or preserving his own livelihood, the chief caves. In his mind, there isn't a choice.

Candace shifts her eyes from Beto to watch Carlos and Ocho enter the parlor. Not seeing her husband, she calls, "Jax, are you coming out?"

Carlos pats her on the arm as the three men pass her. "He's fine, Mrs. Parks. And don't you trouble yourself with us. We'll see ourselves out."

Outside the home, Carlos instructs Ocho to put some research in motion.

"You think it's yours," Ocho asserts as they stride to the car.

"We'll find out," Carlos replies. "I won't rest until I know for sure."

Ocho scowls, unsupportive of his brother's line of thinking. "Man, you should just leave that trick alone. It's better off not knowing. I'm trying to tell you, I know what I'm talking about."

Carlos gives Ocho a brotherly pat on the back. "Better to not know? Now, is that how I operate?"

Ocho shrugs off his hand pugnaciously, and the two brothers take a few playful swings at one another, unperturbed by the Parks watching "discreetly" from their living room window. Shaking his head, Ocho starts to make the calls.

***

Yawning, Shannon smooths the tiny blanket over C-Lo, the nickname she'd playfully given her three-month-old now fast asleep on the sofa cushion next to her in the den. She's fighting to keep from nodding off herself in a pitiful attempt to watch her favorite TV show when there's a rap at the door.

Having dozed slightly, Shannon sits up on the sofa and listens. The knock repeats. She glances at the clock displaying 8:35.

In a huff, she heads to the front door, rather annoyed with these visits now. Just as she suspected, her landlord's college son, Michael, who lives in the casitas across from the tiny courtyard they share, is standing under the porch light, flashing his carefree grin.

She disarms the alarm and opens the door, expecting that he wants to borrow something, as usual.

"Yes?"

"Hey! Sorry to bother you. Got any mustard?" he asks.

"Mustard? Michael, you could've awakened the baby with your knocking. I'll give you some this time, but listen. I'm not the local convenience store. Go get your own supplies, hear?"

With a goofy smile, Michael assures her he's done for the night. Snickering, Shannon plops down on the couch and takes her TV show off pause.

The sound of the doorbell causes her head to pop up from another one of her unplanned naps. She squints at the clock through heavily laden eyes and ascertains it's sometime after 11. Angrily, she looks at the front entrance, visible from her seat in the den, and prepares to give Michael a sharp piece of her mind.

Rising from the sofa, Shannon dons her robe, and walks purposefully to the door. Even in her sleepy stupor, she instinctively takes a quick glance out of the side window panel before unlocking the door, and that's when her heart jumps into her throat.

Carlos.

Shannon can feel the color drain from her face, and a myriad of emotions wash over her as questions flood her mind. *What is he doing here? Could he know about the baby? If he doesn't, how would he receive the news?*

They stare at each other for several seconds without speaking. Movement in her peripheral vision makes Shannon tear her eyes away to swiftly survey the area. An unrecognizable guard stands across the small courtyard next to the window of the casitas where Michael lives.

Carlos calls her attention back to him and probes pleasantly, "Seems like you were expecting someone else?"

Not knowing what to say, Shannon doesn't respond.

"Shannon? Is this how you treat a... friend from long ago?"

Wishing she had time to get her thoughts together, she disarms the alarm and raises her hand toward the lock, but notices the guard peer into the window of the casitas and look around.

"Are you going to leave me standing out here, Shannon, or perhaps there's someone inside waiting to attack me like last time?"

Carlos' tone has an alarming edge to it. Her hand hovers over the lock. The guard peeks into Michael's window again, his behavior antsy and collusive. Shannon shifts away from the door.

Her nervousness morphs into uneasiness. Nearly a full year has passed since she'd last seen Carlos, and she was finally beginning to make peace with the idea that he was truly out of her life. Her prayers for the opportunity to redeem herself with him had seemingly gone unanswered. Yet, here he is, a welcomed sight for worn eyes standing outside her door, and something is holding her back from letting him inside.

Could be my own insecurities. Could be God, Shannon thinks, challenged as usual in discerning the Lord's voice from her own. *Regardless, he is not coming in here. Not tonight, at least.*

"Now is... not a good time," she asserts. "You should leave."

Shannon resets the alarm and steps out of view. *What am I doing? This is what I've been praying for—an occasion to reunite with my child's father—and I'm potentially blowing the only chance I may get.*

Battling her disquieted spirit, she adds, "You can call me. My number's still the same."

Carlos irritatedly motions to the guard. As they recede, Shannon glances out the window, pining at the thought of letting him leave. To her surprise, Ocho steps into view, and she speculates why he seemed to have been standing out of sight.

Relieved to have stood by her initial instincts, she watches everyone exit the courtyard, but with the casitas obstructing her view of the street, she's unable to see the men get into the car. Waiting vigilantly by the door, she looks for vehicle taillights to pull away from the front yard, but none appear. All is dark and still.

For safe measure, Shannon moves quickly through the small, single-story house verifying that all the doors and windows are locked. When all accesses are secured, she scoops C-Lo into her arms and whisks him into her bedroom.

Sitting down on the bed next to the baby's bassinet, she exhales a pinned up sigh of relief and gazes into C-Lo's cherubic face. As she places him inside the bassinet, she longs to sleep so peacefully. *Very unlikely now...*

An eerie feeling brushes across the back of her neck. Shannon spins in time to see a shadow cross her bedroom's door to the patio. Gun in hand, she rushes to get a look outside through its oval glass insert. Nothing is visible in the darkness.

But it shouldn't be dark out there.

Wondering why her timed patio light isn't on, Shannon tries to calm her nerves and remain rational. *The shock of this unexpected visit must have me off kilter and imagining things.*

Not convinced, however, she continues to scan the windows for movement. Seeing no one, she grips the door knob, intending to inspect the patio light fixture. *On second thought, I'll check it out in the morning. Hopefully, it's just a blown bulb.*

A seething Carlos calculates his next move as he waits for the remaining guards to climb inside the car. As far as he is concerned, whatever ambiguity he once had about whether Shannon was purposely keeping the baby's existence from him had just been eliminated. He didn't take too well to being disrespected or being kept from getting his way, and she had essentially done both.

***

Gun and telephone within reach, Shannon lies on the bed cradling C-Lo, trying to sort out her thoughts. Despite her tiredness, she's incapable of closing her eyes. Fleetingly, she thinks of searching her Bible for scriptures about peace in anxiety, but worrying seems easier. When the sun begins to rise and C-Lo's cries insist that she "rise and shine," too, it is clear. Worrying had been a waste of time.

Checking that bulb, she's relieved to see there was no foul play. "It just needs replacing," she says aloud through a yawn and decides to take a somewhat-needed trip to the grocery store. She and C-Lo hadn't been anywhere in a few days and getting out of the house might help her stop replaying the unnerving scene from last night over and over in her mind. *Besides, I would really feel better if I stopped to pick up another bulb for that patio, too...*

Maybe I should take some precautions. She picks up her cell. "Michael, you up? I was thinking... you need groceries, and I could use help with the baby. Had a rough time sleeping last night, so driving me around is the least you can do, buddy."

Although not the primary reason I'm coercing him to go, it's still the truth. He doesn't need to know more than that.

As the doors of their second stop slide open and the desert heat smothers them, a classmate of Michael's, who he's obviously enamored with, makes her way inside. He strikes up a youthful conversation, and Shannon mimes for him to pop the trunk remotely.

Dizzy with her own thoughts, she pushes the noisy grocery cart ahead to his car and sluggishly begins unloading the few bags in the frying sun. She doesn't notice the hand grab her baby carrier from the shopping cart until it's too late.

Shannon's scream and knee-jerk reaction to lunge for C-Lo stop short. Behind the carrier, a gun is shielded for only her to see. As she looks into the man's face, he mouths sternly for her to cooperate before revealing his cowboy drawl.

"AAA is on the way. You'll get a ride. I'll stay with the car until the tow truck gets here," he says, putting on a show for any nearby witnesses. Lowering his voice he tells her, "Grab a couple of those sacks."

Shannon obeys, her insides gripped by invisible, steely fingers as she swings her combination purse-diaper bag over her shoulder. Jerkily, she picks up a grocery bag in each arm. *Dear Jesus, please don't let this guy hurt my baby!*

"Now, walk in front of me toward that car over there. Don't look back and don't make a scene."

She looks in the direction in which he'd nodded his head, unable to believe this is happening in broad daylight. *Come on, Michael—somebody, please see this!* Doing as told, she stops when she approaches the black limousine waiting on the next aisle.

"Open the door and get in," he tells her before crossing to the other side of the car. She watches over the roof of the limo as he opens the door and places her baby inside. With help nowhere near, she has no choice but to comply.

Quickly, Shannon tugs the door and exposes a man's pants leg resting on the seat. She peers in anxiously and stifles a gasp. Smiling at her is Carlos, calmly holding the baby carrier next to him.

Climbing inside, she glares at him in speechless disbelief. The door shuts behind her. Carlos motions with gloved hands for her to have a seat across from him, which happens to be between Ocho and another burly guy. Ocho sneers at her.

She sits, trying to gather her wits about her. She is keenly aware that Carlos wants something severely, having shown up uninvited to her home and now—obviously not at peace with being turned away—forcing a meeting with her at gun point. *What would he be willing to go to such great risk for?* Terrified, all she can hear is Jaxson's warning to not get involved. *In what?*

Shannon opens her mouth to speak, and Carlos quickly presses his forefinger to his lips, gesturing for her to be silent. He then motions to the two men beside her. The unknown guard reaches for her grocery bags, while Ocho tugs at her purse. She resists letting it go, only to have it torn away from her. The guard begins riffling through her bags perfunctorily as Ocho passes her purse to Carlos.

"What the hell is going on, Carlos?" she demands.

A gloved hand clamps over her mouth tightly. Carlos teems with tightlipped disapproval at her disobedience, but continues searching her bag thoroughly. Shannon tries prying the fingers away from her mouth, but it's futile. Her head is being pressed against Ocho's chest and she can feel his vile, hot breath blowing the top of her hair. To Shannon's dismay, the limo begins to drive off slowly.

Still silent, Carlos nods to Ocho, who begins groping her indiscreetly. Meanwhile, Carlos takes her gun from her purse, clears its chamber and stashes it in his coat. Determining her to be free of wire taps and weapons, Ocho announces, "Seguro."[3] and removes his hand from her mouth. Recognizing she is grossly disadvantaged, Shannon can only glare at him in disgust, uncertain of the extent of danger she and her baby are in.

Carlos gives Shannon a quick once over, his disdain for her not precluding him from observing she is still as beautiful as the last time he'd seen her. He notices she has picked up weight—probably even twenty pounds or so—yet it doesn't detract from her looks at all. *She indeed must be the apple of my eye,* he muses with bitter irony. He finds himself considering how this enhanced, more curvaceous Shannon would feel. Swiftly, he rips his gaze away in an effort to dispel the thoughts flooding his mind.

As they pass the store, Carlos mentions absently, "Whole Foods. You drive far from home to go grocery shopping."

Clearly disinterested in small talk, Shannon petitions, "What are you doing, Carlos?"

Turning his eyes back to her face, the scowl there helps him refocus. "I thought I'd arrange another meeting, since the one yesterday was cut so short. Maybe you're ready to talk now, Señorita?" He turns to look at the sleeping baby next to him. "Who is this handsome little guy?"

Tersely, Shannon replies, "He's my son."

Carlos holds the carrier steady with his right hand while reaching in with his left to stroke the baby's soft hair. "Your son. He's a good looking kid. What is *your son's* name?"

Shannon fidgets with her ear in silence. He looks at her astutely.

"What? I can't know your son's name?"

"Why do you need to know his name?"

"Wow. Is it so terrible for me to know his name?"

---

[3] Clear.

Checking her temper, she asks thinly, "What is it you want, Carlos?"

There is a tense pause before he proceeds. "A lot has happened since we last saw each other, yes? You have to admit, it is rather surprising to see you with a baby. Are you married now, as well?"

He leans forward and takes her hand, ostensibly looking for a wedding ring. Shannon snatches away her hand.

"What do you want?" she insists.

Growing irritable, Carlos punctuates his response. "I waa-n-t information."

"What information?" They stare at each other.

"Where is his father?"

Shannon looks out the window then defiantly back at Carlos without answering. Pompously, Carlos continues, "Maybe that wasn't a good question to ask. How about this one. *Who* is the father?"

It is evident that Carlos suspects or already knows that it's him. What Shannon can't surmise is what his intentions are and consequently she remains silent. Observing her refusal to acquiesce to his prodding, Carlos provokes her further.

"Or do you even know?"

Feeling as though she is boiling inside, she responds sarcastically, "I sure don't. If you must know, he was adopted." Carlos glares at Shannon, then it's his turn to look out the window.

His head snaps back toward the baby carrier. Shannon jumps and is seized by the two men flanking her. Straining to see, she watches with trepidation until Carlos' glare transforms into a smile.

The baby's tiny hand clasps onto one of Carlos' fingers dangling above the carrier. His bright, brown eyes fix on the father he doesn't know as he flashes a toothless smile, and now that he is awake, the resemblance is unmistakable.

Carlos looks back at Shannon and resumes, "Couldn't be. He looks too much like someone I know. What a shame, lying on your own son. You could save us both some time by just telling the truth. For a change. Who is the father?" Snidely, he adds, "I'd like to ask him how he achieved this."

Unable to bear anymore, Shannon breaks, shouting, "He's some jerk-off that didn't want to hear what I had to say months ago!"

"Jerk-off!? Terrible. Do I know this guy?"

"Take us back."

Carlos' apparently controlled demeanor only masks the fact he is out of patience. Angrily, he calls to the driver, "STOP THE CAR!" Realizing they are near the grocery store again, Shannon thinks with relief that he's going to let them out. Instead, he tells the driver something in Spanish and turns to Shannon. "I just had a change in plans."

He reaches into Shannon's bag and retrieves her phone. "Call that boy you were with and tell him you got a ride. Be convincing. I know you are good at that. The cowboy will verify that he's the one who answers the phone. Let's hope he does."

Shannon takes her phone and presses redial.

"Hey! Sorry. Still over here... you know, talking. I'll be there in like two minutes!" Michael explains.

"Actually, I saw a friend, too... and decided to get a lift. Handle your biz. Just don't forget your groceries are in your trunk."

She places the device into Carlos' outstretched hand.

From it, he dials his number, answers, then puts both phones on mute. "What is happening right now is a conversation between you and me about how good it was seeing me yesterday and how you are suddenly in need of a favor."

He hangs up and mentions coolly, "You know what that was, don't you, Señorita? An alibi. How nice that I'm willing to help you out with a ride now that your little friend has become otherwise engaged. The ball's in my court now." He tosses the phone battery out the window. "I don't take orders from you."

At his instruction, they drive on. Beto's face appears in the interior window.

"Not a good idea, Los," he states.

"I didn't ask you."

"Where are you taking us?" Shannon struggles to look out the windows. "Where are we going?!" She is ignored as several barbarous statements take place in Spanish. "WHERE ARE WE GOING?"

The other guard puts his hand over her mouth this time, seizing her face roughly. In a thick Spanish accent, he tells her, "Shut up, if you know what's good for you."

She tries to fight him off, but Ocho helps subdue her. Carlos diverts his eyes with indifference, and the brutes don't release their grip on Shannon until the limo begins to slow down.

As soon as her lips can move, she implores Carlos, "Please, don't do whatever it is you are planning, if it's not taking us back home. My son, who his father is—none of it should matter to you. We don't affect you whatsoever, so—"

"Are you going to tell me the baby's name, now, Señorita?" "Just let us out right here. I don't care where we are. I'll find a way back home."

There's a snicker from Ocho. "She wants out, Los. We should just let her out," he says. Looks are exchanged between Carlos and Ocho. Carlos runs a hand over his hair, causing a few previously groomed locks to spring out of place. In a strained tone, he asks, "What's the father's name?"

Stubborn silence.

Leaning forward to stare Shannon in the face, Carlos is unrelenting. "What's... the... father's... name?"

"Why do you care!?"

Without hesitation, Carlos says, "I'll answer that. I believe—" He sits back in the seat before continuing, "...I have a vested interest here."

The limo stops.

Shannon yells, "GO TO HELL!!"

Unscathed, Carlos replies, "No, I don't plan on going there. But, I do plan on taking what's mine."

Shannon follows his gaze onto the airport tarmac she presumes is private and cringes at his next statement.

"So, you can either come along cooperatively or watch *your son* get on the plane without you."

"Are you threatening to take my son?"

"No. I'm offering you a ride."

"A ride? I don't understand... What are you going to do, Carlos?"

"First, I'm going to call my lawyer."

Lifting the baby carrier, he steps out of the limo. Ocho follows suit, leaving Shannon in the other guard's painful grip. She calls out in a panic, "Wait! Don't leave with my baby!! I'll cooperate. Please!"

Tears stream down her face as she struggles wildly with the guard holding her back. She hears Carlos command, "Sul, let her go," and footsteps tap against the pavement.

Sul growls in her ear, "Don't make a scene," before he shoves her away. Scampering from the vehicle, Shannon hurries behind Carlos as he walks purposefully toward the familiar Global 6000 already prepped for departure.

A Private Flight

[11]

Aboard his private aircraft, Carlos leads Shannon through an upscale galley with beautiful lacquered cabinetry and custom countertops. It opens into a plush, mid-sized main cabin with seating for nine passengers. The interior is elegantly designed with matching lacquered trim throughout. He steps aside to let Shannon pass and hands her the baby carrier.

"Sit there," he says, pointing to a seat at a table for four. Shannon takes one of the stately, two-toned leather chairs facing the front of the plane and places the carrier in the window seat adjacent to her.

Ocho steps in front of Carlos, partially blocking her view. He attempts to speak in hushed tones, but Shannon overhears.

"Man, what are you doing right now? This is risky and stupid."

Bristling at the word "stupid," Carlos responds, "If I wanted the opinion of a child, I would have asked for it. There is a reason *I'm* in charge. Tell Moises we're ready for takeoff."

He leaves Ocho, who slinks into the galley hot under the collar, and stands behind the aisle seat facing Shannon. "This side," Carlos tells her, inferring she should move. She complies, switching to the opposite side of the table and moving the baby likewise. Carlos sits down in the seat where she was and regards her coldly.

Intending to capitalize on Ocho's failed attempt, Shannon tries her hand at persuading him. "Carlos, think about what you're doing. This is abduction."

"Should I be worried?" He stares as she tries to continue.

"You're making a big mistake—"

Carlos takes a deep, menacing breath and exhales. "Shut up... your mouth."

She does.

She focuses on calculating a viable plan of escape instead, assessing the exits and whereabouts of the other people on board to describe in detail to the authorities.

Looking around, she recalls the aircraft terminology she learned from a previous case. *If facing the cockpit, the right side of the plane is the starboard side and the left is the port side, which is the side Carlos and I are sitting on. To the rear or aft of the plane is a secondary cabin with at least two additional seats facing each other on the starboard side.* Two unfamiliar men occupy those seats. *Any potential passengers opposite them are obscured from my position.*

At the front of the plane, starboard side, Beto sinks into the chair facing the aft and reclines. Over her shoulder, directly behind the window seat C-Lo rests in, Shannon can see the back of Sul's right arm as he buckles up facing forward. There are no seats behind her chair or Carlos' chair, and their chairs are the only two that extend slightly into the center aisle—which means she is easily accessible. As she looks around, all eyes seem to navigate to her from time to time. *Making it to one of the exits successfully with the baby in tow is highly implausible.*

Carlos breaks into her thoughts. "I'm not some street level detective work, Señorita. I'm much higher than that. You're wasting your time trying to figure out how to get off this plane."

He pulls some documents from an attaché case. Ocho reappears and sits in the aft-facing seat across the aisle from them. With a detectible amount of resentment, he informs Carlos, "We're cleared, here and over there." Carlos nods in comprehension, ignoring the attitude, and with eyes fastened to his papers, he warns Shannon, "You should strap the baby in."

She looks at C-Lo and swallows, perceiving that once the plane takes off they may never be seen again. *God, what do I do?* Shannon grabs the handle of the car seat ambitiously as the plane begins to taxi. Carlos looks up at her and cocks his head in anticipation.

Out of the blue, the words, *"I will never forsake you,"* flutter in her mind and an indescribable peace that defies logic passes over her. Taking that as an answer, she hurries to secure the carrier with the seat belt.

No sooner than they leave the ground, C-Lo begins to fuss inconsolably, probably from an uncomfortable combination of cabin pressure and hunger. Shannon ventures to speak. "I need a private area to nurse. Where is the restroom?"

Disinterested in anything other than the paperwork in front of him, Carlos answers, "You can feed him right here. We've all seen a baby being fed before."

Livid, Shannon gets herself prepared as discreetly as possible, hating the subjection and the powerlessness she feels. Not one man with a clear view of her has the decency to look away, either.

Once the flight is underway, everyone gradually begins to shift about the plane. Despite her personal need to use the restroom, Shannon remains seated, keeping a close eye on the baby. An hour later, however, she can't hold out any longer.

"I have to pee. Can I use the restroom now or should I just go right here?" she asks Carlos, successfully getting his attention.

The corner of his mouth begins to curl, while a thousand silent insults seem to hurl back and forth between them in their stares. He calls out, "Beto!"

"¡Si!"

"Take her to the restroom."

Beto begins walking Shannon to the front of the plane, and Carlos grumbles, "*Not* the one in the front. By the *cockpit*. In the back!"

Quickly, Beto redirects Shannon the other way through the secondary cabin. Inside, Ocho is stretched out fast asleep on the divan to her right, undisturbed by her entrance, but her presence interrupts the card game in play to her left. Doing her best to ignore their lascivious gawking, Shannon pushes the restroom door.

Beto warns her, "Don't lock it."

As told, she closes the door and turns to face the fanciest restroom she's ever seen on a plane. Opposite the entrance is a standup shower, and within it is another door. Wondering who or what is on the other side, Shannon cautiously relieves herself. She flushes the toilet, hoping the noise will camouflage the sound of her snooping, and sneaks a peek inside what turns out to be a fairly spacious storage area.

Eyeballing the luggage stacked around the room, she's tempted to rifle through some pieces in hopes of the off-chance someone had packed a cell phone.

"'Ay!" Beto bangs on the door impatiently.

I can't risk being caught. "Washing my hands!" Shannon yells, rushing back into the restroom.

***

According to Shannon's watch, three hours and forty-seven minutes have passed since they took flight. Carlos returns from the galley, stops at the credenza in the middle of the room, then squats beside her seat. He presents a drink he'd prepared, making no effort to conceal the truth.

"This is to assure you remain ignorant of our whereabouts. It's harmless."

Naturally, she refuses and pulls the baby carrier in the adjacent seat closer to her.

"Drink it."

"I'm breastfeeding. I can't drink that," Shannon protests, hoping to garner some empathy on her behalf.

Carlos is unmoved. "Drink it. Or, you can choose another way." He motions to "Sul" standing nearby, who exposes the butt of his gun on cue. "That leaves a nasty knot. This will be much better for you."

They stare obstinately at one another.

"Sleep... like you did the night we made love."

Slap!

Shannon glares brazenly at Carlos as his head unwinds back in her direction. *If I'm going to die, it will not be without honor.*

His jaw clenching in anger, Carlos glances up at Sul and begins to stand. The guard moves behind Shannon.

In a split second, she feels Sul's arms encircle her neck in a chokehold. With cat-like reflexes, Shannon pushes her feet off the table in front of her, utilizing a hapkido defense technique to thrust her body in the direction Sul is pulling her. Feeling his own force used against him, he stumbles backward, yanking her over the top of the seat.

They fall to the floor and begin to wrestle in the aisle. Shannon gets two stinging blows in and manages to palm his cell phone from his front pocket before Carlos and Beto converge on them. She slips the phone into her bra as she's pulled to her feet.

Embarrassed that Shannon made him look bad, Sul shouts threatening expletives her way. As Carlos restrains her, she sucker punches Sul in the face, and he pulls his gun on her in a rage.

Spinning Shannon away from Sul, Carlos positions himself between them and shouts, "PUT THAT GUN AWAY! You shoot it off on this plane, we're all dead, *idiot!*"

Infuriated, Sul complies, but he rushes Shannon. Urgent, angry Spanish words and frantic activity swirl around the cabin, and her left cheek is struck so hard it feels like her entire face disintegrates. She witnesses an arm swing away from her in a rapid, backhanded motion and hears a loud smack, followed by Carlos calling her name. As she sways in his arms, his concerned face comes into view.

    Before Shannon can determine who punched her or who else had been hit, a cloth covers her nose and mouth in an unshakeable grip, and the terrified cries of her baby fade as she blacks out.

The Arrival

[12]

A bump in the road. The accelerating hum of a car engine followed by a sickening mixture of too many different men's colognes. Slowly, Shannon begins to regain consciousness as they pull uphill onto a long, winding, gated driveway. Someone's arm is around her holding an icepack to the side of her face, and she realizes she's laying on Carlos's shoulder. She looks up at him, wincing.

Her memory returns, and she recoils from him, scooting toward the limo door. "I can't believe you hit me!"

"Correction. You hit me. Then later, *he* hit you," he says, motioning to Sul sitting across from them.

She scowls at both men, and Sul shrugs as if he was just doing his job. Briefly, she observes with gratification the bruising she'd imparted on Sul's left side before he slips on sunglasses. She ponders the unexpected cut on the right side of his face, as well.

As usual, a surly Ocho sits by, looking at her with disgust. Scanning for the baby, she's relieved to see him asleep comfortably in his carrier. Carlos tosses the ice pack onto the small bar top and gives Shannon an assenting nod that the baby is fine.

Whirling around her head in an attempt to catch some landmarks outside the car, Shannon grimaces in pain. With her body twisted toward the door, she pats herself discreetly. Unsurprisingly, the phone she'd stolen is gone. Carlos leans over to retrieve some medication from the console and begins to speak again.

"Since we are on the subject...." The ring on his right hand flashes as he grabs Shannon's chin forcefully and turns it toward him. "Don't ever strike me again. Am I clear?"

Head and cheek throbbing, she squints uncomfortably at him. Carlos tilts his head and raises his eyebrows, awaiting a response. She swallows with difficulty. His grip tightens as he slowly nods his head, encouraging her to answer in the affirmative.

"Yes," Shannon sputters.

Releasing his grip, he turns back to the bar console and pours water into a glass. The car slows at the top of the hill in front of a sprawling four story mansion with garages for five cars. They pull into one, a tandem space long enough to house the limo. When they stop, he offers her the medicine and glass of water.

"Maybe you'll listen this time and take the Motrin for your head. You'll need it."

After a moment, Shannon pops the pills in her mouth and swallows some water. They exit the car.

The swiftness of their pace and the pain in her head makes it difficult for Shannon to take note of her surroundings effectively, but she does recognize that they take a small elevator up one floor and exit into an antechamber. She is guided through a spacious breakfast nook into a wide hallway, past a second elevator, and halted near what appears to be a study. Leaving the others in the hall, Carlos pulls Shannon into an office and closes the door behind them.

The room is beautifully decorated with ornate bookcases lining the nice-sized sitting area. A large flat screen TV is suspended there, opposite a hulking desk. Two overstuffed chairs face the desk, and on the wall behind it hangs a portrait of a young Romero family ranging in skin-tones from strikingly pale to deeply dark. Of the many faces, Shannon recognizes but a few in their youthful state. There are no windows in the room, just two doors—one behind the desk area and the one they entered through.

Carlos sits the baby carrier in one of the chairs and instructs Shannon to have a seat. Leaning against the desk, he states pointedly, "You came to me some time ago begging for a chance to talk. Now, I'm ready to talk. So, let's talk. How long were you planning to go without telling me about the baby?"

"You bastard! You kidnap me and my son at gun point—terrorize me and endanger my baby—because now you are ready to talk?? A year later? Is this what you brought me here for? Yeah, good luck with that!!"

She looks away in disgust and immediately regrets her words. With no idea where his thought process is, it would be wise to keep her temper in check. As she feared, Carlos snatches her arm and begins shoving her to the door.

"Your choice. I'll draw my own conclusions, and we'll see how you like the results. In case you didn't know, my resources are vast, I have a great attorney, and I've always wanted a son."

"What do you mean by that?"

Carlos continues to navigate her toward the door. "To put it bluntly, I have no use for you. You're a waste of my time."

"Wait! I'll talk. You want to know if I was going to tell you about the baby. I was. And I tried, but I couldn't get through to you."

Carlos stops abruptly. He walks to the desk and wakes the computer. With a few keystrokes and a click of a button on the keyboard, the handful of messages she'd left last year with the call center begin to play. He scrolls through a few.

"Sounds like you got through to me just fine. No messages about a baby, though. What else are you going to come up with, Ms. Moore?" he asks.

Shannon is amazed that he has her messages saved. *All this time...*

Confused, she says tentatively, "I didn't want to leave something like that in a message."

All this time, you shunned me. Purposefully! Her anger bubbles over. "I couldn't confirm those messages were reaching you if I NEVER heard back from you!"

"I'm sure you have ways of tracking me down, don't you, Ms. Moore?" Carlos incites.

"Why should I have to track you down? Obviously, you didn't care to know what I had to say then. Why does it matter now?"

Carlos sits down in the tall office chair behind the desk and crosses an ankle over the knee. "Contrary to what you may believe, I'm not one who enjoys having kids that I know nothing about. We may cross paths one day. Now, you tell me, why does a lying, undercover trick—who doesn't even like men—decide to have my child anyway?"

Shannon's mouth opens, but no words come out.

"You can't say?" He laces his fingers and rests his hands against his abs. "Perhaps you were investigating me and things went a little too far. Then, you find out you're pregnant and can have that baby you always wanted, except in this situation you wouldn't need the help of a fertility clinic. Or, maybe he's not my child at all, but you work for someone who would make it very profitable for you to entangle my name."

Infuriated, Shannon dismisses the forewarning he'd given her inside the limo and lunges at Carlos, only to be dodged and slammed harshly on top of the desk. His face displays shock at what he's done, but it's short-lived as she rises up aggressively again.

Pinning her, he confronts her face to face. "NO MORE LIES. Was this your plan or someone else's?"

Shannon's head throbs like it's about to explode. She stares at him, utterly flabbergasted after listening to him say such heartless, caustic things. She doesn't believe he deserves to ever hear the truth, but the rage from the pain and humiliation he's caused send the words flowing from her mouth uncontrollably.

"Get away from me! I hate that I ever met you!" she yells, struggling wildly to free her arms so she can knock his block off. "I was never involved in a case concerning you. I got involved with you because I wanted to—was dumb enough to. I left my job, moved nearly 3,000 miles away and had your baby because I chose to! Whether you believe me or not, consider you came looking for me. Whatever conspiracy theories you have because of your own involvements and paranoia, I have nothing to do with them. And THAT'S the truth."

Shannon continues to struggle against his unrelenting pressure, fighting until she breaks emotionally. Out of breath, she stares into the eyes that had once lit a sensual fire inside her and whispers, "I was crazy enough to love you, and you didn't deserve it. You never deserved it."

Carlos' grasp loosens and she's able to slip away. He steps aside, allowing her to slide from the desk to the floor. She's unable to subdue the heavy sobs emerging from deep within, a display of emotion more embarrassing than anything else she could imagine at the moment.

"Just let us go," she says, not daring to look in Carlos' direction. She feels him observing her as she wipes her tears and tries to regain her footing. Rubbing both hands over his hair, he continues to stare indecisively, then as if sparked by something, he moves to the baby carrier, picks it up, and grabs Shannon's arm. Forcefully ushering her to the door, he mutters, "Too late for that."

They join Beto and a young man strangely familiar to Shannon outside the office. As the four of them stand in the corner of the "L" shaped hallway, a plump, late middle-aged woman emerges from a doorway at the end near the second elevator. Almost simultaneously, an attractive, heavily-endowed younger woman dressed in a silky, thigh length robe advances from the other end. She stops short when she sees Shannon, and the reciprocated vibes are instantly threatening and unfriendly.

Shannon's attention is reclaimed by the older woman's exclamation, "¿¡Es eso un bebé?!"[4] She clasps her hands excitedly over her mouth and her house-shoes click eagerly toward the baby carrier. She peeks. "¡Oh, tan bello! ¿Cuál es su nombre, Carlo?"[5]
Carlos stares at Shannon a few seconds before responding in English. "Carlos Antonio. His *name* is Carlos Antonio."
The woman looks up at him dubiously. Shannon may not understand Spanish, but she can certainly read their non-verbals and intonations.
"¿Él es su hijo?"[6] she asks with bated breath.
Waving her off, Carlos cuts to the matter at hand, his Spanish flowing like one long word. "No questions right now, Tia. I need you to buy the baby... whatever babies need. And get her some clothes to wear, also." He addresses Shannon. "Do you need anything in particular? I don't have time to play games, so I suggest you speak up now."
Shannon tries her best to think through the fog in her head. She comes up with something practical and something useful. *Hopefully in helping us escape.* "Some diapers. And a Baby Bjorn."
Puzzled by her request, Carlos asks, "A Bjorn??"
The young man volunteers enthusiastically, "It's a baby carrier you strap on. I seen it before."
Shannon looks at him with disdain, preferring he'd kept his comment to himself. She observes his nervous energy and the unwarranted, silly smile plastered on his face, and remembers where she'd seen him. He is the overzealous man she mistook as restaurant staff during one of her dates with Carlos. It was the one and only time she'd seen this guard around, and Shannon surmises why that is probably so. *He's a strange bird.*
"Something to help you be hands-free, Ms. Moore?" Carlos chides. "Nice try." To the one called "Tia," he says in Spanish, "No harness type carriers, please."
He hands the baby carrier to the glowing woman, who gladly accepts, then he takes Shannon by the arm once again.
Over his shoulder, he issues stern instructions in Spanish to both guards and the woman as they journey to the elevator.

---

[4] Is that a baby!?

[5] Oh, so handsome!! What is his name, Carlo?

[6] He's your son?

"They don't leave this house. Someone is to stay by her doors at all times. And do not be careless. She's crafty... and trained in combat."

"*Heh, heh*. Sul," Beto sniggers.

Suspicious of plotting behind her back, Shannon turns her head to keep C-Lo in her sights and catches the mixture of curiosity and shock on the faces of the two she didn't know. *Why are they giving me those looks?* she obsesses, wishing she'd paid a little attention in Intro to Foreign Language to at least understand a *few* words.

The elevator doors close, then retract onto another wide hallway one level above. The path ahead fades, unlit at the far end. Moonlight trickles narrowly across the floor through unseen windows. Walking briefly forward, the group turns left through an archway granting access to a set of deeply recessed double doors.

As Carlos reveals the room where Shannon is to stay, he informs her to call his aunt, "Delia," and to buzz the intercom if she needs anything. When Delia seems satisfied the room is in order, she leaves, happy about a baby being there, and pulls both doors closed behind her. Carlos sits on the side of the bed and looks at Shannon holding the baby.

"This is not the way I wanted you to come to my home."

I could not care less about your feelings! Shannon's inner voice screams. But she keeps her lips sealed. Carlos gets up to exit and pauses.

"By the way, this place is heavily monitored, so it will be a waste of time trying to leave."

The door closes. Shannon follows him and cracks one of the double doors to peek out. Beto stands up from a recently placed chair in the alcove, and she shuts and locks the door. *For whatever good it might do.*

Turning around, she surveys the room. She tries one set of double doors. It's the closet. Another set of double doors reveals a private bathroom suite. She moves to the windows, peering through the sheers hanging over each one. No identifying landmarks are visible anywhere. Just trees and darkness.

Unlocking the last door in the room, Shannon looks out onto a private balcony and is engulfed by intense humidity. Not ten seconds later, a guard steps from beneath the balcony to peer up at her while holding his ear piece. Covering C-Lo in her arms, she quickly retreats.

Stay calm, Shannon. Just figure out your location.

She remembers Carlos once saying he had a home in Florida and surmises from the humidity that that must be where they are. *But what city?* She picks up the TV remote from the nightstand, clicks the power button, and turns up the volume. Spanish. She flips to another channel. Spanish. Impatiently, she begins surfing for any news channels and discovers the stations are all in Spanish.

It dawns on her. *We probably aren't even in the states anymore.*

C-Lo begins to fuss, and as Shannon looks at him in her arms, she thinks, *How apropos.* She feels like joining him in a good cry. Instead, she gets down on her knees and prays.

The Longest Night

[13]

Determined not to close her eyes the entire night, Shannon sits by the coffee table, exhausted and on edge. It is now 11:37 and the breakfast tray Delia brought around 9 this morning lies cold and basically untouched on the stand by the door. After scouring all areas of the room for anything she could modify into a concealable weapon and finding nothing, she'd inspected the tray just for the presence of eating utensils. Needless to say, they had been conveniently eliminated.

Beginning early in the morning, annoying interruptions brought on by several, possibly timed deliveries of items for her and the baby served to slow her methodical search and wear her down. To keep focused, Shannon concentrates on the knocks at the door.

This time, however, there isn't a knock. The door handle jiggles, causing Shannon to jump. Without waiting for her to respond, three key tones sound, the door unlocks, and it swings open. Shannon springs, baby in arms, like a cornered cat. In walks Carlos along with a man she has never seen before.

"This is Dr. Valdés," Carlos introduces. "He's here to clear up this little ambiguity between you and me and do a paternity test. You can either cooperate or we can take him elsewhere and get it done."

"A test is not necessary," Shannon admits. "He's your son. You know he's your son."

"You and I both know he's my son. But it still needs to be done. For legal reasons."

The doctor attempts to reassure Shannon by adding in a heavy accent, "It's really a simple procedure." He begins to lay out implements.

"Why do you have a needle?" Shannon asks. "You only need to swab his mouth to obtain DNA."

The doctor pauses. "Yes. But we need his blood type, too."

"You are NOT sticking a needle in my son."

Carlos walks over to Shannon and speaks quietly. "Do not make this more difficult. I'm sure you wouldn't want the baby getting hurt because of some foolish behavior on your part."

Backing away from him, she turns to the doctor and spouts, "Listen to me! He forced me on a plane against my will by threatening to take my son and is now holding us captive here. Please, help us get out of here!"

The doctor looks blankly at Shannon, then proceeds in broken English. "I... not here to get involved in this argument from you. I only here to perform a medical test."

"What do you mean, you can't get involved?" she yells. "I just told you we were abducted! A crime! It's your duty to report any suspicious or potentially harmful incidents. We are in danger here!"

"I see no evidence of harm here. In fact, is clear to me you are well taken care."

Shannon looks at the doctor and Carlos in horrified incredulity. Carlos appears unfazed by her outburst. The doctor turns to Carlos. "I can step out if you need."

Anticipating the worst after taking that half-baked risk, a dozen or more potentially ill-fated scenarios flash through her mind. Carlos speaks. "Are you done with the stunts, Shannon?"

"He's not really a doctor, is he?"

"Oh, he is a doctor. Here to do the medical testing I requested."

"What proof do I have that he is, and that that's all he's doing?"

"You'll have to trust me." To the doctor, he instructs, "Vamos a proceder."[7]

They advance. It feels like the world is closing in on Shannon, but fighting and trying to run with the baby would be useless and foolish, just as Carlos had said. Surrendering C-Lo, she looks on helplessly and prays they won't hurt him.

Once the men depart, she paces, wracking her brain for a plan to seek help quickly and safely with a baby. *I need weapons, and I need a way to carry C-Lo hands-free.* Formulating an idea, she removes the bed sheet and spreads it on the floor.

Instantaneously, a door opens. Ocho—the last of Carlos' henchmen she'd expect to have guarding her door and the first one she'd suspect to do her the most harm, if given the opportunity—

---

[7] Let's proceed.

steps into the room. Shannon scurries away in fear of another attack, but he remains by the door.

"What are you doing?"

"It's... for the baby," Shannon offers, wondering how much of her room is under surveillance.

Distrustfully, he takes his leave, and Shannon's eyes shift from floor to ceiling in search of hidden video cameras. Moving to a remote corner of the room, she presses herself against the wall, places one foot onto a chair and boosts herself upward for a better view.

Ocho bursts in again. "Get down from there!"

Off balance in her haste to step down, Shannon knocks over the chair and twists her ankle in the process. She contorts, trying to mask the pain and appear poised for battle should he come any closer. He doesn't, but the threats in his words are very clear.

"I don't care to babysit. I come in here one more time, you will get hurt. And by the way, you may have suckered Sul back there on the plane, but it won't go down like that with me."

His glare is a mix of lust and contempt. Hating to be in his oppressive, harassing presence, Shannon scowls, suffering for want of an escape.

Thankfully, Ocho exits, but this time when the door closes, she crumples to the floor. Her situation appears hopeless. They are watching her every move. Letting off steam with a muffled scream, she pounds the floor with her fists.

Her tantrum is truncated by noises at the doors. Two awkward knocks and the door on the left opens slightly. Shannon tenses.

Delia and Ocho have a short, animated conversation in the doorway before a resolute "¡Abre la puerta!"[8] resounds. Delia pushes past Ocho's attempt to bar her entry while returning his look of disapproval with her own. She places the food tray on the stand, and they continue to argue in Spanish.

"I'm not going to let the girl starve," she says defiantly.

"You shouldn't come in here—for your own safety. Give one of us the tray and we'll put it in the room," Ocho insists.

"Nonsense!" Turning to Shannon, Delia says, "If you need anything, you just ask me."

---

[8] Open the door!

Apparently having had the last say, she exits. Ocho trails behind her, leaving Shannon hankering to understand what had been said.

Hours later, Carlos returns. Without acknowledging Shannon, he looks around the room, from the sheet on the floor to the overturned chair to the untouched lunch platter. As if he has seen enough, he journeys back to the door and pauses with his hand on a handle.

"It would be wise to make yourself comfortable. You may be here awhile," he advises.

"Where is *here*?"

Carlos steps through the doorway with his eyebrows raised mockingly, and Shannon hobbles after him. "We're not in the U.S. anymore, are we? *Are we*? Carlos, answer me!"

The door closes in her face.

She yanks it open, and a new guard stands up from his post. He does a double take when he sees Shannon, but she doesn't notice. Staring angrily at Carlos' back, she demands, "Answer me."

Carlos whirls around, but remains composed. "No. You answer me. Tell me, what did you find when you were researching me?"

"For the last time! I was not research..."

She falls silent, recalling the phone call she'd made to the bureau. *He can't know about that, can he?*

"Ah! Maybe it's coming back to you now?"

Shoes tap across the large, marble tiles, announcing the arrival of another presence. Delia steps into the short hall and says cheerfully, "¿Tiene hambre, Señorita?"

"'Are you hungry?'" Carlos interprets.

He reaches to take the tray from Delia, who kindly refuses to hand it over. She smiles and gracefully makes her way past them into the room to set down the tray. She removes the cover for Shannon to view. Despite her famished state, Shannon rejects the offer and turns angrily back to Carlos.

Delia looks uncomfortably from Carlos to Shannon. "Entonces... voy a dejarlo aqui en caso que cambie de opinión."[9]

"Eat," Carlos commands.

"No!"

---

[9] Well, I'll leave it in case you change your mind.

"Suit yourself." He beckons Delia from the room. "You'll fold eventually."

***

Over the next forty-eight hours, Shannon observes as much activity as she can. A guard is posted outside her door in shifts at all times. Each of them stand up every time she opens the door, so she gathers that she can't leave the room.

As time drags by, familiar guards are gradually replaced with new ones, but she soon recognizes one guard consistently assigned to the night shift. Yendris. The only one who bothered to introduce himself. *Unlike the others, a courteous knock always proceeds his entry...*

Three times a day, Delia cheerfully delivers food, which Shannon notes is always consumable without the need for utensils, most likely at Carlos' instruction. Receiving the usual refusal, she leaves concerned. It troubles Shannon to come off rudely to someone who seems to genuinely care, not to mention wasting food that looks and smells tasty while her stomach protests. However, having been threatened with drugs once already, she isn't trusting anyone or anything. Her only goal is to find a way to safety, and the only way to do so is to remain alert.

With anyone able to walk into her room at any moment, Shannon is constantly on guard, toting C-Lo in the carrier wherever she goes—whether it's to the restroom, to wash up or to walk from one side of the room to the other.

Spurning the guest bed, she strategically positions herself in an armchair against the wall to discourage sleeping. Fear of the unknown keeps her from closing her eyes for any length of time, but she slides the antique wooden serving stand in front of the bedroom doors as a precaution anyway. *If I do fall asleep, the sound of this scraping across the travertine should wake me up.*

The days pass. Sleep deprived and hounded by hunger pangs, Shannon loses track of what day it is. She guesses it's been three, maybe five days since they got on that plane, and she's no closer to knowing Carlos' objective for bringing her and C-Lo here. Each day, C-Lo grows more irritable and difficult to pacify, but despite her exhaustion, Shannon refuses all Delia's attempts to help.

As the trays continue to appear and her energy depletes, Shannon begins picking out pieces of fruit and other foods that don't appear to be tampered with. Unfortunately, by this juncture, she is too weak and undernourished for it to matter.

One morning, sometime before sunrise, the moment Carlos predicted arrives. The strenuous, endless task of caring for her baby under duress, in conjunction with not sleeping or eating enough, finally takes its toll on her. Delia and Yendris enter her room and are met with a barrage of excruciating baby cries as Shannon sits bedside cradling C-Lo in her arms. She doesn't appear to notice anyone else's presence. Yendris covers his ears, unable to stand another shrill screech, and looks to the one he'd sought to fix it.

Delia sits next to Shannon. Gently, she tries to coax the baby from her while Yendris stands nearby. Instinctively, Shannon moves the baby. Sensing the staunch resistance, Delia does just as she had numerous times before and leaves the room, except this time she returns within a few minutes on the phone.

"Un momento..."[10] she says into the receiver before gingerly offering the phone to Shannon. Shannon doesn't take it, so Delia puts the phone on speaker.

"Hello? Shannon? Listen to me very carefully. If I wanted to kill you and take the baby, I would have done so already. Think about it. You won't do the baby any good if you can't function, and I'm sure that's not what you want. I can either force him from you or you can let Delia take him, you understand? Am I understood?"

Shannon slumps down on the bed and looks up miserably at Delia. The woman waits patiently through the baby's piercing cries for Shannon to cooperate. *He's right. I can't go on like this.* Faintly, she replies, "Yes."

Delia rubs her reassuringly on the arm as she hands C-Lo over. The last thing Shannon remembers before rolling over on the bed is sweet silence.

---

[10] One moment...

Aunt in Trust

[14]

Shannon's eyes fly open, and she sits up, disoriented. As she takes in her surroundings, she realizes she hadn't been having a nightmare. She and her son are really being held captive... in Carlos' home. Daylight filters through the window sheers, so she perceives she must've been asleep for a couple hours. She turns toward C-Lo's bassinet and her memory is jarred. *He's gone!*

Racing from the bed in a panic, she slings the double doors open, anticipating resistance as the overzealous guard springs energetically from his chair. She's poised to fight. He displays that crooked smile of his.

"Where's my son?!" she blurts, proceeding to push past him without waiting for a reply. The guard doesn't stop her, but steps aside, motioning for her to go right ahead. She rushes from the room and halts, not knowing which direction to take.

Straight ahead, stairs lead below, and to the far right is an elevator. Between the stairwell and the elevator there is a wide hallway, and to the far left, past two tall double doors, appears a foyer of some sort. Behind her, she hears the guard say, "They're downstairs," as he walks up.

Shannon's socks skid across the cool, marble floor tiles and down the spiraled stairwell to another wide hallway below. Intuitively, she follows the sound of Spanish television coming from one of the open archways flanking the hall and enters the room. C-Lo reclines in a bouncer, smiling as Delia leans from her seat on the sofa and lovingly coos, "¡Carlito, *Carlito!*"

Shannon lifts him into her arms and snuggles him close. Pleasantly surprised, Delia rises from the sofa, talking excitedly in Spanish.

"Oh, you're awake, and you finally came out of that room! I was beginning to get so worried. You slept for a day and a half! Yes, yes. The baby's fine. He's been eating well—the formula—and playing and smiling. Oh, he's such a happy baby, so wonderful, so handsome!"

Shannon shrugs slightly in confusion. "I—I don't..." she begins, then abandons the effort and looks to the guard. "What did she say?"

Delia also turns to the guard. "Yoan, dile lo que acabo de decir."[11]

Yoan scratches his forehead, struggling to recall what Delia had rattled off. "She said you slept for a day and a half. And... uh, the kid was okay."

Shannon is taken aback. *A day and a half?* She can't believe she was out that long. She turns to Delia and cups her hand in one of hers. "Thank you. Very much. Thank you."

Delia pats her hand lovingly and modestly waves off her thanks. "¡Claro!"[12]

She takes Shannon's arm and begins walking from the den into the hallway.

"¿Adónde vas?"[13] Yoan questions Delia.

"La voy a llevar a la cocina a buscar algo para jamar. Ella debe estar muriendo de hambre por ahora,"[14] she replies.

"¡Ella puede jamar en su cuarto!"[15] Yoan objects, blinking rapidly.

"Ella puede jamar conmigo."[16]

Shaking his head at her obstinacy, Yoan follows closely behind. They head left from the den for a few feet and turn right into a bright, spacious kitchen. Delia picks up a few plates and continues through an open archway into the adjoining breakfast nook. In the center of a large rectangular table prepared with multiple place settings sits a scrumptious looking spread of food.

She informs Shannon in Spanish, motioning expressively with her hands as she speaks, "I cooked some lunch. Ropa vieja, tamales, moros, platano, and some vegetables. It has squash and corn. A salad is there, also. But I understand if you don't want to eat my cooking. It's no problem. Also, I put a microwave and a small refrigerator with some frozen breakfasts, lunches and dinners in the room for you. It's whatever you want."

---

[11] Yoan, tell her what I just said.

[12] Of course!

[13] Where are you going?

[14] I'm taking her to the kitchen to get something to eat. She must be starving by now.

[15] She can eat in her room!

[16] She can eat with me.

Again, Delia looks to the guard to translate. Overtly agitated with his new assignment as an interpreter, Yoan rolls his eyes and huffs. His aunt folds her arms in front of her, and when he catches the look she has in reaction to his attitude, he twitches noticeably and quickly straightens up.

"She said she c-cooked. Some food. And put some food in your room," he recounts, brushing a hand over his curly afro.

Shannon quells the desire to laugh at their interaction. *Delia appears to have a way with the men of this household, and it's probably best to stay in her good graces. I wouldn't want her to think I was laughing at her.* Having found C-lo safe and content in her care, Shannon has admittedly garnered a tremendous amount of respect and appreciation for Delia in their short acquaintance, as well.

Surmising that any ill intent toward her or the baby would have been easily achievable over the past few days, she sits at the table receptively. Delia makes Shannon and Yoan plates, then fixes one for herself.

She sits next to Shannon, and it's obvious she wants to converse. However, the language barrier is an issue. They smile awkwardly at one another every now and then, and when they finish eating, Shannon compliments Delia's cooking in the most effective way she knows how.

"Mmm!" she says.

Delia laughs, waving off Shannon one more time.

Fingering the fork in her hand, Shannon turns to Yoan. "I need to speak with Carlos. Where is he?"

Yoan grins. "He's not here."

"When will he be back?"

"Don't know."

Shannon rises from the table and looks around, trying to recall the way to Carlos' office. One of the breakfast nook archways grants her visibility of the same hallway into which she descended from the stairs near her bedroom, so she knows it's close by.

Yoan stands, as well, and Shannon catches a glimpse of the pistol beneath the buttons of his shirt. He grabs her by the arm and states, "You must be ready to return to your room."

Suspecting him to be unstable, she decides to heed the intimation, and they excuse themselves from Delia's presence. Later that evening, though, she peers from the room to brave another inquiry. "Is Carlos back yet?"

Her question, although posed politely, strikes a nerve with Yoan. "L-Listen, he's out the country, lady! D-Don't keep asking me!" An incredulous look spreads across Shannon's face. *Carlos brought us here and LEFT us?* "I need to speak with him *now.*"

In heightened irritation, Yoan's English becomes garbled, yet he continues to sport a half smile. Nervous twitches punctuate his words. "I'm only make sure you no leave these house! Ev'rythin' else, talk-ay to 'im. Wh-WHEN he g-gets back!"

Shuddering herself, Shannon closes the door and slips the fork she hopes will not be missed into a more secure location.

As she retires for the night, she tries in vain to recall scriptures that will bring comfort or hope to her situation, before remembering the pocket Bible that she keeps in the diaper bag for those late morning dashes to church. She prays it's still there and is allayed to find that it is. Flipping the pages, she looks for the words she knows are somewhere in Psalms 38 and reads aloud, "Make haste to help me, O Lord my salvation..."

The next morning, Shannon rises early, plotting her course of action. *If yesterday was any indication that I'm not confined solely to this bedroom, I have every intention of making myself familiar with as much of this rambling mansion and its occupants as possible until I can slip out undetected.* She looks out the window at the sparkling, tear-drop shaped pool below and contemplates just the person who could most likely make an afternoon exploration happen. But first, she has to meet her for breakfast.

Shannon wipes her mouth with her napkin and scoots back in her chair, gazing around the room. "This is such a lovely home," she tells Delia. "May I have a tour?"

"Hah! No. Absolutely not," Yoan voices.

Shannon puts on her best subtly dejected performance. Delia turns expectantly toward Yoan for a translation. He stalls, so she prods, "¿Y bien? ¿Qué dijo ella?"[17]

Don't you lie.

Yoan closes his eyes. He mutters something in Spanish.

"¡Aye, claro!" Delia gushes. "¡Sí! Vamos a mostrarle la casa."[18]

Excitedly, the matriarch rises from the table, and Yoan can do nothing other than tag along respectfully. Shannon picks up the baby carrier as Delia leads the way, *all according to plan.*

---

[17] Well? What did she say?

[18] Of course! Yes! Let's show her the house.

Exiting the breakfast nook through one of its other archways, they enter a lush, tropical indoor garden with foliage climbing trellises two stories high. Delia plucks away a few troubled leaves that catch her eye and continues to the exterior. Glass double doors open onto a poured concrete exterior balcony framed by colonial concrete railings. From the balcony, they descend stone steps to the ground level and arrive at the pool. Across from it stands a quaint two story guest or, perhaps, pool house.

The pool and its surrounding areas are conveniently covered by mosquito netting elegantly draped from the roof of the main house down to the roof of the pool house. Beyond the netting spans acres of rolling, uncluttered lawns and gardens separated by some sort of leveled sporting field.

Passing the inviting mass of water, they reenter the main house through another set of double doors and access the recreation room, replete with a large, mahogany bar, pool table and various gaming activities one would expect in a pool hall. Shannon is guided from the rec-room into the same hallway she remembers entering on the night of her arrival. The small elevator they'd used then is to the right, next to a narrow stairwell. *So, the garage must be behind that door on the far opposite end,* she presumes, hoping the tour ventures in that direction.

They do turn left, but stop at one of the doorways along the hall. Delia smiles with anticipation as she stands in front of it and says, "For some reason, I think you'll really like this room!"

She waits for Yoan to translate, prolonging her own suspense, before she pushes open the door. A full line of gym equipment awaits them. Eyeing the punching bag, Shannon marvels at the woman's intuition and figures she should make use of this room if she gets the chance. *Strengthening myself during this ordeal would be wise.*

Shannon peeks in at the hot tub and misting room and smiles supportively at Delia. "Nice!" she says.

As if she understood, Delia responds in Spanish, "Wait until you see the workspace for arts and crafts. Now, that's my favorite! I can sew and paint—"

"Tia," Yoan interrupts. "Es todo. Porque si seguimos más adelante, pasamos la línea."[19]

They exchange looks and, for the first time, Shannon watches Delia acquiesce.

---

[19] That's enough. We're going out of bounds.

Yoan tells Shannon, "The tour is over."

She thinks quickly for a reason to stay around the house and stops Delia as they prepare to leave. "I'd like to sit by the pool, if that's okay. It's really hot, and the baby and I have been inside for God only knows how many days. I promise, I won't make any trouble," she says.

She flashes her most convincing smile for Yoan to translate.

Thankful for Delia's influence, Shannon kicks her legs around in the cool water and wipes the perspiration from her brow. The poolside view allows her to scope out a considerable stretch of the rear and side grounds, and she examines her surroundings casually, but carefully.

The first and second levels are subterranean on one side of the house and she surmises that Carlos' windowless office must be on one of those two levels. She locates her bedroom windows on the third floor and ponders how the interior of the home is so beautiful compared to its weather-worn exterior. Nevertheless, the place is every bit as elegant as she would expect a home owned by Carlos to be, perhaps lacking nothing. Under different circumstances, she could really like it here.

The soothing ripples of the water beckon Shannon in. Yoan perches nearby on a chair, watching her faithfully, which gives her an idea. She looks over at C-Lo playing contentedly with the toys dangling from the carrier's handle then back to Yoan. *Time to see who's paying attention.*

She goes for it, clothes and all, thrusting herself into the shallow end of the pool with the biggest splash she can manage. Yoan jerks upright, seized by another jittery attack, but he soon realizes her action is harmless. After he settles down, he seems somewhat amused by the woman splashing around in a flowing top and ankle length skirt.

Hoping to learn where any other watchful eyes may be, Shannon quickly scans the area looking for movement and faces to poke around walls or appear behind windows. Someone spies around the corner of the house. Curtains wiggle on the lower level of the pool house as well as on the fourth floor of the main house.

Everything else is still, confirming for Shannon that most of the eyes on her must be via video surveillance. *I have to find that room!*

The spy, a girl probably in her pre teens, slowly inches her thin, undeveloped frame into their proximity from the side of the house. Having caught a glimpse of the girl staring at her from a distance the day before, Shannon now has a better view of the pretty face framed by a short, wavy bob.

Shannon offers her a smile and wades to the side of the pool to check on C-Lo. Returning the smile, the girl stands shyly by for awhile before seemingly stirring up the courage to come sit beside them. When she speaks, it is surprisingly clear, her accent negligible.

"Hi. May I see the baby?"

Shannon turns C-Lo's carrier around for their new visitor, who coos, "Ahh! ¡Hola bebe Carlito!"[20]

I keep hearing that word. "Carlito. What does that mean?" she ventures.

It turns out the girl is talkative and happy to share her knowledge. "It's a nickname for Carlos! But, Tio's nickname is Los, so that's how you can tell the Big Carlos from the Little Carlos. When we hear Carlito, we know we're talking about the little one."

Nodding, Shannon smiles at the girl's cute explanation of how they differentiate between dad and son. The youth is bursting with curiosity.

"You are from the U.S.?" she asks timidly.

Shannon nods again. Suddenly, the questions begin to flow in rapid succession.

"Are you going to live here with us now?"

Shannon manages a small smile. "No... I don't think so."

"Why not?"

"Uh... because... I have a home somewhere else."

Wide-eyed, the girl asks, "Is your home bigger than this one?"

Shannon laughs, "No. Not even close."

Before the girl can verbalize her next question, Shannon interrupts. "Wait a minute, young lady. I don't even know your name."

"Oh! Sorry!" she giggles. "My name is Yunaisys."

"So, Yunaisys, what about you? Where do you live?"

"I live here with my dad and Tio."

"Who's Tio?"

Yunaisys laughs. "Uncle Carlos!" C-Lo babbles, recapturing Yunaisys' attention. "He's so cute!"

A woman's sharp voice calls from above. Both Shannon and Yunaisys look up to see the other woman who was present the day

---

[20] Hello, baby Carlito!

of Shannon's arrival standing on a fourth floor balcony. She calls again to Yunaisys in Spanish.

"Is that your mom?" Shannon asks.

"She is not my mom," Yunaisys retorts, her pleasant aura turning somber as she excuses herself.

The woman watches Yunaisys until she reaches the house. She then cuts her eyes at Shannon and disappears.

Curious about the exchange, Shannon starts to climb the pool stairs and glances down at her clinging clothes. Dropping back into the water, she looks skeptically at Yoan.

"Hey... think I can get a towel?"

New Information

[15]

The next morning, Yunaisys bounds into the breakfast nook pursued by the same woman from yesterday. The woman greets Delia reservedly, but ignores Shannon. Delia speaks and turns to receive a distracted hug from Yunaisys. It's obvious the girl can hardly wait to speak with Shannon and hurriedly joins the rest of them at the table. The woman, on the other hand, chooses to linger around the kitchen, conspicuously keeping her distance from Shannon.

Yunaisys drops her school bag onto the floor, and the first words from her mouth are, "What happened to your hair? Yesterday, it was curly and now it's es-straight."

Shannon chuckles at Yunaisys' brazenness. "I flat ironed it. You don't like it?"

"Oh, no, it's nice! Can you do me?" Yunaisys' eyes sparkle like a kid enamored by a new toy.

"I can, but your hair is beautiful just like it is, perfect for a young lady your age. How old are you anyway?"

"I will make ten in two weeks. Tio's going to make me a big birthday party!"

Attempting to conceal the disdain Shannon has for Carlos, she musters, "Oh, that's really nice."

"You're so lucky," Yunaisys raves.

"Why do you say that?" Shannon asks, trying to follow the youngster's train of thought while keeping a watchful eye on the woman glaring in her direction every time she speaks.

"I want to marry someone just like Tio when I get older. He's so handsome and nice. And rich!"

Shannon wishes she could tell the girl how wrong her priorities are. Instead, she replies, "I see. Tell me, who is the lady in there?"

"That's Carmen, Tio's assistant."

The girl's body language screams a lack of fondness for the woman, and although Shannon has her own opinions, she wonders why. Carmen calls Sul, the guard currently assigned to Shannon, into the kitchen. Briefly, Shannon relives the morning's unpleasant discovery when she opened the bedroom door and found him on duty. *Lord only knows what would've happened had he not backed away non-threateningly and I'd been forced to play my cards too soon.*

Sul and Carmen chat in a clandestine manner, glancing back at Shannon periodically. Above the rim of her coffee cup, Delia's eyes glint with dissatisfaction as she, too, observes their rude behavior. She gets up to take Shannon's plate into the kitchen and pours a second serving of coffee. As Yunaisys piles more food onto her plate, Shannon slides a knife into her lap and probes further.

"Yesterday, you said you live here with your dad." She tips her head toward Sul. "Is that him?"

"No, that's Uncle Ramon."

Inside the kitchen, Delia has a few stern words with Carmen and Sul, after which she makes her way back into the breakfast nook.

"So, who is your father?"

Delia reclaims her seat, and Carmen whispers something else to Sul.

"¡Te dije, no puedo hacer nada al respecto!"[21] he yells and turns away to refill his coffee cup.

Bristling like a diva, Carmen's fair skin turns siren red and she lifts her chin on her way out, slicing Shannon with a dirty look once more. Distracted by the hubbub, Shannon misses Yunaisys' response.

"What was that again?" she asks, as everyone's eyes in the breakfast nook return from the kitchen scene.

Yunaisys' reply comes in between chews. "His name is Aimé... but... everyone knows him as 'Ocho.'" Delia promptly rebukes the girl for speaking with her mouth full.

That repulsive man is this child's father? Shannon thinks, shielding her face against the unfavorable expressions trying to escape. *If Yunaisys thinks he's spectacular too, I'll be mortified.*

"The other guy that's usually with me—the one who looks like he's in his twenties. He has to be the baby of the bunch, right?"

---

[21] I told you, I can't do nothing about it!

Yunaisys' face puckers. "Uncle Yoan *is* the baby, but he's almost FORTY! He's just a big goofball."

"*Forty*? What!? No way!"

"Hey!!" Sul yells, disrupting the mirth as he halts beside Yunaisys' chair. "You're talking too much."

Shannon tenses, not sure of what Sul will do to Yunaisys. The pre-teen's eyes roll and the pouting begins, and Shannon breathes a sigh of relief. *If the girl isn't scared of him, it's a good sign he's not violent toward HER, at least.*

Sul turns to Shannon. "Let's go. The person you need to be talking to is waiting."

The office chair swivels around to face Shannon. Amazed at the effect the mere sight of her still has on his libido, Carlos appraises her form before motioning for her to sit. He turns his attention to his computer. "I trust Delia has made you feel welcomed and you've had everything you needed in my absence?"

"All except a ride to the airport. I've been as welcomed as I could possibly be while surrounded by your goons who repeatedly threaten my life, one of whom—standing right outside that door—recklessly pulled a gun on me and endangered ALL of our lives. So, thank you very much for your 'hospitality,' but our leave is long overdue."

"Is that how they teach you to negotiate on the police force? It's not very persuasive." Carlos snickers. "You and *my son* will be staying here awhile, if not indefinitely. I suggest you start making yourself comfortable with the idea."

"You think I would want to stay here? You're crazy. You don't control *me*, Carlos."

"Is that right? Well, I just assumed you wouldn't want to be separated from him." Carlos glances at C-Lo. "Because he's not going anywhere."

They stare rigidly at each other. Shannon takes a ragged breath. "We can work out some sort of arrangement—"

"The arrangement has already been worked out. You'll stay here until you're ready to tell me what I need to know."

"There's nothing to tell!" she snaps, envisioning the knife in her possession aiming for his jugular.

Ignoring her, Carlos calls Sul inside. "Take her back to her room."

Shannon shrugs her arm away from Sul, and he doesn't hesitate to grab her into a painful bear hug. He squeezes her torso so tightly she can barely breathe, yet the focus of her prayer is that the knife doesn't dislodge and hit the floor.

Carlos' eyes flash angrily. "Put her down!"

Shannon drops to the floor, coughing violently.

He stands up from his chair and moves in front of Sul. Placing a menacing grip on the back of Sul's neck, he looks him intently in the face. When Carlos speaks, his tone is eerily reserved. "¿Puedo confiar en ti, hermano? ¿Qué estás haciendo, eh?"[22]

Sul drops his head. "Si, Los. Perdonamé."[23]

Carlos tips his head toward the door, and the guard takes his cue to leave. He attempts to assist Shannon to her feet on his way out, and she retracts her arm, glaring at Carlos accusingly.

Carlos offers a token explanation. "He's just upset about how you manhandled him before. It'll pass."

"You *can't* be serious," she counters. "That man wants to *kill* me, and you are keeping me here so that he can."

"Well, then. You should be on your best behavior." He picks up the baby carrier and waits by the door. "Shall we?"

***

Shannon pounds the bed with her fists and flops over, weary of expending so much mental energy trying to devise a plan to get away, only to come up with nothing. She stares despondently into the darkness of the room. Devoid of answers, all she has is the constant accusation of something she had never knowingly been a part of.

A concept hits her. *I can use what Carlos believes to my advantage.* She runs to the door.

Yendris looks up. "What?"

"I need to speak with Carlos. It's urgent."

He shakes his head, his long ponytail swinging gently. "He's gone."

"What do you mean, he's gone?"

"He's gone," Yendris repeats. Striking hazel eyes that Shannon had been blind to before observe her deflated expression. She turns to go, and he adds, "He should be back tonight. Try later."

The information is unexpected. She's positive she wouldn't have received any of Carlos' itinerary from the others and looks over her shoulder as she closes the door. The Latin sentry tosses an easygoing salute her way.

---

[22] Can I trust you, brother? What are you doing, *hmm*?

[23] I'm sorry.

Yendris had unknowingly given Shannon a ray of hope. While none of the guards can be trusted, she'd seen compassion in this one's eyes, and that made her feel just a little better about having him assigned to her. By far the nicest and least threatening of all the guards, she wonders if Yendris might ultimately open up some doors for her. *Literally.* Picking up her hungry baby, Shannon prepares to breastfeed and wait for Carlos' return.

Knock, knock. "Shannon?"

She looks up. According to the clock on the wall, it is ten minutes after 1 in the morning, and C-Lo is still in her arms. They had fallen asleep in the arm chair. Yendris raps on the door and calls again.

"Coming," she responds quietly, laying down C-Lo and covering up before answering the door.

"He's back. Thought you'd like to know."

Yendris has dimples! Shannon notes, unprepared for her own reaction. *He should smile more often.*

As if hearing her thoughts, his eyes dip then resurrect. "So... now you know." The dimples resurface.

There's an awkward silence while the two regroup.

"Yes... Thank you." Shannon rushes to transfer C-Lo into his carrier and returns to the doorway.

Leisurely, Yendris escorts them downstairs into the spa area of the gym. Upon their entry he announces, "Here she is, Boss," and steps away. Shannon places the carrier on the floor beside her.

"Nothing like a hot, relaxing soak right after a stimulating workout," Carlos proclaims, stewing deliciously in the vigorous bubbles. "Care to join me? No? Okay."

Carlos takes a sip from his glass of rum, unhurried despite the sense of urgency Shannon's pursed-lip demeanor conveys. The water sloshes about him as he rises from the tub in the nude. His harmonious physique steaming, he stands within a breath's distance from her. She can smell the rum.

"You want... something, Ms. Moore?"

Determined not to be intimidated, distracted, or provoked by his strapping, virile splendor, Shannon focuses on his face and holds her ground, declaring what she came to say. "You believe someone is investigating you. And I wasn't. But I can help you find out if someone is."

Carlos snorts. "You can help *me?* And how would you do that?"

"I have contacts. At the bureau and in special ops."

"Contacts? Now, we're getting somewhere," Carlos responds, still beaming with mischief. Turning his head slightly for another sip, he says, "Tell me about these contacts."

"First, I need your word you'll let us go unharmed, and second, I'll need access to a computer."

Carlos laughs outright. "I believe you have contacts. I also believe allowing you to contact them would be unwise. And furthermore, I could never promise to let you go."

An undercurrent in those last words combined with his penetrating gaze makes Shannon quiver. Her core tightens, warming involuntarily as Carlos lifts his hand and brushes his finger softly across her cheek. He continues to speak.

"But, here is the deal I propose. You write down all the names of these contacts, and I'll research them."

He takes a gulp from the glass, and Shannon waits for him to continue. When it's apparent he has no intention of saying anything else, she asks, "And?"

"That was it," he says, finishing off his rum.

"So, what is the benefit for me?"

Carlos draws so close his lips tickle her earlobes. "If they come out cleared, so do you. Now, if you'll excuse me."

He reaches over Shannon intentionally and removes his towel from the hook. When he exits the room, Shannon exhales.

Nostalgia

[16]

Having had a difficult time sleeping, Shannon arrives to breakfast later than usual. Of course, as fate would have it, Carlos—the man who tormented her dreams the entire night in ways she once enjoyed in the past—is sitting at the head of the table. Carmen is also present, her scantily clad breasts positioned closely beside his arm, and she halts mid-sentence when she sees Shannon approach. Yoan barrels ahead to the table to help himself to a plate of food, and Shannon loiters, aloof, cuddling C-Lo against her shoulder.

"Good morning," Carlos says and stands to remove the chair on the other side of him.

Shannon doesn't budge, disinclined to join the party. He smiles wryly and waits. Unwilling to appear intimidated by anyone present in the room, Shannon takes the seat proffered. Carlos picks up her plate.

"What would you like to have today?"

Carmen's stippling stare is palpable. Avoiding her leer, Shannon scans the platters in the center of the table, but refuses Carlos' help.

"I've got it," she says, propping C-Lo up on the side of her lap and pulling at the plate.

Carlos relinquishes it. "I was just trying to give you a hand."

Shannon picks up a serving spoon. "Thanks."

He sits and watches Shannon bullheadedly fix her plate with one hand. "I see that aspect of you hasn't changed."

Shannon gives no reply. Carlos reaches over and lifts C-Lo from her lap.

"I told you, I have it. I can eat and hold him at the same time," Shannon asserts, attempting to retrieve the baby.

Carlos blocks her hands. "Relax. Enjoy your meal. I think I can handle holding him while you eat."

He turns his attention from the flustered mother to the bright-eyed, drooling baby in his lap. Carmen shoots up from the table, catching the table cloth and sending the dishes clanging. She glowers at Carlos, who ignores her. Startled by the ruckus, Shannon drops her fork on the table. When she picks it up to resume her meal, Carmen tosses her soiled napkin into Shannon's food.

"Hey!!" Shannon exclaims as Carmen storms from the room. Yoan looks questioningly at Carlos, who turns to look at Shannon.

"Do you have that list of names for me?" he asks, plucking the napkin from Shannon's plate.

Counting backward, Shannon stares at her food and takes several deep breaths. Calmly, she meets Carlos' gaze.

"No," she says. "Giving you the names of my contacts will turn up nothing. And then you'll claim that I didn't give you the pertinent ones. So, I figured it's a moot point."

C-Lo babbles happily as he dandles gently on Carlos' knee. Carlos smiles and centers on the baby. "I'm impressed. Very clever deduction, Ms. Moore. However, what you haven't given valuable consideration is the chance those names may actually validate your position. And send you free to go."

He's patronizing me. "Yeah, so... it's like I said. Guess we'll just be here with you forever in this merry web you have."

Carlos stops bouncing C-Lo and looks at Shannon.

"I wouldn't mind that," he says. He turns to Yoan. "What about you, Yoan? Do you mind Ms. Moore being here?"

Yoan looks up with his mouth full of food. "Aw hell." He grumbles something else unintelligible, swallows, then blurts, "Yes, I mind!!" Picking up his plate, he walks into the kitchen, twitching and murmuring, "I don't want to be g-guarding this chick f-forever!"

Shannon jerks her head around for Carlos' reaction. He stares blankly at his brother, then gets up from his chair to hand C-Lo to Shannon. Their eyes meet, and for the first time in seemingly forever, Shannon sees something there other than disdain or derision for her. The moment, whatever it was turning out to be, is quickly severed.

"¡Tio!"

Yunaisys dashes into the nook and Carlos has only seconds to brace himself for the hug she slings upon him.

"Tio, I want to show you something!" she exclaims, tugging at his arm.

"Yunaisys," Carlos says warmly. "Do you see anyone else in the room?"

"Oh, sorry!" she says. "Hello, Señora."

"Hi, missy," Shannon responds, and Yunaisys quickly refocuses on Carlos, adamant about her surprise. *The girl is truly enamored with him*, she thinks as Carlos is guided from the room.

Shannon checks her surroundings. Yoan wanders the kitchen scarfing down food, but is now engaged in an entertaining phone conversation, as well. No one else is in sight...

Snuggling C-Lo, Shannon creeps from the breakfast nook down the hallway toward the end where she has not been allowed to go. Sounds from the television in the den flood the atmosphere as she passes one archway. She stops, thinking she hears footsteps approaching from the direction in which she is heading. Guardedly, she continues a few more feet and reaches the second archway entrance to the den.

In the kitchen, just a few feet ahead of her, Yoan laughs, and Shannon stops in her tracks. *I should have a viable plan and escape route before I risk a move.*

Abruptly, she changes course. Delia looks over with a smile and welcomes her visitor with a pat on the sofa cushion. Shannon obliges, plopping down beside her. She tucks C-Lo under her shirt and begins to feed him, figuring she should probably appear as innocent as possible. Oblivious to any ulterior motives, Delia smiles and says, "Ponte cómoda, mija,"[24] before turning back to her novela.[25]

All of a sudden, there is a clipped yell and scrambling noises emanate from the breakfast nook. Just as Shannon anticipated, Yoan barks into his headset and footsteps patter into the hallway. He glances into the den, panic-stricken as he races past. Skidding to a stop, he returns to the archway to stare at Shannon.

Delia's in the middle of lamenting an occurrence on her show when Yoan clutches his forehead angrily and hollers, "¡HAY, hay!"

She jumps. "¿Que paso?"[26]

---

[24] Make yourself comfortable, my daughter.

[25] Spanish soap opera

[26] What's going on?

Ignoring her, he mumbles into his headset and walks briskly to the sofa to sit ominously next to Shannon. "What do you think you are d-doing, lady?!"

Shannon doesn't get a chance to respond. Delia scoots to the edge of the sofa and waves Yoan away. "¡Levántate! Dale a la niña un poco de privacidad,"[27] she fires at him, passing Shannon the throw from the arm of the couch just as Beto and Sul enter the room.

"How'd you lose her?!" Beto yells at Yoan.

"She just d-d-disappeared, man!"

Delia stands up. "¡Rigoberto! ¡Yoan! ¿Qué está pasando?"[28] she demands of the two.

"Esta bien, Tia."[29]

Hearing the voice from behind, Delia turns to face the adjoining study. Carlos appears and stops in front of her. They speak in Spanish.

"The guys just had a little scare, is all."

"Well, they're giving me a scare, behaving like this! And the poor girl... How is she ever going to feel comfortable here when they act that way?!" Delia drops her forehead onto his chest melodramatically and sighs, "Oh, my God!"

Carlos hugs her, but peers down at Shannon.

"That was a rousing stunt, Ms. Moore."

Shannon glares at him, having had her fill of insults this morning. "So much for making myself comfortable. Excuse me for that," she says, securing the throw across C-Lo with one hand while she pushes from the sofa with the other. Carlos releases Delia and moves to restrict Shannon's progress.

"I guess I have to ask who will be escorting me to my room."

"Me," he says, nodding his head. He places a firm arm around her waist. "This way."

Yoan gets a shove from Beto, and all the brothers trail behind Carlos and Shannon as she's relocated upstairs. Carlos steers her through the study where Carmen and Yunaisys hunch over homework. Carmen begrudgingly refuses to look their way, but Yunaisys grins broadly as they pass. *If those two only knew the truth about the man they hold so dearly...*

---

[27] Get up! Give the girl some privacy.

[28] What is going on?

[29] Everything is okay, Aunt.

The brothers remain in the main hallway griping indistinctly while Carlos reaches from behind Shannon to open one of her bedroom doors. On a Hail Mary, she spins around to face him, placing the two of them inches apart.

Carlos' hand lingers on the handle behind her hips, his smirk revealing his enjoyment of the delicate position she created. He is too close, the physical pull overwhelming, and the intrusive eyes of the spectators unsettling. Her pelvis tingles at the smell of him. An uncontrollable craving to be taken to the heights once more washes over her.

Carlos observes her mouth move as she tries to formulate words that will speak louder than her body language. *Don't lose focus, Shannon. He is holding you here against your will.*

She psyches herself up to make her demands, but ends up whispering. "If your goal is to have me killed by one of your thugs, then keeping me here is the right plan. But if you care anything about your son or him having his mother, get us out of here."

Carlos swings the door open in response.

"Listen to me," she says. "No one wants us here."

"Oh, now, that's not true."

He gives Shannon an evincing look that takes her by surprise. She averts her eyes, perceiving for the first time that he may have another reason for keeping her around. *Something else masked by that intense anger...*

She backs inside the room self-consciously and slams everyone out. On the other side, Carlos' Spanish words are smug. "Nothing to worry about. She's not going anywhere." The brothers erupt in laughter.

Complicating matters further, Shannon spots a circular box on the nightstand beside the bed. Wondering how long it had been there, she peeks inside and lifts out a gorgeous, pearl white, cross-front monokini with chrome accent rings.

***

Shannon stirs restlessly in the darkness, watching the minutes flicker by on the clock. Unanswered questions swirl in her brain, stumped by another of Carlos' stealthy departures. *His arrivals are just as mysterious,* she thinks, recalling the gift.

Stealthily, he'd watched me take that dip in the pool, and stealthily, he (or someone else) had slipped into my room to leave a swimsuit during the night while I was asleep. While that had been a nice gesture, other intentions might not have been. Shannon rubs her temples to fend off the headache creeping in.

Consumed with thoughts of who or what else may have materialized while she was vulnerable, she gives up on the idea of getting any shut eye. Envisioning Yendris outside her room, she wonders if perhaps he'd let her work off some of this energy.

Shannon rises from the bed, deciding it's worth asking.

Inside the gym, the swaying punching bag makes her workout much more difficult, but she pounds against it as best as she can. She can see Yendris watching her in the mirror whenever she glances at C-Lo for signals of stirring.

Suddenly, he stands, and Shannon cringes. *What is he doing?* As he walks toward her, she continues to strike the bag with reservation, preserving what little strength she has left should she need it.

Yendris grabs the bag and steadies it. He nods for her to proceed.

He's spotting me, Shannon realizes and nods a relieved "thank you" in return. Punching rigorously, she pounds away at her thoughts and, for a welcomed change, sleep comes easily that night.

Imminent Danger

[17]

Tiring of Delia's afternoon novelas, Shannon migrates from the den through the adjacent study in search of signs of Carlos. Yunaisys sits at the desk doing homework. Carmen monitors the child from across the room while flipping pages of a magazine. She drops the gossip publication guiltily at Shannon's appearance.

It must be her job to watch Yunaisys, Shannon speculates as she stops by the desk. She's greeted with a wide smile. Taking great delight in disrupting Carmen's state of mind by her intrusion, Shannon prolongs her visit with casual dialogue.

Meanwhile, Carmen grabs Yoan by the arm as he tags along into the room, significantly more mellow and perhaps less concerned with Shannon's flight risk than the day before. She begins whispering, and Yoan looks annoyed. Shannon gloats at his response, itching for just five minutes alone with the skank. Flashbacks of the dirty napkin in her plate are still fresh in her mind.

Shannon turns her attention back to Yunaisys. "Hey, yesterday you drug Carlos off, and I thought you stashed him somewhere. But then, he popped back out. Today, I've been looking for him all morning, and he's nowhere to be found. Did you hide him?"

Yunaisys giggles. "Noooo!"

Shannon leans over conspiratorially to whisper, "Well, where is he?"

Yunaisys is tickled out of breath, but finally manages, "He's gone to work!"

"Oh," Shannon says. *Does that mean Carlos is out of the country again?* She changes the subject. "What are *you* working on?"

"Math and English."

Shannon looks over her work briefly and notices she's writing an essay. "Can I read it?"

"It's time to leave," Yoan interrupts, poking his finger against the girl's papers to remind her of her task. "She has to pay attention to her work."

Yunaisys pouts, and Shannon tries to smooth things over. "Maybe I can read it when you finish? Would that be cool?"

"Yes!" she responds. "I'd like that very much."

The rest of the day seems like it will fade without Carlos' return. To pass the time, Shannon meanders around the house and grounds, venturing as far as she is allowed, often quelling the ever-mounting desire to break away with her need to know the truth. By the end of the day, she's bubbling over with anxiety and seeks another diffusing trip to the gym. Again, Yendris is happy to oblige.

He trails loosely behind while Shannon navigates the still, dimly lit hallways. She opts to take the stairs to the second floor, pass through the breakfast nook, and pick up the next flight to get to the gym below. Although the route makes lugging C-Lo's carrier more arduous, she figures the more muscle exertion, the better she should sleep.

As Shannon descends the stairs to the first level, she halts midway. Muffled moans and groans travel faintly through the walls, and although Shannon can't be sure, it sounds like a couple having sex. Unsure if she should proceed, she listens for confirmation, taking the opportunity to switch the baby carrier to her other hand.

Yendris reaches Shannon and stands next to her on the stair. He places a shocking hand on the small of her back and takes the carrier handle in the other.

"I can help." He smiles, obviously under the impression that carting a sixteen-pound, three-and-a-half-month–old baby around was the reason Shannon stopped.

He doesn't appear to hear anything. Shannon smiles back, and his gaze lingers. He seems to want to say something else, but before he can, she turns a distracted ear to the wall.

"What is wrong?" he asks.

"I just... thought I heard something."

Both of them listen.

"Guess it was nothing," Shannon concludes. Tucking the corner of her lip between her teeth, she accepts Yendris' assistance. He motions for her to continue ahead.

Cautiously, Shannon rounds the corner of the stairwell into the hallway, and walks past the rec-room entrance. As she nears another door on the left, it hurls open. Startled, she jumps aside to avoid colliding with an equally stunned Ocho. He pulls the bathroom door behind him, but not in time to prevent Shannon from glimpsing Carmen inside. His visage ignites.

Run!

Shannon dashes back toward Yendris, but she's quickly outpaced. Ocho catches her by the elbow and jerks her around. *Come on, God,* Shannon prays, and right at that moment, everyone turns to look as the door to the garage opens. An irritated guard pokes his head inside, criticizing Ocho in Spanish.

"Where've you been? I'm back from my break fifteen minutes, *waiting* and *waiting,* looking around for you! Why is the control room locked anyway?"

"¡Ya voy!"[30] Ocho snarls, flustered.

Concerned, Yendris asks, "You locked the control room and there's no one in there monitoring the grounds right now?"

Shannon is surprised by Yendris' dialogue with Ocho in English. It's almost as if he didn't want the other guard to understand. Handing Shannon the baby carrier, he steps in front of Ocho collusively with a warning shake of his head. "No time to get sloppy, hombre."

"It's all under control!!! Just a bathroom break, man!" Ocho bellows, angrily brushing him off and narrowing eyes at Shannon that dare her to utter a word.

Clearly annoyed at his inability to behave how he would like, he tosses Shannon's arm away and backs out of the hallway into the garage, sneering at her the entire time. Wanting to get as far away from him as possible, Shannon scraps her visit to the gym and heads back to her room, a skeptical Yendris in tow.

With each retreating step, Shannon's conscience cries out louder, *I've got to get us OUT of here.* Yendris hurries to catch her.

Hoping Ocho's presence is an indication that Carlos also returned, she blurts over her shoulder, "Where is he? Where is Carlos?"

"He's not here—Why are you running?" he pants, tugging Shannon by the arm to slow her. "Hey! Stop! Calm down. It's okay."

Yendris stares at Shannon intently. Although she would like to believe him, she knows things are not okay. She could see it in Ocho's eyes.

Overwrought, she spends the night spying on the activity outside her door, praying that Carlos—and not Ocho—will show up. Long after Yendris and Yoan change shifts, Shannon continues to

---

[30] I'm coming right now!

keep watch, and even in the absence of a direct threat, she represses every inclination to leave her room, until mid-afternoon.

Clutching C-Lo on her hip, she cracks the door, stir crazy for information. Yoan nods in the chair, his Adam's apple bobbing each time he gulps down a sneaky snore trying to escape.

Shannon calls, "Yoan?"

"Eh?" he replies, his head popping up. Focusing on Shannon, he flashes that crooked smile and clears his throat. "A little nap," he admits sheepishly.

"I see," she responds, forcing a smile in return in hopes of fostering some camaraderie. "I guess Carlos is back by now, huh?"

"Nope!" He yawns, leaning so far back in his chair that the front legs lift dangerously off the floor.

Dejected, Shannon stands there trying to determine what to do next. Now more desperate than ever to find a way out, she wants to try her hand at exploring more of the home, but she doesn't want to chance crossing paths with Ocho. Yoan yawns again and sets the chair legs back onto the floor. His movement spurs her next question.

"You ready to get going?" she asks nicely.

"Yuh," Yoan replies, blinking the sleep from his eyes. He stands and heads for the stairwell as usual, but Shannon stops him.

"Yoan, I already ate lunch in my room. I was hoping to see some of the rooms on this floor. Maybe hang out around here, you know? Before heading down?"

Yoan scrunches his nose in thought as he stares at Shannon in a semi stupor.

"Like, what's over there?" she says, pointing to the left to help him out.

"That's just the library," he answers blandly.

"Can I see it?"

Reluctantly, Shannon contemplates whether she may have to violate her morals and seduce him, but at the perfect time, C-Lo tugs at her shirt. A few buttons unfasten, exposing a sizable portion of the skin of her milk-filled breasts.

Yoan angles for a better view, his nostrils flaring. His hand gravitates in her direction, but she obstructs his movement by brushing off the crumbs sticking to his shirt. However, exploiting the opportunity, she links her elbow with his, giving him an eyeful.

She tugs coyly. "The library?"

Yoan takes a second to consider. *I could go for his gun right now, if I didn't have C-Lo in my arms,* Shannon thinks.

Shrugging, Yoan mutters, "Yeah, I don't care."

He leads her to the tall double doors and twists both handles. As the doors sway ajar, Shannon pushes her way into an expansive room lined with books on shelving from floor to ceiling, polished off with a fancy rolling ladder.

"Oh, my," Shannon says. "Who is the reader?"

"'Los, I guess. It sure ain't m-me!" Yoan snorts and then snickers.

Shannon swallows a laugh, beginning to find his quirkiness comical. She moseys by the desk in the center of the room and skims through the mix of English and Spanish titles sitting on top. *Three windows, a fireplace, a couple of chairs. No computer in sight.* Turning to face the double doors again, she sees the formal living room straight ahead.

"Look at that beautiful, humongous mirror," she exclaims, exaggerating her excitement slightly as she takes off in that direction. Passing between the formal entrance and the grand wrought iron and wooden railed spiral staircase that ascends to the floor above, Shannon pauses to admire the elegant decor. Surreptitiously, she examines the fourth floor landing overhead.

Moving along, she steps down into the open, sunken living room and shifts C-Lo to her other side. Expressing a deflecting exclamation of awe, she runs her fingers along the edge of the elaborate, decorative mirror hung above the fireplace mantle and inspects the windows to her left. She can see the front yard, the driveway, and a long, snaking path of stairs leading to the ground level, and she realizes that she and C-Lo have been staying on a floor with direct access to the outside the entire time.

Yoan remains near the open foyer area as she ventures to the right and steps up into a formal dining room nestled among tall columns. C-Lo squawks gleefully, perhaps because of the refraction of the chandelier, and Shannon nuzzles his warm, lightly toasted cheeks.

"You like this room, huh, my little guy?" she coos.

"What?" Yoan asks.

Shannon pokes her head around a column and replies, "Just talking with the baby!"

He mutters something incomprehensible, so she continues to look around. The room boasts an immaculate fireplace, as well, and Shannon wonders if any of the fireplaces in the house have ever been used. In the corner, a door separates the occupants of the room from the unknown.

Vacillating between checking where it leads or continuing into the hallway to the right, Shannon chooses the latter, more intrigued by the two sets of double doors there. Glancing at Yoan, she tries the first set with the curtains. They are locked, of course.

"There's nothing out there. And I'm hungry," Yoan informs as he approaches.

I'm sure the aromas coming from the kitchen have him salivating, but that's exactly where I don't want to go, Shannon thinks. The probability of running into Ocho there is very high.

"Can I stay..." she begins her request, then quickly reconsiders. *He let me do this much. I'd better not aggravate him.* She smiles pleasantly. "Let's go down. Following you."

Yoan doesn't hesitate to make his way along the hallway, bringing them full circle in front of the elevator near where they began. Apparently no longer in the mood to take the stairs, he presses the call button.

When the elevator opens onto the floor below, Yunaisys spots Shannon exiting and races from the study entrance to greet her. The backpack she's wearing bounces wildly behind her as she picks up speed.

Yoan extends his hand in warning. "Hey! Watch what you're doing before you run us over, you n-nut job!"

Ignoring her uncle, Yunaisys skids to a stop in front of Shannon.

"Señora, will you like to help me with my English homework?" she asks.

Carmen steps hastily into view in the distance, clearly tracking Yunaisys, and Shannon presumes the woman's charge must have just arrived home from school.

"I'd love to, Yunaisys, but only if it's okay with your... guardians." Shannon looks to Yoan who shrugs ambivalently, but when Carmen shakes her head sharply, he says, "No, she can't help you."

Yunaisys is combative. "Tio told me I could ask her! If you don't believe me, call him."

Shannon smiles, admiring the girl's feistiness. She takes Shannon's hand and pulls her toward the den quite a distance before Yoan stops her. Carmen bristles, refusing to look Shannon in the eye. *Is she aware I know her dirty secret?*

"No!" Yoan tells Yunaisys. "G-Go with Carmen and work on s-something else." He tries to be authoritative, but the girl is determined. He folds. "For now."

Grimacing at Yoan, Carmen cups Yunaisys' shoulder with a guiding hand. The girl doesn't budge.

"He did say it!" Yunaisys assures everyone. Only then does she allow Carmen to lead her into the study. Cheekily, Yoan turns to Shannon.

"Looks like you g-got yourself a job to do. After I eat."

The girl may be just the leverage I need to get away from here, Shannon thinks. "It will be a pleasure."

Pomp and Circumstance

[18]

After hearing, "But, why? I don't understand," for nearly an hour, Shannon finally drops her head into her hands and peeks over at Yoan. He grins, well aware of the frustration.

"I think this is good for today, young lady," Shannon says.

Yunaisys folds up her notebooks and stuffs them into her pack. *No objection there.* Shannon chuckles quietly, and out of curiosity, she asks, "Who normally helps you with your English here at home?"

Yunaisys confides, "Tio has a tutor here for me two times a month. She flies from America."

"Is that right?"

"¡Si! She also teaches me dance."

"She does?"

"Un huh! I have the best uncle ever! I wouldn't want to live with anyone else. He's so wonderful!"

"I'm glad you're so happy with your uncle, young lady," Shannon manages.

"Aren't you?" comes the girl's perceptive inquiry. Shannon purses her lips, not wanting to answer. "Why you don't like here?" Yunaisys persists.

"Let's say, your uncle... brought me here even though I didn't want to come."

Assuming Shannon is referring to living in Cuba, Yunaisys nods in understanding. "What's it like in the U.S.?" she asks dreamily.

Shannon pauses, grappling with how to answer such a broad question. "Well, there are lots of people living in the cities. Lots of businesses. Plenty of different climates. It's definitely a huge nation—"

"I can't imagine living someplace where everyone is wealthy."

The girl's face is filled with longing. Hating to vanquish her fantasy, Shannon replies, "No, my dear, everyone in the states is not wealthy. Believe me, we have plenty of poverty."

Yunaisys' eyes lock on Shannon. "Not like us. Tio says Americans eat three times a day. With La Libreta,[31] you'll be lucky to eat once a day outside this house. If it wasn't for Tio, most of our family—and a lot of others, too, would be starving—"

Nervously, Yunaisys looks around as if she just said or did the unthinkable. Before Shannon can ask what's the matter, she stands.

"Um, thanks. I gotta go."

Yunaisys exits the room, and Carmen lurches into action, a mutually undesired pursuit. Contemplating what could be troubling the girl, Shannon mentally replays what was said. Only one comment stands out to her, and it is surprisingly pleasant. *So, Carlos is a benefactor here in Cuba, too,* she paraphrases, unaware of the reticent smile teasing her face as she recalls the award dinner from so long ago.

The growl is unexpected. *"You. Out of your room—AGAIN!"*

As quickly as her smile came, it vanishes. In the doorway is Ocho's horrifying grimace. Shannon smothers a scream. His glazed over, dilated pupils assault every feminine aspect of her body. He staggers dangerously closer, pinching often at his nose, evidently inebriated and high on drugs. She inches backward, trying to assess the best response.

She looks over at Yoan calmly flipping through a hot rod magazine and wishes she could trust him to come to her aid. "The boss said I could come down," she remarks.

Ocho blows up. "The boss!!? *I'm* the boss. I'M THE BOSS!!" he yells, thumbing his finger at himself while he glares back and forth at Shannon and Yoan.

Looking up in amusement, Yoan tosses his magazine onto the coffee table and uncrosses his legs, twitching with excitement. "Ha! Hell if you are!" He snickers at Ocho's self-promotion.

"Shut up, you moron," Ocho grumbles. He casts a threatening glance at Shannon under the shroud of Yoan's cackle.

---

[31] The distribution system by the Cuban government that subsidizes rations of staple food items and household goods based on the exact family composition. Shortages are frequent and distribution is often delayed or unavailable.

"I'll be sure to let *the Boss* know how you feel when he gets back," Yoan says, continuing his mockery. He springs suddenly to his feet, which makes Ocho flinch.

Looking Yoan up and down, he grunts, "You freak."

"That's what your w-woman told me last night!" Yoan gyrates his hips and cackles wildly as he wags his tongue erotically at Ocho.

Repelled, Ocho turns to leave the study. Likewise, Shannon abandons Yoan, still caterwauling and gyrating for an invisible audience, and moves quickly into the den to retrieve C-Lo. Hoping to find security in Delia's presence once more, she decides that staying in the open is probably her best bet at the moment. One thought echos louder than any other. *Until I find an escape, keeping my distance from Ocho is imperative.*

For the remainder of the day, Shannon sticks by Delia's side, even offering to help make dinner. The matriarch's eyes dance at the companionship around the kitchen island; Shannon washes, dices and slices the items placed before her and the great-niece fires off translations so the three can chat. Yunaisys immerses herself in the opportunity to play grown-up and dotes on C-Lo like he's a baby doll. Yoan, content to be near the food, commandeers a chair by the wall in the breakfast nook and leans the legs off the floor, whittling debris from his teeth with a toothpick. It doesn't take long for him to get on the phone.

Suddenly, the serenity in the room is fragmented by what Shannon perceives are indecipherable words squawking from Yoan's radio. The Spanish speakers seem to understand.

"¡¿Que!?" Yoan yells, thumping the chair legs onto the floor.

Yunaisys looks at Shannon. "Someone's breaking in!"

Shannon lifts C-Lo from the girl's arms, and Yunaisys sidles closer to Delia in fear. As Yoan listens for more information, Delia powers on the monitor in the kitchen with the remote. All eyes look at the suspended screen to witness a pair of legs catapult the 8-foot stone fence somewhere along the property's perimeter. Seconds later, Ocho reaches the wall and scales himself above it for a look. He drops to the ground when Beto runs in the scene.

Wishing she could hear what is being said, Shannon eyeballs the edgy conversation taking place between Ocho and Beto. Yoan puts the radio to his mouth and says in Spanish, "Which one of those..." He glances at Delia. "...chumps do you th-think it was?"

The radio is quiet. Before their eyes, Beto and Ocho's stances transform into that of two roosters in a cock fight. They get in each other's faces. Ocho nudges Beto with his shoulder. Beto bumps him back.

"¡Oye! ¡Mira, *mira!*" Yoan hollers through the radio. Slowly, the aggression subsides, and the radio comes alive again. "Yuh," Yoan replies into the transmitter, then announces to the room, "We need to secure the grounds." Walking to the doorway, he remembers Shannon. "Now what am I s'posed to do wi' you?"

***

"You're back!" Shannon exclaims, shocked by the unexplainable sense of security Carlos' presence brings as he enters her room the next morning. She has to suppress herself from running to throw her arms around him, but she doesn't restrain the anger in her words.

"Carlos, if you won't take us home, take us somewhere else. Take us with you. You cannot leave us here."

He closes the door behind him and faces her with a furrowed brow. "What happened?"

"I'm a sitting duck for Ocho, or anyone, for that matter, to stick a knife in my throat!" she spurts, overwhelmed with pinned-up emotion.

"What happened?"

"It's not safe here. And he doesn't want me here. He's made that very clear, and we just need to *go.*"

Leisurely, he approaches Shannon. "Shannon. Calm down and tell me what happened."

Perhaps hearing her name helps her to refocus because she begins to recount. "On top of this place almost getting robbed last night—"

"Robbed?"

"Yes. You didn't know?"

He looks at her. "What else?"

"As if that isn't enough?"

"WHAT ELSE?"

"I went to the gym the other night and... surprised Ocho by being down there while he was...in the bathroom, and there was some commotion about nobody manning the control room—" Shannon stops, feeling she may have alluded to too much.

"And?"

"This isn't fair keeping us here. It's too dangerous, especially when you're not around. I never know when you're here or if you're even going to come back, Carlos."

"TELL ME WHAT HAPPENED. Did someone come in here? Did someone hurt you?"

"We need to get out of here, *got it?*"

Abruptly, Carlos walks away, scratching his five o'clock stubble in frustration. He turns his attention to the baby swaying gently in his motorized swing. Squatting next to him, he watches with adoration as C-Lo drools and gnaws his own fists with delight. Carlos knuckles him playfully in the cheeks a few times and a furtive smile breaks through his anger. C-Lo's youthful gums gleam, his arms and legs flailing excitedly from the roughhousing.

Watching the father-son moment, Shannon is caught off guard. Flooded by the injustice of their incongruous familial situation, her eyes moisten. *It shouldn't be this way.*

Carlos cuts into her train of thought. "For some reason, you don't want to tell me. But, do know that I will find out."

He turns to look at Shannon, eyeing her suspiciously, before noticing her damp eyes. His eyes dart elsewhere, looking for something more tolerable to view as he aggressively ruffles his hair.

Recognizing the flustered mannerism, Shannon wonders, *Is that an indication that he cares or that he doesn't?* Banking on the former, she takes another earnest stab at rationalization.

"Carlos, C-Lo and I have a life, you know. He's due for his immunizations. My landlord is expecting his rent. I'm going to lose my home, my belongings—irreplaceable things that mean a lot to me. I have bills to pay. Please, we just need to go home. People are looking for us."

Shannon prays her last sentence is true. The reality is she had nothing more than acquaintances there in Las Vegas and, aside from her landlord and his son, she suspects no one is looking for them at all.

"I'm not concerned about your bills," Carlos states. "Nor would I care if they have a search party started on your behalf. Which they don't. No one is looking for you. I can say that with absolute certainty."

"How can you be so sure?"

"For one, your landlord has been paid—for this month and the previous month, too, by the way—and all of your bills are now current. Paid for out of your own checking account. So, Señorita, from the outside looking in, you're on vacation."

"Do you think I don't keep track of my finances? You're lying," Shannon asserts. "And even if you did hack into my accounts, there was no money available to pay anything. I know that for a fact."

"Actually, the fact is, I made sure you had money in your account."

With no way of knowing if he's telling the truth, Shannon doesn't know what to think. *If nothing about our absence appears dubious to those who may be concerned, then Carlos is right. No one would be looking for us.*

Managing to sound almost compassionate, Carlos says, "You really have no idea who you're dealing with. I thought you were a super detective." He shakes his head scornfully and tosses a patronizing, "You're welcome" over his shoulder as he turns to leave.

"You expect me to thank you? Screw you."

Carlos stops, chuckles.

"There's no reason for you to keep us here," Shannon insists.

"Certainly there is. And you're not leaving here until I learn what I need to know."

"I'm innocent of what you think I've done. Do you want me to lie, to make up something to tell you?"

Reaching for the handle, Carlos turns his head, his eyes piercing her intensely. "No. You've done enough of that already. By the way, decent people only use kitchen knives and forks for eating."

He closes the door.

Sure enough, the pair of utensils she'd stashed under the fuzzy covering of C-Lo's swing had left the room.

Things Fall Apart

[19]

At 5:30 in the morning, Shannon rolls over in bed defensively, awakened by the sound of the door opening. Carlos walks in, fully dressed, clean shaven and smelling freshly showered. He tells her, "You have forty-five minutes to get ready."

"Where are we going?" she whispers anxiously, forcing her vocal chords into gear. She palms the backup knife under her pillow.

"You told me Carlos needs immunizations. So, we're making a visit to the pediatrician." Shannon stares at him blankly. "By the way, afterwards, we'll probably take a little trip to our capital building. It's time my father met his only grandson. Wear something appropriate—"

Both bedroom doors fling open, and Ocho rushes into the room. Shannon grips the sheet to her chest, swiveling her legs to the side of the bed in a seated position. Her heart pounds fiercely. Carlos doesn't even look at him, but rather closes his eyes in anticipation of Ocho's announcement.

"What is it *now?*" he snaps.

"The shipment to Dubai. Intercepted," Ocho informs, glancing at Shannon. "They made off with a crate of SCAR-Hs." Carlos' eyes open and glint with rage.

FN SCAR military rifles?? What's he doing with those? Shannon conjectures as Carlos glares at the bearer of bad news. In a silent fury, he exits the room, and Ocho trails fast on his heels.

Left behind to speculate, Shannon complies with the command to get dressed, but once the afternoon is well underway, there is no doubt Carlos has vanished without her. However, it was not before he made sure to alert his staff of her sleight of hand—a skill which, absurdly, Yoan found impressive. He'd joked over breakfast, "To get one over on me, you've got to be good."

Anxious to acquire any updates, Shannon reconvenes to the study on the pretense of tutoring Yunaisys, a convenient activity granting her visuals to both Carlos' office and the front driveway.

Only Shannon, Yunaisys and Yoan are in the room, for Carmen, incapable of influencing Yoan with her whims, had made her exit soon after they came down.

Vigilantly, Shannon peers out the window, awaiting a response from her disinterested student. In lieu of answering the question, however, Yunaisys jumps up from her seat on the bench.

"Wait one minute! I'll be right back," she exclaims.

Yoan, who had been dozing, lifts his head, and they both watch Yunaisys run from the room. Several minutes later, she returns, holding a laptop. She places it next to Shannon and lifts the screen. The computer wakes.

"I want to show you this website! My friend told me about it today at school," she says. She rummages through her papers on the desk and sighs. "Aw, hold on. I got to go get the paper." Once again, she dashes out.

Shocked, Shannon looks at Yoan, calculating if this could be her golden opportunity. Chin tucked to his chest, he appears to have surrendered once again to his drowsiness.

With no one else in sight, she risks it. Hoping to God no one is monitoring the girl's Internet activity, she swiftly launches the browser, accesses her email site and logs in. Typing "Jax" into the recipient box to populate his email address, she hurriedly inputs a cryptic message. "SEND HELP. HERE IN CUBA. ABDUCTED BY CARLOS. THIS IS N—"

Shannon doesn't finish the message. Hearing footsteps approach, she hastily presses send and glances back at a comatose Yoan as she waits for the transmission to complete. She quits the browser just as Yunaisys returns.

Waving a scrap of paper in her hand, she slides onto the bench, alerting Yoan with the noise. He looks up, and Shannon promptly closes the laptop.

"Yunaisys, we should finish your homework first, and then we can play," Shannon instructs.

Throwing her head back, Yunaisys whines, "But, I wanna take a break!"

"Come on, now. You're a big girl, Yunaisys. We're almost done."

Yoan observes the two of them, but doesn't seem to notice or care that the laptop is there. He picks up a magazine and crosses his legs. Shannon bows her head in thanks.

***

The next morning after breakfast, the household is thrown into a frenzy. Voices can be heard outside barking orders and disseminating information all around the perimeter of the house as an enraged Carlos, Ocho, Beto, and Sul swarm past the den archways into Carlos' office. It is a homecoming unlike any Shannon has seen.

Yoan stands up frantically, dithering between staying put or leaving his post until Beto's face reappears in an archway seconds later. He whistles for Yoan to join the rest of the brothers, and the office door bangs shut.

Shannon, Delia, Yunaisys and Carmen all gravitate toward the hallway to peer out curiously in the aftermath. Whispers of what is plain to everyone travels in waves; something has gone terribly wrong. *But I'm the one who needs to be worried,* Shannon laments. Undoubtedly, Carlos discovered her email.

The ladies sit in silence awaiting some news. Shannon weighs her options. *They left me unguarded. Should I try to run or gamble staying? What if this is a trap to test whether my guilt will make me flee? Then again, perhaps I'm not the only one in the room with cause for concern...*

Shannon's eyes drift to Carmen rigidly poised in the chair with her heels bouncing nervously above the floor. Next, she looks from Delia wringing her hands in her lap to the terror plastered on the face of the great-niece leaning against her.

There is no point in continuing down this path, Shannon resolves. *The only concrete answer is held by the men inside that office, and until someone comes out or goes in, no one in this room will know anything.*

Frazzled, she remains seated like the rest. She doesn't wish to draw attention to herself, but she wonders why Delia won't at least go to the door and inquire. Shannon can't stomach the sheepish behavior.

Finally, three of the brothers emerge from the office. Beto and Sul approach Delia and speak quietly. She nearly faints, and they end up assisting her from the room. Overhearing their dialogue, Carmen escorts Yunaisys diplomatically from the room, as well.

On pins and needles, Shannon stares awkwardly at Yoan. His look is begrudging.

"You need to get back to your room."

"What's going on, Yoan?" she asks. He ignores her, so she repeats the question.

"None of your b-business!"

"No, please, I need to know what's happening."

"Sh-SHUT U-UP!" Yoan hollers, convulsing violently.

C-Lo shivers in Shannon's arms, sputters, then rapidly revs into a full blown wail. Yoan ducks his head at the scowl she gives him during her mothering efforts to soothe the baby, but he is relentless in forging ahead to the bedroom. He slams the doors, and the lock clicks. Inhaling sharply, Shannon grabs the handles, suspecting the obvious.

Panic washes over her as she calls, "Hey! Why are you locking us in!? Would somebody tell me what's going on?!"

Silence.

She pounds the doors, yelling for someone to come.

No one does.

***

At nightfall, Shannon is still coldly secluded. She's missed lunch and dinner, and no one has come near her room. Shannon is sure she is now a threat and a target. *They've probably been plotting my demise.*

Unable to handle the exclusion a moment longer, she resumes banging on the doors, anticipating the effort to be futile. However, Yendris answers.

Shocked, Shannon drops to her knees and peeks under the doors to make sure. "Yendris!" she says, scrambling to her feet. "I'm locked in. Would you unlock the door, please?"

"Can't do that, Señorita," he responds coolly.

"I need to speak with Carlos."

"He can't be bothered right now. What you need to do is be quiet and wait."

Shannon doesn't like the sound of that. Frowning at his uncharacteristically heartless manner, she steps away from the doors, eager to verify for herself—in person—where she stands with Carlos. She spies the intercom.

Hoping to reach Carlos' room, she presses the master bedroom button, thinking it would be icing on the cake if he actually answers. He does.

"Carlos, I don't know what's going on, but I have something urgent to speak with you about."

"Now is not a good time, Señorita," he slurs through the crackling speaker.

"Now is a *great* time," she insists.

The crackling stops. He doesn't respond. She presses the button again. Still no response. Losing her composure, Shannon mashes the button repeatedly, resulting in an annoying tune of beeping tones.

"Stop it!" Yendris yells through the door.

"I'm not going to stop buzzing until he LETS ME OUT!" Shannon declares, depressing the intercom button for Carlos to listen in.

The intercom hisses, and Carlos' words hinge with impending regret. "Have it your way, Señorita... Yendris! Bring her."

The doors unlock and the room goes silent. Hesitantly, Shannon exits the room with C-Lo in her arms. Ocho enters the archway. Alarmed, Shannon freezes, but his glare is directed at Yendris.

"What are you doing?" he asks tensely between his teeth. "You're supposed to keep her *in the room.*"

Yendris pushes Ocho backward, creating some space away from Shannon. He whispers something to Ocho that adds deep displeasure to the grimace already imprinted on the man's face. Shannon is able to catch the last sentence: "We'll have time."

Again, the words don't sit well with her. Ocho appears to acquiesce to Yendris' advice, but he journeys with them up the grand spiral staircase to the master suite on the fourth floor.

Without announcement, the door clicks quietly as Carlos unlocks it remotely. The three plus baby enter the master bedroom foyer. Shannon progresses into the sitting area and stumbles to a halt.

Carlos is seated on the sofa, staring straight ahead, holding a nearly empty glass of rum in one hand and a TV remote in the other. Between his legs kneels Carmen. Stupefied, she jerks up her head before gathering enough wits to turn her face from the intruders in shame. She scrambles away from him. Carlos continues to look absently at the television.

Mortified, Shannon sputters, "Oh G—... Really Carlos?? I can't bel—"

From the half-stifled chuckle behind her, she surmises that Ocho is delighted at the dual degradation experienced by both women in the room. She turns to leave. Carlos calls after her.

"Didn't you DEMAND to speak to me NOW, and I said NOW was not a good time? So, NOW I will try to split my attention. Please, let's chat." Carlos' accent is considerably thicker, brought on by the excessive alcohol he's consumed. He finally turns to look at her just as she throws a dagger glance back at him.

"You disgust me!"

Loathing herself for the betrayal and disrespect she feels even though Carlos, her captor in this whole fiasco, is not, and probably never was, hers to claim, Shannon tries to push past Ocho blocking the door. She has no reason to feel anything besides hatred for Carlos and yet she does, her cheeks burning red with devastation moreso than embarrassment. In her struggle, she catches Yendris watching her, but he turns his eyes to the wall.

"Get out of the way!" Shannon cries out. Ocho doesn't budge. "Let me OUT!"

He sneers at her in response. With Shannon's back to them, Carmen whimpers to Carlos, "You let her in here to disgrace me?"

The words in English don't escape Shannon's keen hearing or shocking notice, but she resists turning around. Carlos observes Carmen icily.

"Get out," he slurs.

"I'm trying to—" Shannon begins, but Carmen's escalating emotions drown her out. Shannon realizes his command wasn't intended for her.

"Why are you treating me like a da—"

"GET OUT!"

Exasperated, he waves them all away. Yendris moves to do so immediately, but Ocho is intentionally slow clearing a path for Shannon's exodus. Carlos pours himself the last of a full bottle of rum and gulps it down. As soon as Ocho gives Shannon an angle, she rushes past her antagonist, chased by his blatant laughter at her humiliation. Ocho exits after Yendris, but not before taking one last look at Carmen as she dons her mini robe.

Behind them, glass shatters against a wall. Ocho and Yendris pause briefly. Seconds later, Carmen runs from the room, scampers across the hall, and slams a door somewhere in the distance.

"Los?" Ocho calls.

He's answered by more shattering glass, most likely the bottle. In a race to reach her room before tears fall, Shannon continues down the stairs. She thinks of changing course, but with two guards following her, she knows she wouldn't get away.

Lying on the bed next to C-Lo, she rubs away the anger and humiliation filling her eyes. For several minutes, Shannon doesn't hear the tapping at the door. Finally, Yendris calls her name, and she sits up nervously.

"Yes?"

"If you need it, I... have some tissue in my hands. Just say the word."

Huh? Foggily, Shannon considers the sweetness of his offer—right up until the door opens and he steps inside.

"Wait! I'm not going to hurt you," he asserts, palms showing. He sits silently next to Shannon on the bed for a beat. When their eyes meet, the dam breaks, and Yendris chances a comforting hug.

Shannon gives in to the solace there in his arms and leans against his chest. She doesn't come to her senses until his lips press against hers.

Instantly, she stands up. "Get out of here."

"Not a good idea, I guess."

"No, it was not," she snaps at his downturned head.

As Yendris walks swiftly from the room, there is no doubt in Shannon's mind that her problems just got exponentially bigger.

***

The next day, Shannon pokes her head through the bedroom doors with a request for something to eat. The refrigerator in her room had become bare since she began to eat downstairs and Delia stopped stocking it. She figures, *if I am now being starved, then it will be clear that I was the cause of yesterday's upheaval.*

Yoan stands. "I'm not your servant. You know where the kitchen is," he tells her with that smile she can't quite read. As usual, he heads for the stairs. *Not in the clear, but a good sign, I guess.* Warily, she follows.

The breakfast nook is occupied by the regulars. Delia sips a cup of black coffee. Yunaisys sits next to her at the table shuffling crumbs on her plate, and Carmen leans against the kitchen counter in a daze. Shannon can't help staring with disdain at the one caught on her knees, but Carmen doesn't even notice. Gratefully, the men she really wants to avoid are absent.

Puffy eyed, Delia greets Shannon with a weak smile and motions to a plate of pastries and a pitcher of milk on the table. Shannon pulls out a chair, and Carmen disappears into the kitchen. She places the baby carrier in it and takes the seat beside C-Lo.

This isn't the spread Shannon has grown accustomed to, and she knows whatever the news was yesterday must have greatly affected Delia. No sooner than she thinks it, the woman starts crying, looking beyond Shannon as if something set her off. Turning, Shannon sees Carlos above her, and instinctively, she tries to bolt.

Gripping her by the arms, he signals her to stay seated, but she refuses, producing a brief up and down battle of wills. It ends when Carlos looks Shannon intently in the eyes.

"I'm sorry. For my behavior. I'm sorry."

Assaulted by images from the night before, she stares at him, unfazed and utterly repulsed. "Don't apologize to me for the *filthy* human being you are. And let go of *my son,*" she snaps in front of all the eyes and ears in their midst. Unable to retract her words, she lifts her chin in defiance, almost daring him to strike her. What follows is not retaliation, but a nod of agreement.

"I deserve that. You stay. I'll go." Carlos takes the newspaper from Carmen, who'd sidled over to him, picks up a pastry from the table and walks out.

Delia calls after him in Spanish, "Carlo, stay! Have some coffee. Please."

He ignores her and knocks Carmen's hand away as she tries to grab his arm. Shaking her head anxiously, Delia busies herself with gathering the extra place settings on the table. She bursts into tears again near the kitchen archway, and Yoan, who had yet to take a seat, goes to console her.

"¡Yunaisys, vamonos!"[32] Carmen calls.

Shannon can feel Yunaisys' eyes boring into her skull, yet when she looks over, the girl stares into her plate. "I'm so sorry you witnessed that, Yunaisys," Shannon says.

"My Gran-pa is dead."

Stunned by the girl's volunteered information, Shannon exclaims, "Oh, Yunaisys, I'm so sorry!" She pieces together the family tree in her mind. *This would mean Carlos' father and Delia's brother was—*

"Killed. Two nights ago."

The reason behind what transpired from yesterday to today.

Yunaisys' words slice Shannon to the core.

"¡Vamonos!" Carmen cries again.

"Who... *How* would you know a thing like that?" Shannon asks, unable to believe an adult would share such news with a child.

She reels on Shannon. "Because I just know!"

Shannon is speechless.

Yunaisys persists in ignoring Carmen. "Why are you so mean to him?" she demands in her non-sequitur manner. Shannon realizes Yunaisys is speaking about Carlos.

---

[32] Let's go!

"It's... complicated, Yunaisys," she attempts, watching Carmen leave. "I guess the simplest explanation is that we both weren't honest with each other in the beginning and now we are dealing with the consequences."

The look she receives tells Shannon her answer isn't good enough. Like the others, Yunaisys vacates the room.

Housecleaning

[20]

Ducking her head, Shannon climbs into the black Soviet-built GAZ model limousine as directed by the two guards with her. They join her, and the three of them wait inside the historic vehicle as Carlos, his aunt, his niece, and all of his siblings, including the newly acquainted sister, receive condolences from family and friends. The morning's event replays in Shannon's mind.

The funeral had been packed, yet the vibe among the attendees was strangely cold and sorrowful. Despite not wanting to bring attention to herself, Shannon looked around often, the skin on the back of her neck crawling with foreboding. Carlos had, in no uncertain terms, made it clear that she be on her best behavior—patting her down before they proceeded—and she knew she was being monitored closely the entire time.

The majority of Carlos' household and staff were also there, and Shannon surmised that was probably the reason why he had refused to leave her behind. Minimal staffing at home meant greater risk for her. Only she couldn't conclude whether the concern was more with her escaping or with protecting her and C-Lo from danger.

As Shannon sat uneasily next to Carlos during the ceremony, she wondered what kind of man his father had been. A few of the women wept, but all except one of the men refused to shed a tear, and he was someone she'd never seen before. Visions of her own estranged father came to mind, bringing an unwelcome introspection of her unforgivingness and guilt—which, naturally, she suppressed. *Still too embittered to address those thoughts...*

Cautiously, she would glance at Carlos, hoping that he wouldn't break emotionally—for her sake. After learning what had shaken up the household, Shannon spent the following days contemplating not only their safety, but the justification for Carlos' drunken indiscretion. In their current circumstance, the conflict for the one she abhors, yet somehow, still loves, would be unbearable.

Actually, Carlos had kept his eyes carefully averted from Shannon, and he seemed preoccupied with his surroundings and his time piece. Apparently, she and he both shared an urge to conclude the service, perhaps because of the same ominous perceptions.

Her reflection fades away as Carlos approaches the window. Observing his stoic demeanor, Shannon is overwhelmed with the urge to pray for his well-being, something she had not done on his behalf in a long time.

The limo door closes, and Carlos settles in beside Shannon. Still refusing to look at her, he heaves a weighty sigh and, after a beat, instructs the driver to go. Stubbornly, Shannon looks away, sickened by her inability to withstand even the first small display of emotion he's shown.

***

As the exterior garage door rolls shut, Carlos lifts C-Lo and leads Shannon to a doorway inside the garage. At last, they enter the room she's been hoping to find for weeks. She takes in the wall of monitors and the two guards in front of the large security console and, with dismay, confirms her assumptions that the entire property is under surveillance.

Carlos critiques the monitors also, asking information of the guards in Spanish. They respond well enough to his liking for him to proceed into the house, but Shannon can tell he's unusually wary. *Something is definitely awry.*

Carlos escorts Shannon and the baby to the room. He places the carrier near the door and then glances behind the closet doors, inside the bathroom, and onto the balcony, unmistakably checking for foul play, which serves to heighten Shannon's apprehension. She takes C-Lo from the carrier into her arms.

Apparently satisfied with his findings or lack thereof, Carlos heads out without a word. After a momentary delay, Shannon runs after him, catching up at the grand staircase. Above, she sees Carmen waiting possessively along the balcony railing.

Shannon clutches Carlos' rock hard bicep to stop him. He turns halfway to look at her, and she takes two steps up to get eye level with him.

"Was he murdered?" Her inquiry is gentle, her intention not to grind open wounds. *I just need to know for sure.*

Finally, Carlos looks her in the eyes, and the pain she sees him withholding is heart-wrenching. Forgetting her own agenda, Shannon says what comes naturally.

"You don't have to be tough all the time. Let it out, even if it means... in the shower, with the water running over your face."

The corner of his mouth turns up slightly at her advice, but the smile never makes it. "What makes you think I don't do that already?"

Shannon surprises herself by pulling Carlos into a brief, half-embrace with her free arm. She presses her cheek against his, and immediately his hands encircle her waist, pulling her closer. Straining to keep her physical responses in check and stay the course of providing consolation only, she pulls away. She's met with a perceptive gaze.

"I'm very sorry, Carlos... about your loss."

He looks away and extends his forefinger to C-Lo, staring tenderly at the baby as the little fingers clutch onto his. Disregarded, Carmen looks on enviously from above.

"Please," Shannon implores. "Let me in on what's happening. I know it's more than the obvious."

Hearing Shannon's words, Carlos disengages and proceeds up the stairs to his room. He denies Carmen the pleasure of accompanying him with a wave of his hand. She throws Shannon a vile look, and as both ladies reluctantly retreat to their own spaces, Shannon discovers her escort, Yendris waiting—*watching*—off to the side.

She is too disconcerted to remain in her room. Yendris is initially uncooperative, but late in the evening, she convinces him to seek out Carlos. As they near the rec-room where he supposedly is, a high-pitched rant assaults their ears. Reactively, Yendris holds back Shannon to ascertain what is happening.

Carmen is audibly upset. The two pause unnoticed in the hallway and watch the woman intrude on a brotherly game of pool, fussing hysterically at Carlos about something Shannon cannot understand. A smirk creeps onto Yendris' face.

"Things are not the same!" Carmen sobs. She punctuates her words by drawing invisible check marks in the air with a manicured finger and then erases them with both hands. "I see how you look at her. I see how you treat her, but you avoid me! You refuse to talk to me! You do everything to keep from having a baby with *me*, but you did with that Black trash. You disgrace me in front of the whole family, having her by your side at the funeral. She's beneath you. She doesn't even love you! I do. I'm here. I'm here for you. She shouldn't even be here."

Carlos responds heartlessly—and in English to further infuriate her. "You're saying you no longer want to be here? Yes, I agree. Go work for someone else. You should leave right now."

"No! No! Carlos, please!" she cries, rushing toward him.

He holds out his pool stick to keep her at bay. Ocho swivels on the bar stool, presenting his back to everyone as he downs his drink. Yoan balances on two chair legs, grinning from ear to ear. Sul, always ready to react, watches the scene carefully from his propped up position against the wall. *Hmmm, no Beto,* Shannon notes.

"GET OUT!" Carlos yells, his eyes glinting with disgust as Carmen continues to press her way toward him. Sul steps in, extending a straight arm to thwart her progress, but strangely, Carlos seeks assistance from the bar instead.

"Take her out of here," he commands, catching the one occupying the stool off guard.

Ocho stiffens then quickly downs another serving before sliding off the stool. He looks pissed, but obliges, and with Sul's help, he corrals the distraught, love-sick, wailing woman. He begins dragging her out mercilessly, which is when they all become aware of Shannon and Yendris' presence. Carlos lowers his eyes and resumes lining up his shot.

Carmen's torrential sobs pause long enough for her to hawk up a good-sized projectile of spit for Shannon. Twisting her body, Shannon shields C-Lo from the savage and barely avoids the spray in their direction. Yendris drops the empty baby carrier he was toting for Shannon and steps in between the women just as Carmen lunges away from Ocho. *The jerk loosened his grip on purpose...*

The pool stick thuds on the table top, and Carlos advances in their direction. Carmen swings wildly, hurling obscenities at Shannon until Ocho wrestles her into submission and the two disappear into the garage.

Seeing the situation under control, Carlos retrieves the pool stick and returns to the three balls left on the table. His question joggles Shannon.

"What can I do for you, Señorita?"

I don't believe it. Once again, he's going to ignore the white elephant in the room? Flustered, she can't remember what she had prepared to say, so she says the first thing that comes to mind.

"I didn't expect to find you playing pool on a day like today, and it seems no manner of inappropriate behavior can tear you away."

"I couldn't sleep," he says, focusing on his shot.

"You know, it's a good thing C-Lo didn't get hurt just now."

Carlos stands agitatedly, but before he can respond, she walks away. *Another few feet, and I'll be inside the gym and he, out of my sight. He won't be the only one working off sleep-depriving anxiety tonight...*

"You look beautiful," Yendris says, disrupting her punching rhythm.

Shannon glances at her sweaty, disheveled image in the mirror and laughs him off. "Yeah, right!"

"No, you are, and if you were mine, I'd protect you, treat you like a queen, not a prisoner."

Compelled to smile, Shannon pounds the bag forcefully, keenly aware of Yendris' willingness to continue overstepping his boundaries.

***

The workout didn't have the tranquilizing effect on Shannon that she had hoped. She lies on the bed for hours, her thoughts grating her nerves like fingernails against a chalkboard, until the muffled sounds of a skirmish kick up outside her bedroom entrance.

Shannon slides from the bed to listen. The wooden guard chair creaks with the shifting of body weight. Too wary to open the doors, she lies down on the cold tile trying to spy beneath them, but she can only make out that someone is sitting there, as usual. Shannon knows she wasn't hallucinating.

She stands and calls hesitantly, "Yendris?"

"¿Si?" is the reply.

Shannon cracks the door. It isn't Yendris.

"Who are you? Where's Yendris?" Shannon demands, masking her surprise.

"Yendris?" he repeats, a blend between a question and an answer.

"Yes. Yendris."

"No Inglés."

***

The next morning, Shannon opens the refrigerator and removes some fruit she had stashed from the kitchen. She goes into the bathroom to rinse them off and absently stares at her bloodshot eyes in the mirror. Last night had only proven useful for surveilling the doorway in expectation of more activity. As Shannon blinks away the sting, Carlos' haggard reflection appears over her shoulder. She whirls to find him standing in the doorway holding C-Lo.

"What?" Shannon asks.

Carlos' expression is indiscernible. He returns to the bedroom, and Shannon trails anxiously after. With dread, she watches Carlos plop C-Lo into a seated position onto the activity blanket on the floor and take a seat in the chair next to him. Crossing an ankle over his knee, he reclines pensively, his eyes adhered to Shannon as if assessing what to do.

"Carlos, what is it? What is going on?"

His finger taps against the armrest.

"Is there something I should know?" she asks.

Cocking his head to one side, Carlos states, "I should ask you the same question."

He knows something. She places the fruit on the bedspread, seeking out words to tread lightly. "Are you referring to the scuffle outside my room last night?

Carlos' eyes burn into hers, but his tone is non-committal. "Scuffle? You saw something?"

"I didn't see it, but I heard it, and when I checked, there was someone different guarding my room. What is going on? Are we in danger?" The finger taps a rhythm. "What happened to Yendris?"

"Why do you ask about Yendris?"

Shannon tries not to misstep. "I'm used to him being here every night."

Carlos' temples pulsate. "Yendris was a traitor, one who didn't know how to keep his hands to himself."

"Was? What did you mean, was? Did something happen to him?"

Carlos smooths the hem of his pants leg from his calf to his crossed ankle. "What kind of man do you think I am, Ms. Moore?"

"A man who wou—"

"Don't answer that. I've had enough bad news lately."

"Did something happen, Carlos?"

"Are you asking me about Yendris again? You should be worried about yourself."

Shannon swallows hard, rendered tongue-tied by his threat.

"Has the pendulum swung all the way to the other extreme now, so that you lust after every man who shows you some attention?" Carlos demands, rising from his chair to stare her in the face. "Were you in love with him, too, Shannon?"

Shannon's brain reconnects with her tongue. "No, I was not."

"Then the kiss was just business?"

The smoke has finally cleared.

"It was a mistake. A misjudgment," she admits, crumbling under the pressure of his scrutiny. "And I know I was wrong for not being honest with you about where I was when you met me, but you don't have to keep throwing it up in my face. It's not like you were exactly transparent, either."

"I told you there was more to me to learn. You, on the other hand, assured me there was nothing else unusual to know about you."

"That's the past. God sees me *trying* to live the right way now. What can you say?" She looks away and mutters, "Jaxson tried to warn me—"

"Things aren't always what they seem, Señorita," Carlos reprimands. "You should stop trusting in the wrong people. People like Yendris and Jaxson." He smirks. "He actually scolded me for letting you get that cry for help out."

"What are you talking about?"

"You know specifically what I'm talking about," Carlos responds, calling up some data on his cell phone. "But I'm positive you won't believe me, so please, take a look for yourself."

He shows her correspondence from Jaxson, which reads, "I received an email from Det. Moore. I hope you've contained the situation. If this gets out, I will have to get involved, so don't let it get back to me."

Shannon looks up, crushed by the blow, and lashes out at the only person she can, the one with the smug countenance standing before her.

"You're the most selfish, arrogant, evil—"

Carlos draws dangerously close. "Careful what you say, Señorita. If I am all those things, then that's not wise."

Shannon glares at Carlos, devastated by what he'd revealed. Not only that, but every secret she had hoped to hide had been exposed.

Mercifully, he departs, relinquishing Shannon to a winless battle with her tumultuous thoughts. Jaxson's betrayal, Yendris' disappearance, the father's possible murder, C-Lo's well-being—and her own—all hang in the balance and, as much as she hates to admit it, Carlos is the sole person juggling it all.

Shaking, she picks up C-Lo and cuddles with him on the bed until she falls asleep, exhausted from wondering what will happen next.

Release

[21]

C-Lo, purportedly in dire need of attention, awakens Shannon from her rest an hour or so in. His diaper is wet and he is hungry, but his vocal chords require no assistance.

Lovingly, she tends to her son and starts him on a gentle sway in the swing. Bathed and satiated, his pleasant manner returns, and she doesn't have to wait long before his eyelids yield to their heaviness. Relocating him to his bassinet, Shannon takes the opportunity to tend to her own needs.

As the sun begins its late afternoon decline, Shannon's energy wanes in tandem. Relishing the stillness of the room, she lies down once more for a cat nap, but the act of sprawling across the bed seems to cue resonant rhythms and hypnotizing vocals that penetrate her bedroom walls.

Baffled, she peers out the window onto the festivity dancing in and around the pool house below. A live band performs jubilantly as party goers groove, drink, laugh, and converse. Colorful lights accentuate the beats, casting rainbow shadows across the mill of people, and the pool ripples with vibration. Shannon steals a glance at the clock. *4:32 p.m.? Reckon, they start early in this household.*

She spots Carlos, and, within seconds, he is looking at her. He calls Yoan to him. After a few words, Yoan disappears, only to reappear at her door. Fearful of why she is being summoned, Shannon refuses.

"You don't have a choice," she's told.

Yoan escorts Shannon and C-Lo to the party, and by the time they arrive on the grounds, Carlos has roamed inside the pool house.

The room is rife with cigar smoke and ruckus, and reeks of stale rum. It certainly isn't the place for a baby to be. Frankly, despite the intrigue of Cuban culture she's never seen, Shannon doesn't want to be there, either.

Carlos extends his arm toward her, welcoming her to come to him. His gaze roves down her tank top, over her shorts, to the silver anklet adorning her delicate ankle, then travels back up to her face.

Shannon's stomach does a somersault at being on display, but she forces herself to keep walking. Once in range, he wraps his arm around her shoulders, pulling her close. Shannon ices over at the contact, unnerved by his behavior. Perhaps sensing it, Carlos removes his arm and reaches for a glass. He offers her a drink, which she declines, so he pours himself another.

"Considering what you think of me, I didn't believe you'd want to come to my party, but after seeing you watching wistfully from the window, I decided to invite you anyway."

"Is this the culture here after someone dies? To party?"

Carlos looks hollowly into the crowd, his haggard aspect increasing rapidly. "It's better to celebrate his life than to mourn his death."

Regretting her caustic dig, Shannon shifts her attention on the partiers. Discomfiting looks of intrigue and disinterest flash her way. Once again, all of the brothers are present, except Beto. *Come to think of it, I haven't seen him since the funeral.* The cigar smoke thickens, and Shannon fans the air around C-Lo.

"I'd prefer to take him back to the room," she says.

Carlos shrugs, and Shannon accepts that as permission to walk away.

***

The afternoon sunlight shines through the window sheers in the living room. Having survived the ambiance of what had to be the longest party in history the night before, Shannon holds C-Lo upright on her stomach and stretches out on the sofa. She intentionally missed participating in all of it, scoffing throughout its duration at the irony of finally arriving on an exotic island only to be confined from its appeal.

Sliding her knees up, she props C-Lo against her thighs and purposes to simply enjoy him for a change rather than obsessing about their safety or the unknown. For fun, she begins telling him a kiddie story and becomes so engrossed she doesn't notice Carlos arrive. He sends Yoan away while Shannon continues to prattle.

"So, the little kitty enters the jungle. Suddenly, a big lion jumps from the bushes and roars. Rawrr!" In her deepest, gruffest voice, Shannon mimics her storybook lion. "What are you doing in my jungle?" C-Lo's head and shoulders bob with laughter at her silly tale, which makes Shannon laugh. "And the brave little kitten says, 'Sorry, Mr. Lion. But I'm lost and can't find my way back to the city.'"

Carlos chuckles at the voices. Shannon cocks her head to see his frame hovering above her at the sofa's end, and her smile shrinks. She refocuses on C-Lo.

Unexpectedly, Carlos slides his hands under her head and shoulders, lifting her in order to sit on the cushion beneath her.

Shannon starts to get up, but he stretches his arm across her shoulders to pin her down. "Please. Don't go."

Reluctantly, she rests her head against his thigh and inhales his light, refreshing cologne. It's quiet.

Carlos suggests, "Let's hear the end of the story."

"There is no end," Shannon mutters. "I was making it up."

He studies C-Lo. "That day... in Las Vegas, I was just going to have a conversation with you and then go. But, when I looked into his face, I saw myself. I knew I couldn't just walk away from this little guy. Or you."

Shannon's heart skips a beat, and she twists her head to look in Carlos' face. Their eyes fix on one another.

"That's why when I learn that one of my trusted staff, charged with protecting my interests, encroaches upon them, I can't let it slide."

Bracing, Shannon forces herself to not look away. He fondles her hair.

"I'm part of a brutal world, Shannon. You may never be able to forgive me or even understand what I have to do." Zoning into the distance, he says, "I know you say your prayers at night... faithfully. Maybe you could say one for me sometime."

Roughing C-Lo's hair, Carlos rises from the sofa. Shannon is dumbfounded as his words settle on her like dust. Then, as clear as day, she hears the Lord say, *"No pridefulness, no anger. Just ask him."*

Doing her best to act obediently, Shannon sits up and blurts, "Why are you still holding us prisoners, Carlos?"

He smirks. "Prisoners in a 16,000 square foot mansion?"

"We're prisoners. You already know I had no ulterior motives for getting involved with you."

"About that, you are correct."

"So, what is it that you still need to know?"

"I need to know how deeply you hate me," Carlos answers. "Because if it's not that deep, it can be fixed. And then I would have hope."

Shannon stands, transfixed. Softened by the rawness of his words yet petrified by the person he is, she despises the confusion of it all. The only words she manages are "Oh, God."

"The cowboy's gun wasn't loaded," he says.

"What??"

"In Vegas. A safeguard in case things went wrong. I'd rather you to have gotten the best of him than for him to have ended up shooting either of you."

She frowns at Carlos, overloaded with information painfully difficult to compute. "And Sul's? On the plane?"

"Now, his was loaded," Carlos says, shaking his head in disgust at his brother's stupidity. Shannon stares.

"No... No, Carlos. You did this. Reckless endangerment. Abuse. Selfishness. A complete failure in judgment. Don't try to make me believe this is something other than what it is. I won't accept it."

Clutching C-Lo tightly to her chest, she flees the room, scurrying from his view and the turmoil, to a place where she can drop to her knees. Her thoughts push against her momentum, and her nearby room suddenly feels far away from the living room.

I can't bear this. Why am I even in this predicament? she demands of God. *The man is a criminal, a kidnapper, a brute, and is probably sleeping with countless women along his travels...*

Yet, Shannon had never been able to stop thinking about the other side of him; the side she fell in love with. The man who was kind, gentle, charming, romantic, humorous. The man she truthfully wants back.

How is it possible to still long for his touch and the command of his presence or desire his camaraderie after all he's put me through, after all he's exposed me to? Am I supposed to simply forgive him and put everything in the past?

She doesn't think she can. *The whole situation is wrong. Believing it could be different, that he could be a good father to his son and a faithful, God-fearing husband to me—a pipe dream,* she concludes. But lying on her bed that evening, flashbacks of the hotel yank at her resolve and she longs for him to walk through her door.

And don't tell me to pray about it, either, Holy Spirit, Shannon spews right before she closes her eyes.

Act III
Life or Death

[22]

Rising with the dawn, Shannon slips out of bed and tip-toes across the floor to the bathroom, grinning at the unusual and coveted occasion of waking before C-Lo. As she passes his crib, her attention is drawn to the swimsuit tumbling from the half open box on the dresser. Still tossing yesterday afternoon's conversation around with the rebuttals in her head, she pauses sentimentally and slides the suit from under the lid.

Looking toward the window, Shannon envisions the pool below. The day is already beginning to swelter. *I could at least try it on.*

Leaving C-Lo in Delia's care, Shannon makes her way outdoors, undresses quickly, and jumps into the aqueous covering of the pool. Without consistent access to a pool or body of water in which to practice growing up, she never learned to dive. In fact, teaching herself to swim became a big feat, and she marvels at her present courage to brave beyond the shallow end.

Two or three ungainly laps later, Yoan stretches and shuffles away. Even before Shannon can pinpoint someone else approaching, she can feel Carlos nearby. He stands poolside in his embossed robe observing her.

Trying to ignore him, she flips on her back spontaneously. She begins floating to the deep end, showing off the suit until she starts to sink in the process. Jerking upright, she sneaks a peek at Carlos. He licks his lips and tosses his garment across the recliner competitively, revealing his own custom-made suit. As he moves, taut triceps counterbalance the biceps bulging beneath his sunlit skin. Shannon's eyes float over his pumped pectorals downward...

"You're getting in naked?"

Outdone by his brazenness, her head swivels around anxiously in search of onlookers.

"Of course," he says. "Only adults here."

Winking, he dives in expertly and glides straight to Shannon's treading legs. Panicking at the thought of being pulled under, she begins beating her way to the pool edge, but she isn't quick enough to avoid being caught. She coughs and sputters between fits of laughter, trying to keep her head above water and kick her legs free from the tickler below.

Not a moment too soon, he relents from his toying, allowing her to reach the side and catch her breath.

"You try'na drown me!" the southern belle gasps, splashing water in his face when his head emerges beside her.

"Maybe you should stay out of the deep end where sharks who chase pretty mermaids lurk."

Carlos migrates to Shannon's other side, and she shoves the water again. Laughing, he swipes the water from his face and pulls her from the wall.

"No, no, no!" she cries, and then they're off, gliding on their backs in tandem, Carlos supporting her with one strong arm as he propels them with a few powerful kicks.

"Relax," he instructs.

Shannon does what she can to comply.

Overhead, a beautiful blanket of blue stretches before them, dotted with pregnant puffs of grayish-white clouds. Reaching the shallow end, they stand, facing each other.

"Well, that was fun," Shannon teases, smoothing the hair from her face before she turns to make her exit.

Carlos gently pulls one of her wrists toward him and glides the fingertips of his other hand along her forearm from wrist to elbow. He then bends and follows the path he just traced with wet kisses. Fighting the sensation, Shannon peels her arm away and hoists a questioning eyebrow.

Sighing, Carlos rubs the back of his neck in frustration. "Shannon... seeing you out here this morning reminded me I need to enjoy what I have. To think, I once had more than just beauty around me—I had wit, intelligence, strength, passion—until that day I let my pride get in the way." Shannon's eyes drop uncomfortably.

He glances above the tree tops, and the sly grin returns. "Get dressed. I want to show you something."

***

Carlos leads Shannon into the fifth car garage and hits the automatic garage door opener as they walk in. Even before the light floods the garage, Shannon's eyes gravitate immediately to the motorcycle parked there.

Assuming it is the surprise, she climbs on the Ducati Monster 796 and examines its features. The model's single round headlamp, simple framing, and custom black matte and silver finish lend to its sleek, classic appeal. "It's okay, I guess," she says.

"I thought you would like it." Carlos watches her a moment. "I've seen how well you can ride, but are you a good teacher?"

Repressing paradoxical feelings of flattery and dismay—one, that he had been watching her that night, and two, that he remembered—Shannon fiddles with the features.

"Are you asking me to teach you?"

"Why not?"

She swings her leg off the bike, shaking her head as she dismounts. "Nah."

"Come on," Carlos urges, straddling the bike. "Give me some pointers. What are the basics, at least? I'm a quick learner."

"It's not that simple."

He lifts the helmet from the side of the bike and puts it on. "Okay, climb on."

"I'm not getting on a bike with someone who hasn't a clue how to ride."

"Just get on." Carlos flips open his visor, his eyes twinkling mischievously.

Thinking about C-Lo, Shannon looks over her shoulder.

"He's with Delia," Carlos says. "He's in good hands."

Shannon stares at him a beat, then in an absurd decision of trust, she climbs on behind him.

"Better put on your helmet," he instructs and fires up the motorcycle.

Bracing herself for major jerking or worse, Shannon grips Carlos around the waist and thinks herself insane to have gotten on the bike. The take off down the driveway is quick and smooth. Carlos, indisputably adept at riding a motorcycle, turns to look guilefully at Shannon. She wags her finger at the hoax.

Waving his fob at the keypad post, they slow for the driveway gate to open, and Shannon asks, "Where are we going?"

"You're teaching me how to ride. Hold on."

They cruise down Carretera Central de Cuba into the heart of the city, passing through tightly nestled dwellings until they reach one of Havana's many bustling business districts. Buses, people, and peddle cabs densify the views while the distinctive lines and curves of vintage American cars dot the streets with restored vibrancy and rusty, faded hues.

From time to time, Carlos plays the tour guide, slowing near sights of interest and hollering a descriptive blurb. "El Capitolio," he informs, as they pass the large, domed structure on the left resembling the U.S. Capitol building in Washington, D.C. "Our Central Park" is on the right.

He names the wide, low-walled, tree-lined promenade dividing the vehicular traffic in two directions along Paseo de Marti street as "Paseo del Prado." Shannon watches the activity of the ample supply of street vendors set up there atop the intriguingly designed cement pathway until her attention is called to the fortress ahead. "Castillo de San Salvador de la Punta."

Their drive along Paseo de Marti ends and the city spills open to meet the expansive ocean bordering the island. "El Malecón," she's told of the broad roadway adjacent to a battered sea wall that "stretches approximately five miles from Old Havana to the Vedado barrio."

He drops down a couple gears on the bike and maneuvers closer to the wall ledge, allowing the sea spray to cool them. A blend of Colonial, Baroque, Neoclassical, and Art Deco structures span the distance. Brown bodies of varying shades dive and jump from the wall edge and the occasional wave splatters its droplets above the sea wall. It is a beautiful spectacle of historic architecture and seascape, and Shannon takes it in.

"This place is breathtaking. The people, the buildings, the views. Just fascinating. It's a trip, though, how some places look on the verge of falling down, yet appear to be occupied, many of them right next to buildings that look brand new."

"They're in the process of restoring a lot of Habana Vieja, but my country still leaves a lot to be desired economically." Carlos muses a moment before continuing. "It's often said, if someone leaves Cuba, they return a king. It holds true. At least, it certainly does for me. But even that comes with a high price. It's imperative that I keep a lot of government officials content."

On the move again, the couple pass three impressive monuments along the Malecón, then turn left off the esplanade onto Avenida Paseo and make their way back into the city thicket. Shannon raises her arms as they coast peacefully to a stop light.

"HOLD ON!"

Carlos' yell is abrupt, followed by "Ah!!" as he flinches. Silenced bullets begin whizzing past them. Adrenaline rushing, Shannon hunches over in synchronization with Carlos, gripping him tightly as he crashes the red light. He burns rubber wildly through the intersection, narrowly missing the crossway cars.

In Shannon's peripheral, a car pulls from the traffic and swiftly makes its way into the intersection. Horns blare, and their attackers emerge behind them, zig zagging aggressively past vehicles. Terrified screams permeate the air as Carlos speeds dangerously along the street, weaving around obstacles and scattering pedestrians.

Gaining some distance, he yells, "Were you hit?!"

"No! Go, go, go!!!"

Another car screeches onto the street, and Carlos leans daringly to miss it. Car engines race behind them while gun fire seems to explode from all angles. Ahead, a third vehicle charges in their direction.

"¡Diablos!"[33] Carlos exclaims.

He makes a sharp right turn onto a narrower street and yells over his shoulder, "Take my gun!"

"Where!?"

"Holster! Left side!"

Deftly, Shannon reaches around his waist, retrieves the semi-automatic, clicks the safety and begins firing. A massive cemetery looms next to them, making her skin crawl as she aims at the killers in pursuit.

The closest car dips and careens into a parked car. The second car swerves to miss it, with the third car right on its bumper. The second and third cars recover ungracefully and attempt to regain some ground. Nearby and remote police sirens add to the swell around them. Shannon fires a couple more deterring blasts at the vehicles, buying the motorcycle some precious distance.

Carlos heads for the river. Skillfully, he glides across the dirt paths and grass of Almendares Park, receiving mixed stares from the few park visitors present. As they approach a couple of drainage ditches, he tosses a warning to Shannon. "Get ready!"

She stashes the gun in her waistband and they both raise from the seat. Carlos maneuvers the motorcycle carefully over the humps, then speeds off again along the river-walk. Under the bridge, he slows to quiet the engine, then cuts through the grass under the canopy of treetops to another side of the park. Easing back onto the streets, they resume top speeds.

"Anyone on us?" Carlos asks, concentrating on the road.

---

[33] Damn it or literally, demons

"No," Shannon replies.

"Were you hit?"

"No! I'm okay!"

She leans against him tightly and the scenery blurs past them along the road, mirroring the swarm of emotions screaming through her mind. When it looks like they have lost all tails, Carlos still doesn't head back. With the pavement continuing to whiz beneath them, Shannon asks, "Where are we going?"

"We can't go home. They'll expect it and just ambush us," Carlos yells into the wind. "And I have to get you into something safer."

Doing well over a hundred miles per hour, they travel far into the country side. With the worst seemingly behind them, Shannon registers a new problem: There's blood gushing from Carlos' left arm. Pressing her hand over the wound, a new level of fright washes over her and, praying even harder, she closes her eyes.

About an hour out, after passing through a city called Artemisa, they leave behind the busier, narrow roads, shared by tractors, Zebu cattle, and pigs, for one less traveled and flanked by dense tropical foliage. The bike slows at one of the tree-lined, dirt road junctions. Carlos takes the path slowly to not kick up much dust and coasts to the lock on an obscured, dilapidated barn door.

Shannon stares numbly at the thatched roof of the barn until she's jolted from her observation by Carlos' command. "Gun," he says, holding his right hand out while turning the combination with his left. Shannon hands it over.

With weapon drawn, he pulls slowly into the suffocatingly hot, rickety barn and pauses long enough to sweep his sights across the shadows before activating the flashlight on his cell phone. After another gander to make sure the place is clear, he straddle-walks the bike next to a covered car. Seemingly satisfied that everything is as it should be, he parks the bike, and Shannon climbs off.

Carlos throws his helmet to the ground, cursing in Spanish. "How did they know?! How did those ratas[34] know it was me on a motorcycle?"

Shannon stands there, aware that he doesn't intend for her to answer. He dismounts and grabs his arm, wincing in pain. More expletives flow as he bends next to a small generator, turns on the

---

[34] Cowards

gas, pulls the choke and hits the start button. The light bulb dangling overhead glows brightly, banishing the darkness.

Shannon removes her helmet slowly and stares at his bleeding arm. Carlos glances at her face, drained of color and another set of profanities flow. "Tell me you weren't hurt."

She shakes her head. "No. I'm fine, but we have to stop that bleeding immediately."

"I know."

Rotating his arm to inspect his injury, he walks to a tool box against the wall and pulls out a screw driver. He uses it to dig a shallow hole in the ground next to the box and tells Shannon, "Pull the cover off the car for me."

Dropping the cover to the ground, she exclaims, "You have a Chevy stashed away in an old barn—with electricity."

"One of the many wise things my father taught me was to have a get-away car somewhere that no one else knew about but me. For scenarios just like this one."

Carlos lifts out a set of keys from the dirt and tosses the screwdriver back into the box. Even though he's trying to keep his left arm still, blood continues to gush from the wound. He unlocks the car and hands Shannon the first aid kit. She gets to work dressing the wound, packing gauze against it.

"How the hell did they know?" Carlos muses aloud. "We never even took off our helmets. There was no way they could recognize me unless they knew to look for me. You..." He stops his train of thought to direct Shannon as she begins securing the dressing with tape. "Make it tight."

"What do you think I'm doing?"

In the excruciating heat, they are both sweating. The conditions aren't helping, and Shannon is starting to get nauseated from the heat and smell of blood. On top of this, the dressing isn't holding effectively.

She announces, "I need something to make a tourniquet. Take off your belt."

Continuing her work on the wound, Shannon says quietly, "So, if we weren't recognizable that means—"

"THERE IS A SNITCH IN MY HOME! ANOTHER traitor! Which explains things falling apart lately. And they will pay. THEY WILL PAY! I'm gonna blow their—"

"CARLOS! I can't finish dressing this wound with your arms flailing."

He looks at her.

"We could have been killed today! Can you just..." Shannon falters, overwhelmed by the afternoon's death-defying experience and her sudden desire to punch Carlos in his injury. She finishes dressing the wound. As her bloody hands begin to quake, Carlos closes his eyes and drops his head.

"I'm sorry. It was... a bad idea to put you on that bike with me, Shannon." He pulls her to him in an embrace.

Holding her hands behind him, she breathes in deeply. "I'm just hap—I thank God He kept us alive. No rider is that good to dodge all those bullets flying at us nor can they have aim that bad."

Carlos' phone resumes its incessant ringing. He pulls away to silence it, and Shannon wipes her arm across her eyes, looking around for something to clean her hands on. There's nothing but the front of her shorts.

When she looks up from her inefficient smearing, she's startled by the blood already oozing from under the bandaging she just applied.

"We need to get you to a hospital."

"No hospital," Carlos retorts. "A bullet wound will draw the police. Plus, they'll want to keep me there, and we don't have the time."

"What do you mean 'we don't have time'? You can't leave that bullet in there, Carlos."

"I'll take care of it! Right now, we need to get back to the house."

"Do you think whoever it is is going to hurt C-lo?"

Carlos doesn't respond. She gets it. *No time for speculation*. He grabs a flashlight from the tool box and flashes it around and under the vehicle. When he opens the hood, she asks in exasperation, "What are you doing?"

"Checking for triggers."

Shannon grabs the sides of her head and prays softly, "Lord Jesus, please help us."

Satisfied, Carlos closes the hood of the Chevy and opens the door for Shannon. He climbs in and turns the key. It cranks, but doesn't fire. He cranks it again. Nothing.

Shannon drops her head in dismay. "The battery's dead?"

Popping the hood, Carlos slides out, and Shannon does likewise to escape the heat. She watches as he pulls a battery charger from one of the stalls, plugs it in, and hooks up jumper cables to the battery. He tries the ignition again. The Chevy fires up.

"Yes!" she exhales. "Props on your forethought."

Carlos begins unhooking the cables and glances at her with a slight smile. "You have to think the plan all the way through. Do me a favor. Throw that cover over the bike."

Gratefully, she obliges and climbs back inside the Chevy.

Full Disclosure

[23]

Neither of them says a word as they pass lengthy rows of sugar cane, tobacco and fruit cutting through the red soil of the farmland on both sides of the road. With the hot air fanning forcefully through the windows, Shannon's stomach settles, and she voices her thoughts to break the ice.

"This old Chevy looks like a modern car on the inside. Have you ever driven it?"

Carlos remains quiet for a minute. "You want to know the story?"

"Yes, very much so."

"Years ago, thinking about what my father said, I purchased that barn under a different name. Then, I drove from Habana to Artemisa, paid cash for a restored '57 Chevy and installed a tracking device—"

"A tracking device. Why?"

"So I would be notified if someone ever moved the car. It wouldn't help to arrive at your getaway car and it not be there, now would it?"

She raises her eyebrows in comprehension. He chuckles and continues, "I bought the tool box, the charger you saw, and a bike—"

"That motorcycle we were on?"

"No. A bicycle. No motor. I drove the Chevy to the barn, locked it up, and rode the bicycle ten miles or so back to Artemisa. I tossed the bike, got in my car and drove back to Havana. My family was irate. No one could understand why I had to go off by myself." He grunts sarcastically. "Kind of like today."

Shannon marvels inwardly at his ingenuity, but instead of admitting it, she asks, "What are you gonna do about your arm?"

Carlos picks up his phone. "I have a doctor in mind."

He dials. There's no answer. He doesn't leave a message. Instead, he accesses his voicemail. Shannon can hear various voices, mostly unidentifiable, leaving messages of urgent intonation.

She assumes they are family members or his crew trying to track him down.

"No one said anything about C-Lo, did they?" Shannon asks.

Carlos shakes his head, then attempts to counter her worry. "C-Lo is fine."

Praying he is right, Shannon soaks up the exterior scenery in contemplation. "Who do you think it is? The snitch, I mean."

Carlos breathes in deeply. She doesn't think he's going to respond, but surprisingly, he discloses, "I don't know who betrayed me. But I'll bet my life whoever the bastard is was also involved in my father's murder."

It was murder. The gears in Shannon's mind tick. "You said Yendris was a traitor—"

Carlos spumes at the man's name.

"Hear me out," she urges. "That wasn't just about me, was it?"

He studies Shannon a beat. "No. It wasn't."

"He had something to do with your father's death." She looks to him for a response even though it wasn't a question.

Carlos opens up. "The snake you cuddled up to slept with my sister to gain access to our father and led our enemy right to him. His foolish moves with you helped me to weed him out quickly." Carlos gets angrier as he speaks. "You didn't notice his absence the night before my father ended up dead, but I have my ways of finding out EVERYTHING that happens in my camp!"

"Who is the enemy?"

Carlos inhales slowly. "Those who would have my family eliminated in order to acquire the long-held positions we maintain."

"But why?"

"The black market. It is very profitable worldwide, Señorita. But here in Cuba, it is so even in the simplest commodities, like food."

"Or guns. Your legal business dealings are essentially a cover," Shannon expounds. "Your primary mainstay is smuggling on the black market."

"I wouldn't say primary. More like a means to an end."

Carlos is reflective as he slows for a group of barefoot, shirtless boys playing in the middle of the unpaved road, their skin taut against their rib cages. "Somehow, they look happy. We looked that way when we visited relatives in places similar to this, too, but it was because we knew we were going home at the end of the day."

Passing the kids, he negotiates the vehicle away from three leathery-skinned, bedraggled farm workers trudging roadside, hauling produce on themselves and their beasts of burden under the hot sun. Carlos scratches his five o'clock shadow that Shannon catches herself admiring.

"Politics have created an enduring hardship for many people in my country," he comments. "Low wages, shortages in food rations and basic provisions, financial inaccessibility to more nutritious options, farmers who meet their production quotas and often watch it rot waiting for the bureaucracy to claim it while their families go hungry. And then there's the systemic judicial retaliation for violators of the regime—even based on heresay... No es fácil.[35] But, there are those of us who've managed to remain on the other side who give back." He looks at Shannon. "A necessary evil for a greater good to manifest."

Shannon lets that steep awhile, recalling Yunaisys' words and subsequent fright. She can't say she agrees with his logic, but at least, there is some clarity. Not until they reach the main road of the approaching city, does she ask, "Is... he dead?"

"Yes."

"Did you kill him?"

"No, I did not. He was caught trying to escape before I returned and someone else took care of him for me. Happy?"

"Who killed him?"

"Why do you care?"

"If another culprit is in your midst, every detail matters."

"Are you investigating, Detective?"

Shannon bullheadedly awaits a response to her question. Carlos obliges. "I trust the person who shot him with my life. He has risked his own more than once to save it."

"But, did anyone else *see* Yendris try to escape?"

"I *see* where you're going with this, but it's not Ocho."

"You said yourself you don't know who it is. I overheard the two of them talking."

"Ocho and Yendris? What did you hear?"

"I don't recall exactly. Something about having time to do whatever it was later. I just know it didn't sit well with me."

Carlos is contemplative, formulating something in the silence. However, his response isn't what she was expecting.

---

[35] The living is difficult.

"You have a chip on your shoulder about my brother, and you're biased."

"You're biased because he's your brother."

"Touché."

The sudden mirth in their banter helps take the edge off. In the silence that follows, Shannon declares, "Well, I know it wasn't Delia."

"Are you kidding me? She's my first suspect."

"Ha! But, seriously... Why do y'all call Ocho, Ocho?"

"I guess the best answer is he always ends the game. Blows up all other moves like an eight ball. We've seen him jump from a three-story building, grab the blade of a swinging knife, even dive in front of gunmen before to turn some bad situations around. All in the name of family honor and respect."

"Well, he certainly doesn't respect your women." Shannon regrets the words as soon as they slip from her mouth.

"My *women?* What do you mean by that?"

"Nothing."

"No, no. You don't say something like that, and then try to clean it up with 'nothing.' Spill it."

Shannon procrastinates. "Okay. I'm pretty certain he was sleeping with Carmen."

Camouflaging his reaction, she can't tell if her statement was news to him or trivial by the look on his face. His expression turns jocular.

"You want an answer."

"What are you talking about? *Ha!* I didn't ask you a thing!" Shannon says, her cheeks growing flushed.

"I've been around women long enough to recognize when your kind wants information. So here it is: Carmen was my personal assistant who over the years began desiring more from me than I had to give. She was never my woman, my girlfriend or even a prospect, but rather, an occasional tool of convenience. So, you can let that assumption go."

"You're telling me you didn't love her at all? I find that hard to believe."

"She's never been the one I love."

Nothing else needs to be said.

***

Carlos swings the car into the driveway and phones the surveillance room, alerting the crew of their arrival in a Chevy. Yoan stands cautiously in the garage doorway waiting to determine that it's actually Carlos pulling in. When he does, he assails him with questions.

"What are you doing riding a motorcycle through the city? Unprotected? Man, we're not kids anymore! Are you trying to make it easy for Goyzo to t-take you out?"

Ocho and Beto enter. Carlos asks, "How do you know it was Goyzo?"

"I saw his hombre, Chucha, d-dead on the news!" Yoan explains.

Brushing past everyone, Carlos mutters, "I don't have much time."

"You want to go after him now?" Yoan asks.

Carlos raises his hand for silence. "Not yet. Tell Delia to bring Carlito down."

He pulls Shannon into the security room. The three brothers try to follow, but Carlos orders, "Everyone out!" They leave along with the two guards inside, and he pulls out a chair.

"Sit. I need your eyes," Carlos says, pointing. "Watch for anything suspicious in those monitors there."

He calls up video footage from 1:15 that afternoon. From different angles, they observe the two of them entering the garage. Checking the other monitors, they see Ocho sitting in the surveillance room, Yoan and Sul roughhousing playfully outside near the pool house, Delia cooking in the kitchen, and staff members working around the grounds. Next, he cues the time period right after they left on the motorcycle, looking for anything that would clue him in on the leak.

They are interrupted by a knock on the door.

"¿Mijo?"

Carlos and Shannon move to the door. As soon as Carlos opens it, Delia's words begin to rush forth, and Shannon gratefully pulls C-Lo into her arms. She returns to her seat, whispering praises of thanksgiving and smothering C-Lo in kisses while Delia continues her loquacious expository in Spanish.

"How terrified I was when I was watching the news break on TV, and Yoan said it looked like the two of you, and I said it *did* look like you, but it couldn't be. My God! I'm so glad you're okay—"

"Yes, we're okay. Now, please, Tia, I need the room." She leaves in a fluster, and Carlos returns to the security console.

The two watch carefully. Everyone used a phone at some point, but nothing out of the ordinary is detectable. Carlos fast forwards to the approximate time of the attack. Delia calls Yoan into the den, ostensibly when she sees the breaking news. He nearly drops his bowl of cereal, and it looks as if he is instructing her to search out other news channels. There is genuine angst on Yoan's face as he races from the den to the garage where the motorcycle should be. Discovering it missing, he immediately runs to the security room, questioning Sul and Beto.

Carlos turns to Shannon. "You see anything?"

"Just that while everyone else seemed to mosey around the property from the time we left until the news broke, Ocho never moved from this spot. But he was gone when Yoan ran in here."

Carlos lowers his eyes half-mast. Lightly, he says, "You keep picking on my brother."

Shannon notices how profusely Carlos is sweating even under the air conditioning. His bandage is now soaked through. "You need to get to a doctor NOW."

"Not yet. I need to know who I can trust."

"Your stubbornness is unbelievable! You're going to die from blood loss if we don't get out of here, Carlos."

As if he didn't hear a word she said, he takes her hand and leads her and C-Lo out of the security room down the hall to the same elevator they had used when she'd first arrived. They take it up to the top floor and enter through a back way into his master suite.

The doors open onto a travertine tiled foyer. To the right lies the master bedroom. A portion of a sprawling bed is visible just opposite the large convex-shaped wall next to where she stands. Straight ahead, down two short flights of stairs, is the sitting room she had visited briefly before.

While Shannon struggles to erase the unwanted visuals from her memory, Carlos enters a few codes into the keypad by the elevator. He proceeds into the sitting room to turn on the TV. The news is broadcasting a short, poorly recorded video of the shootout over and over, a surreal repeat of them racing down a street with gun fire resounding all around, spliced together with footage showing the aftermath of wreckage and body bags—rather indiscreetly, in Shannon's opinion.

Photos flash on the screen of those killed in the shootout. Carlos recognizes one of Goyzo's men, but apparently the rest in the death toll were innocent bystanders. Those identified in connection with the shooting are named next.

"Anything mentioned tying us to the incident?" Shannon asks, burdened by her possible hand in the senseless loss of lives.

"No. But, Yoan was telling the truth."

Carlos scrolls through his phone's recent list and calls again. The recipient still doesn't answer. He dials another number, and Shannon follows him into the bedroom as he exchanges a few words. They pass between the convex wall and the master bed, and she can now see a large convex-shaped fireplace built into it. Carlos presses a button near one of the nightstands, and a panel above the fireplace opens to reveal a replica of the downstairs surveillance monitors. He's placed on hold.

Carlos studies the surveillance monitors. Someone returns to the line. "Gracias," he says hurriedly and hangs up.

Hopeful that he has finally reached whoever can help him, Shannon waits for information. Instead, Carlos begins unbuttoning his shirt and pulling out a change of clothes.

"So... did you reach the doctor?"

"The hospital where he works. He's in surgery. I'm going to him."

"That's crazy. You don't even know if he'll be able to see you. Can't you please get seen somewhere else?"

"I trust him to do what I need and get me back on the road."

Before she can say another word, Carlos buzzes Delia on the intercom with instructions. Shannon runs from the room.

"Where are you going?"

"To get the baby carrier. At least I can strap him in the car."

"Stop! You two are staying here in the suite."

"No, we're not."

"Yes, you are. It is the safest place for you to be. You are less likely to be shot at in here."

Shannon pictures the gunmen from earlier shooting at them with C-Lo in the car. Frustrated, she sits on the steps, squeezing her forehead. "Who are you taking with you?"

"Until I know who tried to have me killed, no one can know my moves."

"So, you're gonna drive yourself to the hospital in this condition?"

Ignoring her, Carlos unlocks the front entry remotely. Delia appears with arms full of bandaging and antiseptics. Gingerly, she removes his shirt and re-dresses his wound with clean bandages. Then, in typical Delia fashion, she dabs excessively at his perspiring forehead. Carlos grabs her hands.

"Tia! Please..." He looks at her intently before proceeding in Spanish. "Keep Yunaisys with you."

His meaning is clear. Nodding anxiously, Delia hugs him tightly and whispers, "Que Dios te bendiga,"[36] into his ear. Clasping her hands over her mouth, she exits the room.

Carlos winces as he dons a clean shirt. He crumples into a seated position on the side of his bed and wipes his brow in agony. Feeling helpless, Shannon looks around. Hoping the bathroom is on the other side, she walks through the only other doors in the bedroom.

She enters a huge room, with multiple doorways throughout, and thankfully straight ahead flanking a hallway entrance are two sinks. She hastily opens drawers and cabinet doors near the sinks until she finds what she's looking for. Returning to the bedroom, she hands the bottle of pain pills to Carlos, who takes a handful of them dry.

"Thank you."

Shannon musters a smile through the bleakness. Carlos finishes pulling on a fresh pair of pants and motions toward a pen and pad lying on a nightstand. She retrieves the pen with her free hand and stoops, poised to write.

"53 5 302 0211. Call me if you see or hear anything. I locked the elevator with a private code, so no one will be able to use it to enter the room. The front entrance is locked the same way." He pauses. "This is very important. If I don't come back—"

Shannon puts down the pen, preparing to interject, but Carlos doesn't give her the opening. "Use the elevator as a safe room. It's bullet proof. Go to the bottom floor. Hit the red button. The doors won't open from the outside. There's a phone on a private line in there, and the number to the police is posted next to it. I know you know what to tell them to get them here in a hurry. There are also limited surveillance monitors behind the wall panel. Use them. And be careful."

Carlos turns to leave, but Shannon grabs his chin so that he faces her. "You come back. *You come back.*"

He moves to go. She grabs his face again and presses her lips against his. She kisses him hungrily, feeling him awaken against her belly. Knowing he's in dire need of medical attention, Shannon maneuvers him away from her toward the door.

"Go," she says softly.

---

[36] May God bless you.

Carlos leans to kiss C-Lo gently on the cheek and ruffles his baby tendrils before walking out. He doesn't look back.

Outside the suite, he directs Yoan to guard Shannon and the baby. Yoan insists on going with him, but Carlos resists.

"I need you to be my eyes and ears here. Stay alert."

The Breach

[24]

Peeking out the sitting room window onto the dark pool, Shannon realizes she's at the back side of the house. Wanting to see the the front driveway, she traverses the bedroom into the bathroom and establishes her bearings. To the left, behind an ajar door she can see a toilet. To the right, behind a closed door she finds another toilet and bidet. Assuming the two sets of slatted double doors cater-corner to where she's standing must be closets, she advances past the sinks into the hallway. On both sides of the short hallway are showers, and at the end is a spa-like area with a four-person sized hot tub and lots of windows along the walls.

Shannon reaches the main window just in time to see taillights flash down the long drive, disappear behind a hill, and reappear briefly at the entrance gate. Closing her eyes, she prays for Carlos to receive the medical care he needs in time and return safely. She snuggles C-Lo closer to her. "It's you and me, little guy," she says, planting a kiss on C-Lo's soft cheek. *Time to get busy.*

Retracing her steps to the front foyer, Shannon acquaints herself with the surroundings, searching for guns and opening every door inside the suite to confirm there are no balconies or otherwise maneuverable ways to gain access. *His guns must be locked up in one of these drawers,* she thinks, contemplating how to pick the locks.

With arms tired of carrying the baby, she lays C-Lo on the bed and keeps a watchful eye on the video surveillance. Outside the main suite entrance, Yoan stands guard. Downstairs, it appears Ocho is pacing the floor anxiously, but then, the activity of everyone visible around the home seems skittish. Despite her fatigue, Shannon tries to pay close attention to everything that's going on.

Observing the master bedroom surveillance, she notices the only images cycling through are windows, select doorways, and the elevator, as far as she can tell. *Carlos must not want his family or crew spying on his private bedroom activity.* Whatever the reason, Shannon is grateful for the veil.

***

"I'm sorry. He's in surgery and can't be disturbed, sir."

Carlos sizes up the charge nurse standing behind the desk. He turns on the charm, shining that gorgeous smile.

"Please, miss, give him the message that Los is here and it's urgent. Do this for me, and I will make it worth your while." He slips several highly coveted CUCs[37] into her hand.

Minutes later, Dr. Valdés comes into the waiting room. "Carlos! Look at you! What is going on?"

"I was hit. During the shootout today."

The doctor snaps, "And you're just now coming to me? You look like you've lost a lot of blood." Immediately, he calls a passing nurse. "This man's been shot. Don't bother with paperwork right now. Put him in surgical suite three; chem panel, X-ray. Anticipate transfusion, one unit of packed red blood cells. I'll be with him as soon as I can. Stay with him the entire time. He doesn't like hospitals, understand?"

"Yes, doctor." The nurse rushes to bring over a wheelchair.

Carlos mouths to Valdés, "Nice."

***

It proves very difficult to stay alert while watching minuscule changes occur on the surveillance monitors and C-Lo's tummy rise and fall in uninhibited slumber. Shannon stands and walks into the sitting room to see if there is any new news. In front of the TV, she freezes, caught off guard at having missed the room's longest wall made entirely of glass.

Could someone be watching me? she wonders, drawing nearer. She overlooks the indoor garden area two stories below. No other rooms share the sitting room view, and Shannon grows confident of their seclusion once again.

She turns her attention to the TV. The same information reported earlier displays across the screen, so she heads back to the bedroom, relieved at not seeing an update with Carlos' face, at least. Passing by the small bar stocked full of booze bottles, Shannon glimpses her blood smeared clothes in the mirror and halts. *It's probably a good time for a shower.*

---

[37] CUC (Cuban Convertible Peso) one of two Cuban currencies used primarily by foreigners or the elect for upscale, private, or imported goods and services. It is worth approx. 1 US dollar and 25 CUP (Cuban Peso, aka Moneda Nacional, used primarily by locals for day-to-day purchases and rationed provisions.)

***

When Doctor Valdés enters the room, he lights into Carlos, whispering out of earshot of the nurse on the other side of the room. "I'm jeopardizing my license. If I didn't owe you my life, I wouldn't do it. I swear."

"I need you to make it quick, Doc."

Examining the arm, the doctor informs, "You'll need anesthesia."

"No anesthesia. Just take the bullet out and wrap it up."

"Carlos, you may be able to withstand the pain of that bullet in your arm now. But when I start to take it out, the pain will be unbearable."

"Just numb the area! I'll be alright."

Valdés complies, administering a Lidocaine injection just above the bullet entry. When he proceeds to clean the wound, Carlos shouts, "Aaghh! Did you numb it? I said numb it!"

"It is numb." Shaking his head with exasperation, he turns and raises his voice to the nurse. "Start a morphine drip."

***

Quickly showered, Shannon returns to the bedroom and digs through Carlos' drawers until she finds a white undershirt and a pair of lace-up gym shorts. As she cinches the strings together tightly, tones sound from the elevator keypad.

Reeling, Shannon leaps toward the monitors for a look. Her heart pounds as she catches the shadow of someone hurrying from the elevator doors downstairs. She waits momentarily to see if the elevator starts to move.

Nothing happens. A sweep of the monitors shows Yoan still at his post, guarding the suite entrance, except now from a chair by the door. She glances down at C-Lo, then moves stealthily into the front foyer for a listen.

"Yoan?" Shannon calls tentatively.

"Yuh," comes his muffled, yet distinct reply.

"Any word?"

"No."

Shannon closes her eyes in an effort to regroup. It's been two and a half hours since Carlos left, and she's done her best to stay calm and not worry. However, she is beyond ready for answers.

Returning to the bedroom and her vigil of the security monitors, it appears nothing else changed in her absence. *Carlos, you better have made it to the doctor.*

She dials.

***

Drowsy and weakened by blood loss, Carlos succumbs to a deep sleep shortly after they start him on the morphine. He doesn't witness Dr. Valdés hard at work, and he doesn't hear his phone ring.

***

He doesn't answer. Shannon keeps glancing between the clock and the video monitors. Every so often, she takes a peek at the muted news channel in the sitting room. An hour later, she calls Carlos again. Still no answer.

The time is getting later and later. C-Lo wakes up hungry, but Shannon can't sit still to feed him. Worried and antsy, she carries the nursing baby to a front window to look out, hoping to see Carlos pulling into the drive. The yard is still and dark. Another try to Carlos, but he can't be reached.

***

Over the headset, Yoan announces his need for a bathroom break.

His relief arrives to the top floor, and as Yoan dashes for the nearest bathroom, he hears, "Go ahead and take a break. I can wait up here awhile."

Yoan nods in affirmation before disappearing around the other side of the hallway.

***

Dismayed at not being able to contact Carlos, Shannon revisits the bedroom, scrutinizing the video monitors again for new activity as she lays C-Lo onto the bed. Nothing looks different, but she had missed the changing of the guard.

***

Carlos lies motionless on the gurney, the work of the medical staff complete.

***

There's a knock. Shannon scrutinizes the low-resolution image in the monitor and perceives it is Yoan standing in front of the door. Yearning for news, she hastens to the entrance and calls, "Yes?"

From the muffled words coming through the door, Shannon barely makes out, "Carlos... back... downstairs."

"What?" she asks.

Footsteps withdraw.

Gingerly, Shannon turns the handle for a peek.

Thwack!

The door slams her hard in the face and a terrifying hand seizes her by the throat. Before she can react, Ocho is pushing his way into the master foyer.

"You are an annoying little whore," he snarls, shoving her into the sitting room. "You shouldn't be here. SCREWING EVERYTHING UP!"

Shannon stumbles backward against the arm of the love seat, launching it a few feet across the tiled floor. Steadying herself, she gauges his next move.

"Now," he informs, "you will do for me what he had *my lady* do for him—"

Shannon throws an upper cut to his chin, dives past and lands an accurately placed kick to his knee. The knee buckles, accompanied by a gruesome pop. As Ocho crumbles, Shannon hesitates, trying to decide if she should run for her baby or for the door.

Screaming for help, she chooses the door, hoping to draw Ocho away from the direction of her child. She barely pulls it open before it's slammed shut against her hand. Shannon hollers and writhes in pain. Ocho yanks her with him to the floor, and the skin peels from her fingers.

He slides her by the throat into the sitting room and slaps her several times. As she struggles to protect herself and gasps for help, he attempts to silence her with his hand over her mouth.

"I'll make you swallow me whole," he threatens, and Shannon sinks her teeth into his flesh. Jerking away his hand, he rears back to punch her in the face. Her eye seems to implode. His fingers clasp around her neck. Clawing at his choking grip, she fights to retain consciousness. She feels his nails dig into the flesh of her stomach as he tears at her over-sized shorts.

His weight shifts to one side, and Shannon senses his accommodation of the maimed knee. In the fleeting space created, she thrusts the palm of her hand into his nose and twists her body from under him. She tries to get to her feet, but he tackles her against the coffee table. It overturns, and they roll, hitting the glass wall.

Shannon is terrified it's going to break. She squirms away, crawling backward on her palms around the coffee table. Ocho shoves the corner of the coffee table into her side, knocking her off balance. Dragging his injured leg, he grips her by the ankle.

"You think you're a tough girl? Huh?" he growls, propping himself on one knee. "How 'bout shooting me?! Shoot *me* now! Not so tough without a gun!"

As Ocho reaches for his weapon, Shannon snatches the glass and wrought iron lamp from the end table near them and smashes it against the side of his head. The high pitched shatter startles C-Lo in the next room, and he starts wailing. She backswings, striking Ocho soundly on the opposite temple.

Disoriented, he falls on top of her, blood running down his face. Shannon positions herself to immobilize him, interlocking her elbow with his. Using her other arm as leverage to roll him slightly, she brings her knee up forcefully into his crotch. He coughs and loses his breath, granting her the opportunity to slam his armed hand into his skull. The gun dislodges and skids under the love seat.

Just as she disarms him, Yoan and another guard rush in. Shannon kicks Ocho away from her, and, as if on cue, he yells at them, "She's trying to escape! *Damn it!* I think she broke my knee!"

Yoan and the guard are frozen, seemingly at a loss. Ocho hollers in frustration, "Catch her, you morons! Don't let her get out!"

Despite the fact that Shannon remains seated with her hands held up in surrender, Yoan snaps into action, pinning her violently to the floor. Ocho pulls out his cell phone.

"I'll inform Los," he says. They listen to him have an abbreviated conversation with Carlos as he hobbles away painfully. At Yoan's instruction, the other guard moves to assist him from the room.

"I'm okay!" he screams, scowling as he snatches the phone from his ear. He waves the guard away furiously.

"Stay with him!" Yoan insists and turns angrily back to Shannon.

"Don't believe him!" she pleads. "I wasn't trying to escape. He attacked me. Please, believe me. Think about it, Yoan. Have I ever tried to run?"

Yoan stares at the third eye rising up on her forehead and the gash across the bridge of her nose. Suspicious about the scuffle, her words give him further pause. Too many things had gone wrong today. He had spent a lot of time around Shannon, and she just didn't seem like she would try to escape this way. Then again, he could be wrong about her.

Frowning, he asks, "What happened?"

"I heard a knock on the door," Shannon recounts. "I opened it, thinking it was still you. Ocho lunged in and attacked me. It's him!

He's the one who leaked that we were on the motorcycle. He was trying to get Carlos killed. And me, apparently."

He looks accusingly at her. "You're calling my brother a traitor?"

Shannon can't tell if she will win Yoan's trust, but she calculates. "He said something about me being a tough girl and taunted me to shoot him, too."

Nothing registers on Yoan's face as he tries to put two and three together. *Clearly, he isn't the smartest one in the bunch.*

She attempts to clarify. "Carlos gave me his gun while we were on that bike. Ocho said it like he knew I shot someone today. I haven't seen any news showing me firing a gun. How could he know that, Yoan?"

Yoan struggles to make sense of it all, but doesn't move to release Shannon. C-Lo continues to wail pitifully.

"I have to get my baby. Please, let me get my baby."

Reluctantly, Yoan lets her go, but he follows her into the bedroom. Shannon says, "I don't understand. I've been trying to call Carlos all night. He never answered, but Ocho reaches him right away."

Quickly, Yoan slides out his phone and dials. The line rings until Carlos' voicemail answers, and it is full—just like when he tried less than fifteen minutes ago. He hangs up and calls again. Still, no answer. Bewildered, he blinks pensively at Shannon and mumbles, "Aw, man. Something's n-not right."

Suddenly, everything clicks, and they both realize Ocho put on a charade.

"Stay here!" he yells, running for the door, and Shannon rushes to lock it behind him.

Taking the stairs two at a time, Yoan attempts to be unsuspecting as he calls into his headset, "Ay, you okay, Ocho?"

Ocho growls back, "No! She broke my leg! I should've killed her. I've got to get to a doctor."

"We'll call a doctor over—"

"NO! Someone needs to *take me* to a doctor right now!!"

Yoan wracks his brain for what to say next. The only thing he can come up with is the mysterious phone call Ocho placed. "What did he say?" he asks.

"What!?"

"What did Los say when you called him?"

"He said he was on his way. But I can't wait for him to come back. I'm in too much pain..."

"Just hold on, bro. I'm coming to help."

Yoan tries Carlos again. This time, there's a groggy greeting on the other end of the line. Relieved, Yoan questions Carlos.

"Did you just talk to Ocho? Just a few minutes ago?"

Gathering his faculties, Carlos replies, "No. I just... got back to my phone. I haven't talked to anyone."

That's exactly what Yoan needed to hear. "We g-got a problem."

Carlos didn't remember falling asleep, but welcomes the phone rousing him. He demands, "Say it."

As Yoan proceeds to tell him what happened, he reflects briefly about Shannon's hunch.

"Where is he now?"

"I think he's downstairs."

"DO NOT let him leave!"

"What do you want me to do with him?"

"Just make sure he doesn't get away! I'm coming now."

Carlos hangs up. He notices the calls he missed and hastily pulls out the IVs. Blood drains from both the transfusion IV and his arm, and Carlos swallows the rise of nausea in his throat.

Lightheaded, he combs the drawers for bandages and finds one. He puts the bandage on one arm and presses some toilet paper from the bathroom against the other to help stop the bleeding where the medication had been administered. Holding his wounded arm in front of him, Carlos slips quietly from the hospital room and makes an unsteady beeline for his car.

***

Ocho tells the guard, "Go find me a cane and an ice pack," but when he's left alone, he moves into the hallway toward the garage. Leaning against the wall, he hops along until he reaches the recessed key cabinet in the hallway reserved for the vehicles in the garage. Grabbing a random set, he continues his hobble toward freedom.

When Ocho steps into the garage, another guard comes out of the security room and tries to usher him in that direction.

"Hey, man, something is happening. The surveillance recording was paused. I turned it back on, but looks like there's a glitch in the system," he complains before taking note of Ocho's injuries. "What—"

Ocho shirks him off. "Not now, you idiot! Help me to the car. Have to get to the hospital." He clicks the key remote and headlights flash. "Here. This one," he says, pointing to the car.

Confused, the subordinate guard supports his boss to the driver's seat.

"Why isn't someone driving you?" he asks.

In frustration, Ocho struggles to get his injured leg in the vehicle. He strikes out and lambasts the unfortunate guard for aiding in his agony as he tries to assist. "Get away from me, you—"

Two guns click. They turn to see Yoan stealthily approaching from the garage stairwell with a barrel in each hand pointed at them.

"What are you doing, bro?" Ocho entreats him. "I need to get to the hospital. I'm dying here."

"Nobody is leaving here until Los returns," Yoan declares. "And I need your guns."

***

Shannon's eyes remain cemented to the video monitors. Ocho and the guard sit in front of the security console with multiple guns pointed at their backs. No one moves for what seems like a lifetime. At last, Yoan stirs and picks up the phone. A few minutes later, a car pulls up the driveway and parks inside. Exchanging words with Beto, Sul, and the other two guards, Yoan exits the room and stands near the car.

She waits with bated breath.

The car door opens. As Carlos rises from the vehicle, Shannon drops to her knees and pumps her fist.

"Yes, God."

The Trial

[25]

Carlos converses with Yoan outside the security room, then leaves him and proceeds inside. Shannon hears the key tones sound, and the elevator begins to move.

With her hand on the butt of Ocho's gun, she waits by the elevator for his arrival. The doors slide apart, and Carlos walks swiftly toward her.

"I kept trying to call, and you never—I thought something happened to you."

Carlos pulls her to him and examines her battered face. His jaw clenches. "Are you hurt anywhere else?"

Removing her make-shift icepack, Shannon raises her injured hand, revealing four swollen, bloody, and bruising fingers. The dread is visible on his face as he waits for her to continue.

"That's it," she says.

Pressing the icepack gently onto her forehead, Carlos takes notice of the destruction in the sitting room. Fury rages in his eyes.

"Let the authorities handle him, Carlos. Let's just go."

"I am the authority."

Flashing an unpropitious look her way, he brushes past to the bedroom, grabs another handful of pain medication and heads to the bar for a drink.

"What if you don't come back?"

Swallowing the pills and liquor, Carlos reaches into a hidden side drawer of the bar. "Here's a gun, in case you need it to get out of here."

Stricken, Shannon watches him board the elevator and disappear behind the closing doors.

***

Carlos stands beside the culprits in front of the security console and prods.

"You say she tried to escape. Let's see it."

"I'm in a lot of pain, Los. I need to get medical attention right away," Ocho says.

"You'll get medical attention. But first *I* need to see that she's lying."

Ocho looks to the guard suspected of abetting his near escape. "Rewind it, Ernesto."

"No!" Carlos snaps. "You do it."

Ocho rewinds the surveillance to the approximate time of offense. Eyes study the monitors. Carlos has him cue it up again, fast forwarding and rewinding several times.

Anxiously, Yoan proclaims, "Nothing there!"

"That's the problem," Carlos says before roaring, "THERE'S NOTHING THERE! Why is that?"

"I don't know. I don't know what happened," Ocho says. He views the guard next to him. "What'd you do, Ernesto?"

"Los, I swear, I had nothing to do with this," Ernesto blabs. "He sent me on a break, I came back and the system was paused. When I saw him, I tried to tell him, but he only wanted me to help him to the car. I don't even know how to pause it, Los—"

"Enough!"

Carlos enters a code into the console. To everyone's surprise, the screens flicker and a separate surveillance feed pops up showing the master suite's interior.

Someone mutters, "How...?" before the room falls silent. Ocho's demeanor, once smugly assured of the lack of incriminating evidence against him, slowly changes to one of impending doom.

"A surveillance system to monitor the surveillance system," Carlos taunts. "Try it now."

Reluctantly, Ocho presses rewind, and there's the commotion. Ernesto rolls away his chair.

Carlos leans into Ocho's ear. "Did you think you could out smart me, big bro?"

Quick as lightning, he slams Ocho's head onto the console. It bounces back up, and blood pours from his nose. Carlos draws his gun. All three brothers follow his lead. Shannon gasps.

Ocho looks brazenly between the guns pointed at him.

Carlos grabs him by the hair. "I don't see her trying to escape, Ocho."

He releases him and steps back. Ocho juts his chin, looking up at Carlos sinisterly, and Carlos roars, "I TRUSTED YOU WITH EVERYTHING I HAVE... WHY?"

"I just couldn't stand to see you win anymore. It was my turn. MY TURN! With dad gone, you gone, it would've been. Goyzo couldn't finish the last, simple job."

The brothers stare at him with mixtures of shock, rage, and repulsion.

"You sided with an enemy and had the old man killed?" Beto asks incredulously.

Sul hisses, "Shoot him already."

"I wish I had've killed your little whore. Her and your little brat. But don't worry, *Los-ito*, I'm not finished yet," Ocho says. Displaying a bloody smile, he spits on Carlos' pants and lunges.

"NO!" Shannon yells, unheard.

The barrels pointed at him discharge. Within seconds, Ocho is riddled with lead. His body slumps to the floor, and Shannon stares, paralyzed.

In one last fit of rage, Carlos kicks Ocho's lifeless body. "I told you you would get medical attention!!! Anyone else want to BETRAY THE FAMILY!?"

Carlos fumes, looking around at those present in the room. He motions for Ocho to be picked up and wipes his sleeve across his eyes. "Get him out of here."

As the guards stoop to assist with Ocho's remains, Yoan asks, "Los, should we have him prepared f-for a f-funeral?"

"Funeral?" Carlos replies, looking at Yoan. "No. Something more appropriate. Call the general. Tell him we'll need his helicopter. I'm dumping this worthless body onto Goyzo's front porch, and I'm kicking it from the cockpit myself."

Carlos dials Moises. "Get the plane ready."

***

Shannon stands, holding the baby tightly when Carlos reenters the master bedroom. He stares tenuously at her, his eyes glistening.

"You were right. Not the enemy, but my flesh and blood." His voice breaks, overwhelmed with emotions he can no longer conceal. "My brother. My closest brother."

Shannon looks woefully at Carlos. She touches her fingertips gently to his cheek.

"For the first time," Carlos confides, "I started praying for God to give me a way out. For you. For Carlo. Instead, it's this. I get in deeper."

Shannon wants to tell him he could start by making different choices. Deciding this isn't the best time for that, she shifts C-Lo to her other side in silence, clueless to what she *should* say. Carlos snaps from his remorse and bypasses them into the bedroom.

"We need to move."

He traverses the suite, pulling small bags from random compartments in the walls, flooring, and furniture.

"You and C-Lo will have new identities back in the states. Get a new career, new friends, start completely over. Never mention me, talk about your past or try to seek out your family—and that includes your beloved Chief Jaxson. I hope you know by now, he's not who you think he is. You must stay alert as if everyone is your enemy. They probably will be because of me."

"Why are you speaking as if we're not going to see you again?"

He shoves the smaller bags into one large duffel. "Because you won't. The less association you have with me, the safer you'll be."

"You want me to spend the rest of my life hiding and lying to C-Lo about who his father is and his family? No. This sounds like you just want to toss us out to fend for ourselves. What kind of man are you?"

"I'm a man who loves you. I'm doing what I should have done, and that was to let you live your lives without being entangled in mine. Trust me, this is best. I will make sure you have everything you need."

"It's too late for damage control now! You brought us here and we are affiliated with you. Sending us away isn't going to change that."

Carlos stops packing to settle on her. "Listen! If these vultures don't think you're of value to me, you'll have better chances."

"But I have your son. I guess he's not valuable?"

Carlos grabs her. "I brought my son here because I wanted him here. With me. Now, I'm trying to fix this mistake the best way I know how. Do you think this is easy for me? The only difference between how you and I feel right now is that I know being around me is far more dangerous than us being apart, and you don't. I know how they think because I'm one of them. You'll be the first targets. You two have to disappear. Now, get what you want to take with you or have it left behind." He lets her go and picks up a pre-packed garment bag.

"What about all your praying for God to give you a way out? Don't you believe that He can?"

"Sure He can. But He won't. There is no other way for me, Shannon. You live dirty, you die dirty."

"Carlos, God turned me away from a lifestyle that was leading nowhere—"

"And then He led you to me."

"You are implying that God wanted these terrible things to happen, and that's not so."

Carlos looks at Shannon judgmentally.

"Or maybe it is," she says. "Maybe we're supposed to learn something from all this. I don't know. I'm still seeking Him for answers, but one thing is clear. I have to *try* to do right."

"And I'm going to help you do just that." He looks into the monitors at the bodies scurrying to clean up evidence downstairs and says, "Time to go."

Carlos walks down the stairs from the bedroom to the sitting room. Shannon follows him.

"I don't want to act like "we" never happened, Carlos."

He ignores her. She grabs his wrist.

"Did you hear what I said? Don't choose this life over us. We can fix this. This is justifiable homicide."

Prying her fingers away, Carlos turns to exit the suite.

"¿Mijo?" Delia's teary face pokes around the entrance door in the foyer. "Yunaisys..."

Carlos freezes.

***

"What do you mean, 'she's missing'? Shannon asks, trailing Carlos as he pulls Delia into the master bedroom.

Ignoring Shannon, he asks Delia in Spanish, "When did you say you last saw her?" He listens to her reply as she nervously dabs her cheeks with a crumpled tissue, then rewinds the surveillance video.

The monitors show Delia and Yunaisys in a room unknown to Shannon, at the time the standoff in the security room occurs. He hits play. The guns fire. Yunaisys covers her face and Delia faints.

"Oh, God! The girl *watched* that?" Shannon exclaims. "Why would—"

"What is this?" Carlos points to the monitor.

They watch closely as Yunaisys pulls out her phone and dials. Then, while all conscious attention is on the activity in the security room, she slips undetected from the house, down the driveway to the keypad, and into a car parked at the front gate.

Carlos zooms in on the silhouettes inside the car.

Yoan and Beto rush into the room.

"We looked everywhere. We can't find her."

Carlos rubs his fingers across his forehead. "You're not going to. She's not here."

Jostled by a thought, he turns back to the surveillance and scrubs through the footage again. Something catches his eye. He lets it roll. In one monitor, a hobbling Ocho sends the guard away then makes a call. In another monitor, Yunaisys answers. Her face stricken, slowly she nods her head.

***

In the garage, he ushers Delia into one car and Shannon toward another. As the ladies separate, unspoken farewells are exchanged in their harried looks. Carlos instructs Yoan and two other guards to wait with Shannon and the baby at the plane.

"Beto, gather the crew. *Find her.* Start with Carmen. Sul, Ernesto, you're coming with me."

"I understand searching for Yunaisys, but what are *you* planning to do, Carlos?" Shannon demands.

He motions for the guards with Delia to get moving before turning to Shannon. "If I'm not there by—" He pivots his wrist to verify the time. "—two o'clock, leave without me."

Shannon doesn't want to hear such nonsense. "If I can start over, you can start over. Don't keep going down this road."

Carlos shakes his head at her naiveté. "I can't start over. Get in the car."

"What you can't do is continue living life this way. God will not keep striving with you. I'm telling you, this grace that you have will run out. You may think that you can't get away from this lifestyle, but you can. We can have a normal life together."

Carlos laughs. "A normal life? Let's just take one part of your flawed philosophy and pretend for a moment that all of the low-life hoodlums and white collar criminals in the world suddenly left me completely alone—to live a 'normal' life. Do you really think I would be able to go work at say... a bank or selling cars? Me?"

He stoops close to her ear and lowers his voice. "You're trying to convince me to walk away from this life that I lead, Mi Corazon, but you're missing something else very importanté. And that is, I like what I do. All of it. I like the power, the money, the prestige. Ultimately, I chose this life, and I built an empire. I will let no one take it from me." He straightens. "These ratas, these escoria—who think they can manipulate my family—must see how I tie up my loose ends. Walking away is not an option. Get in."

"Why not? Why not, if it means being with us? I've learned to turn *to* God when I hurt—not away. He's the only One who can help."

"No need to preach to me, Señorita. God and I have an understanding. *I'm* the one who must fix the problems. He helps those who help themselves."

"Haven't come across that scripture yet, and I've read the Bible from front to back. You need *His* salvation, and you're running."

Carlos shuts the door. "Drive!"

Yoan puts the car in gear.

***

Shannon didn't realize she had been holding her breath most of the time until Carlos and Sul drive up to the Bombadier. Carlos sits next to her, cold, withdrawn, and beyond reasoning, and the turmoil between them rebounds in the silence. The flight back to the U.S. feels more grueling in a sense than the first.

Touching down on the Las Vegas tarmac, with lights from the strip twinkling faintly behind them, Carlos hands Shannon a bag stacked with cash and weapons. A dapper, black-bearded man with a silver, diamond-shaped patch in its center steps from a dark Escalade awaiting their arrival. He slides Carlos an envelope, who takes a peek inside, nods approvingly, then hands it to Shannon and directs her into the driver's seat of the car. While he straps C-Lo into the rear seat, she peers at the driver's license, passports and birth certificates crammed inside. *I can't do this. I don't want this.*

Carlos returns to bend at her window, and Shannon stares at him in silence. It feels like an eternity before he is able to muster any words past the angst on his face. He pinches the moisture from his eyes toward the bridge of his nose, then sweeps his hand briefly across his mouth.

"For what it is worth, I never intended... I hope you can forgive me." His eyes dart to C-Lo in the backseat. "If... "

He stops. Cupping her face with his hand, he kisses her temple and lingers, imprinting the coconut smell of her hair as he smooths a few ringlets from her face.

She presses her hand over his. "Carlos, this isn't the right move."

"Yes, it is." He looks into her face again, and she watches his expression harden. "It's done. There's nothing more to talk about. Get on the highway and leave everything behind. Be smart, Shannon. Disappear."

Straightening, Carlos backs away from the vehicle with finality. Forcing herself to step on the gas, Shannon eases slowly into the uncertainty of her future. In the rear view mirror, through aching eyes, she watches Carlos re-board the plane.

Within minutes, he is gone.

Epilogue

Clicking the safety from her gun, she creeps across the cabin floor in her bare feet. She looks through the peephole at the shadow daring to rap on her door at this hour of night. Her heart races, and her hands turn clammy. She's been tracked down. Again.

No need to run.

For a better view, she cracks the door with the safety chain still connected. Pushing the door closed, she takes a deep breath, then unlocks it. The figure steps inside.

"Are we alone?"

"Yes."

He closes the door behind him and locks it. Carefully, he removes the gun from her hand and puts it down.

Pulling her aggressively into his arms, he says, "I couldn't do it, Mi Vida. I couldn't stay away... I'm ready to trade it all for what's right."

His eyes brim, penetrating her soul. Lovingly, her arms encircle his neck.

"It's about time you said those words."

He runs his hand up the small of her back to her nape, drawing her forehead to the lips she's missed. She lifts her face, and their mouths connect in electrifying reunion as they retreat into the room.

She's back in his arms, just like she'd prayed...

Ringing startles her from sleep. She answers quickly to silence it. The phone line crackles with static.

"Did he make contact?"

A pause. She rolls to her side and says softly, "No."

"I hope you are not lying. A lot of lives are depending on your full cooperation... beginning with the child."

Made in the USA
Monee, IL
17 October 2020